"Chess and fantastic fiction began an enthusiastic encounter with each other at least as far back as Lewis Carroll, and the mating is still in progress. Both contain strong elements of conflict and both are set in worlds where time and space are subject to transformation; the ordinary rules of human existence do not apply. Therefore both tend to appeal to the same kind of mind; an interest in the fantastic is very often a sign of interest in chess, and vice versa. . ."

Fred & Joan Saberhagen

Science Fiction and the "Game of Kings":

PAWN TO INFINITY

PAWN
TO INFINITY

EDITED BY
FRED SABERHAGEN
WITH
JOAN SABERHAGEN

SF
ace books
A Division of Charter Communications Inc.
A GROSSET & DUNLAP COMPANY
51 Madison Avenue
New York, New York 10010

PAWN TO INFINITY
Copyright © 1982 by Fred and Joan Saberhagen

An ACE Book

First Ace printing: June 1982
Published Simultaneously in Canada

2 4 6 8 0 9 7 5 3 1
Manufactured in the United States of America

ACKNOWLEDGEMENTS

"Introduction" © 1982 Fred Saberhagen.

"The Marvelous Brass Chessplaying Automaton" by Gene Wolfe. © 1977 Terry Carr; reprinted by permission of the author and his agent, Virginia Kidd; first published in *Universe 7*, edited by Terry Carr.

"Unicorn Variation" by Roger Zelazny. © 1982 The Amber Corporation, first published in *Isaac Asimov's Science Fiction Magazine;* March 13, 1982.

"The Immortal Game" by Poul Anderson. © 1954 Mercury Press, Inc., first published in *The Magazine of Fantasy and Science Fiction*, Feb. 1954.

"Midnight by the Morphy Watch" by Fritz Leiber. © 1974 UPD Publishing Company for *Worlds of If Science Fiction;* first published in *If*, July-August 1974.

"Unsound Variations" by George R.R. Martin. © 1982 Ultimate Publishing Company, Inc., first published in *Amazing/Fantastic*, Jan. 1982.

"A Game of Vlet" by Joanna Russ. © 1974 Joanna Russ; first published in *The Magazine of Fantasy and Science Fiction*, Feb. 1974.

"Without A Thought" by Fred Saberhagen. © 1962 Digest Productions Corp.; first published in *If*, vol. 12 no. 6 Jan. 1963.

"A Board in the Other Direction" by Ruth Berman. © 1972 Mercury Press; first published in *The Magazine of Fantasy and Science Fiction*.

"Von Goom's Gambit" by Victor Contoski; © 1966 Victor Contoski; first published in *Chess Review*, April 1966.

"Kokomu" by Daniel Gilbert. © 1982 Daniel Gilbert; first published in *Pawn to Infinity*, edited by Fred & Joan Saberhagen.

"Moxon's Master" by Ambrose Bierce. In the Public Domain.

"Rendezvous 2062" by Robert Frazier, first published in *Fantasy Book*. © 1982 by Robert Frazier; published by arrangement with the author.

"Reflections on the Looking-Glass, An Essay" by Alfred Stewart. © 1982 Alfred Stewart; first published in *Pawn to Infinity*, edited by Fred & Joan Saberhagen

CONTENTS

INTRODUCTION

Chess and fantastic fiction (I use the term here to include science fiction) began an enthusiastic encounter with each other at least as far back as Lewis Carroll, and the mating is still in progress. Both contain strong elements of conflict—Emanuel Lasker, one of the great players of all time, defined chess as a struggle—and both are set in worlds where time and space are subject to transformation, the ordinary rules of human existence do not apply. Therefore both tend to appeal to the same kind of mind; an interest in the fantastic is very often a sign of interest in chess, and vice versa.

The games in the stories in this book are not always chess, if we define chess by a certain precise set of rules, and configurations of pieces which are to be moved on a flat board eight squares by eight. But by Lasker's definition the fit is good, because each story in this book recounts a struggle. The opponents are not always the humanity we know, any more than the games are always literally the chess we know; but a board game plays some essential part in each story, and in each some conflict beyond gaming is to be resolved.

Getting this book done has been something of a struggle, too, at times, though mostly it has been a lot of fun. We would like to thank all those who have co-operated and offered suggestions, in particular George R.R. Martin, and Ruth Berman and her friends Dennis Lein and Joyce Muskat.

Start your clocks!

—Fred and Joan Saberhagen

1

THE MARVELOUS BRASS CHESSPLAYING AUTOMATON

Gene Wolfe

Each day Lame Hans sits with his knees against the bars, playing chess with the machine. Though I have seen the game often I have never learned to play, but I watch them as I sweep. It is a beautiful game, and Lame Hans has told me of its beginnings in the great ages now past; for that reason I always feel a sympathy toward the little pawns with their pencils and wrenches and plain clothing, each figure representing many generations of those whose labor built the great bishops that split the skys in the days of the old wars.

I feel pity for Lame Hans also. He talks to me when I bring his food, and sometimes when I am cleaning the jail. Let me tell you his story, as I have learned it in the many days since the police drew poor Gretchen out and laid her in the dust of the street. Lame Hans would never tell you himself—for all that big, bulging head his tongue is slow and halting when he speaks of his own affairs.

It was last summer during the truce that the showman's cart was driven into our village. For a month not a drop of rain had fallen; each day at noon Father Karl rang the churchbells, and women went in to pray for rain for their husbands' crops. After dark many of these same women met to form lines and circles on the slopes of the Schlossberg, the mountain that was once a great building. The lines and circles are supposed to influence the Weatherwatchers, whose winking lights pass so swiftly through the starry sky. For myself, I do not believe it. What men ever made a machine that could see a few old women on the mountainside at night?

So it was when the cart of Herr Heitzmann the mountebank came. The sun was down, but the street still so hot that the dogs would not bark for fear of fainting, and the dust rolled away from the wheels in waves, like grain when foxes run through the fields.

This cart was shorter than a farm wagon, but very high, with such a roof as a house has. The sides had been painted, and even I, who do not play, but have so often watched Albricht the moneylender play Father Karl, or Doctor Eckardt play Burgermeister Landsteiner, recognized the mighty figures of the Queen-Computers who lead the armies of the field of squares into battle; and the haughty King-Generals who command, and if they fall bring down all.

A small, bent man drove. He had a head large enough for a giant—that was Lame Hans, but I paid little attention to him, not knowing that he and I would be companions here in the jail where I work. Beside him sat Heitzmann the mountebank, and it was he who took one's eyes, which was as he intended. He was tall and thin, with a sharp chin and a large nose and snapping black eyes. He had velvet trousers and a fine hat which sweat had stained around the band, and long locks of dark hair that hung from under it at odd angles so that one knew he used the finger-comb when he woke, as drunkards do who find themselves beneath a bench. When the small man brought the cart through the inn-yard gate, I rose from my seat on the jail steps and went across to the inn parlor. And it was a fortunate thing I did so, because it was in this way that I chanced to see the famous game between the brass machine and Professor Baumeister.

Haven't I mentioned Professor Baumeister before? Have you not noticed that in a village such as ours there are always a dozen celebrities? Always a man who is strong (with us that is Willi Schacht, the smith's apprentice), one who eats a great deal, a learned man like Doctor Eckardt, a ladies man, and so on. But for all these people to be properly admired, there must also be a distinguished visitor to whom to point them out, and here in Oder Spree that is Professor Baumeister, because our village lies midway between the University and Furstenwald, and it is here that he spends the night whenever he journeys from one to the other, much to the enrichment of Scheer the innkeeper. The fact of the matter is that Professor Baumeister has become one of our celebrities himself, only by spending the night here so often. With his broad brown beard and fine coat and tall hat and leather riding breeches, he gives the parlor of our inn the air of a gentlemen's club.

I have heard that it is often the case that the beginning of the greatest drama is as casual as any commonplace event. So it was that night. The inn was full of off duty soldiers drinking beer, and because of the heat all the windows were thrown open, though a dozen candles were burning. Professor Baumeister was deep in conversation with Doctor Eckardt; something about the war. Herr Heitzmann the mountebank—though I did not know what to call him then—had already gotten his half-liter when I came in, and was standing at the bar.

At last, when Professor Baumeister paused to emphasize some point, Herr Heitzmann leaned over to them, and in the most offhand way asked a question. It was peculiar, but the whole room seemed to grow silent as he spoke, so that he could be heard everywhere though it was no more than a whisper. He said: "I wonder if I might venture to ask you gentlemen—you both appear to be learned men—if, to the best of your knowledge, there still exists even one of those great computational machines which were perhaps the most extraordinary—I trust you will agree with me?—creations of the age now past."

Professor Baumeister said at once, "No, sir. Not one remains."

"You feel certain of this?"

"My dear sir," said Professor Baumeister, "you must understand that those devices were dependent upon a supply of replacement parts consisting of the most delicate subminiature electronic components. These have not been produced now for over a hundred years—indeed, some of them have been unavailable longer."

"Ah," Herr Heitzmann said (mostly to himself, it seemed, but you could hear him in the kitchen). "Then I have the only one."

Professor Baumeister attempted to ignore this amazing remark, as not having been addressed to himself; but Doctor Eckardt, who is of an inquisitive disposition, said boldly: "You have such a machine, Herr. . .?"

"Heitzmann. Originally of Berlin, now come from Zurich. And you, my good sir?"

Doctor Eckardt introduced himself, and Professor Baumeister too, and Herr Heitzmann clasped them by the hand. Then the doctor said to Professor Baumeister: "You are certain that no computers remain in existence, my friend?"

The professor said: "I am referring to working computers—machines in operating condition. There are plenty of old hulks in museums, of course."

Herr Heitzmann sighed, and pulled out a chair and sat down at the table with them, bringing his beer. "Would it not be sad," he said, "if those world-ruling machines were lost to mankind forever?"

Professor Baumeister said dryly: "They based their extrapolations on numbers. That worked well enough as long as money, which is easily measured numerically, was the principal motivating force in human affairs. But as time progressed human actions became responsive instead to a multitude of incommensurable vectors; the computers' predictions failed, the civilization they had built collapsed, and parts for the machines were no longer obtainable or desired."

"How fascinating!" Herr Heitzmann exclaimed. "Do you know, I have never heard it explained in quite that way. You have provided me, for the first time, with an explanation for the survival of my own machine."

Doctor Eckardt said, "You have a working computer, then?"

"I do. You see, mine is a specialized device. It was not designed, like the computers the learned professor spoke of just now, to predict human actions. It plays chess."

Professor Baumeister asked, "And where do you keep this wonderful machine?" By this time everyone else in the room had fallen silent. Even Scheer took care not to allow the glasses he was drying to clink; and Gretchen, the fat blond serving girl who usually cracked jokes with the soldiers and banged down the plates, moved through the pipesmoke among the tables as silently as a canalboat in fog.

"Outside," Herr Heitzmann replied to the professor. "In my conveyance. I am taking it to Dresden."

"And it plays chess."

"It has never been defeated."

"Are you aware," Professor Baumeister inquired sardonically, "that to program a computer to play chess —to play well—was considered one of the most difficult problems? That many judged that it was never actually solved, and that those machines which most closely approached acceptable solutions were never so small as to be portable?"

"Nevertheless," Herr Heitzmann declared, "I have such a machine."

"My friend, I do not believe you."

"I take it you are a player yourself," Herr Heitzmann said. "Such a learned man could hardly be otherwise.

Very well. As I said a moment ago, my machine is outside." His hand touched the table between Professor Baumeister's glass and his own, and when it came away five gold kilomarks stood there in a neat stack. "I will lay these on the outcome of the game, if you will play my machine tonight."

"Done," said Professor Baumeister.

"I must see your money."

"You will accept a draft on Streicher's, in Furstenwald?"

And so it was settled. Doctor Eckardt held the stakes, and six men volunteered to carry the machine into the inn parlor under Herr Heitzmann's direction.

Six were not too many, though the machine was not as large as might have been expected—not more than a hundred and twenty centimeters high, with a base, as it might be, a meter on a side. The sides and top were all of brass, set with many dials and other devices no one understood.

When it was at last in place, Professor Baumeister viewed it from all sides and smiled. "This is not a computer," he said.

"My dear friend," said Herr Heitzmann, "you are mistaken."

"It is several computers. There are two keyboards and a portion of a third. There are even two nameplates, and one of these dials once belonged to a radio."

Herr Heitzmann nodded. "It was assembled at the very close of the period, for one purpose only—to play chess."

"You still contend that this machine can play?"

"I contend more. That it will win."

"Very well. Bring a board."

"That is not necessary," Herr Heitzmann said. He pulled a knob at the front of the machine, and a whole section swung forward, as the door of a vegetable bin does in a scullery. But the top of this bin was not open as though to receive the vegetables: it was instead a chessboard, with the white squares of brass, and the black of dark glass, and on the board, standing in formation and ready to play, were two such armies of chessmen as no one in our village had ever seen, tall metal figures so stately they might have been sculptured apostles in a church, one army of brass and the other of some dark metal. "You may play white," Herr Heitzmann said. "That is generally considered an advantage."

Professor Baumeister nodded, advanced the white king's pawn two squares, and drew a chair up to the board. By the time he had seated himself the machine had replied, moving so swiftly that no one saw by what mechanism the piece had been shifted.

The next time Professor Baumeister acted more slowly, and everyone watched, eager to see the machine's countermove. It came the moment the professor had set his piece in its new position—the black queen slid forward silently, with nothing to propel it.

After ten moves Professor Baumeister said, "There is a man inside."

Herr Heitzmann smiled. "I see why you say that, my friend. Your position on the board is precarious."

"I insist that the machine be opened for my examination."

"I suppose that you would say that if a man were concealed inside, the bet would be cancelled." Herr Heitzmann had ordered a second glass of beer, and was leaning against the bar watching the game.

"Of course. My bet was that a machine could not defeat me. I am well aware that certain human players can."

"But conversely, if there is no man in the machine, the bet stands?"

"Certainly."

"Very well." Herr Heitzmann walked to the machine, twisted four catches on one side, and with the help of some onlookers removed the entire panel. It was of brass, like the rest of the machine; but because the metal was thin, not so heavy as it appeared.

There was more room inside than might have been thought, yet withall a considerable amount of mechanism: things like shingles the size of little tabletops, all covered with patterns like writing (Lame Hans has told me since that these are called circuit cards). And gears and motors and the like.

When Professor Baumeister had poked among all these mechanical parts for half a minute, Herr Heitzmann asked: "Are you satisfied?"

"Yes," answered Professor Baumeister, straightening up. "There is no one in there."

"But I am not," said Herr Heitzmann, and he walked with long strides to the other side of the machine. Everyone crowded around him as he released the catches on that side, lifted away the panel, and stood it against the wall. "Now," he said, "you can see completely through my machine—isn't that right? Look, do you see Doctor Eckardt? Do you see me? Wave to us."

"I am satisfied," Professor Baumeister said. "Let us go on with the game."

"The machine has already taken its move. You may think about your next one while these gentlemen help me replace the panels."

Professor Baumeister was beaten in twenty-two moves. Albricht the moneylender then asked if he could play without betting, and when this was refused by Herr Heitzmann, bet a kilomark and was beaten in fourteen moves. Herr Heitzmann asked then if anyone else would play, and when no one replied, requested that the same men who carried the machine into the inn assist him in putting it away again.

"Wait," said Professor Baumeister.

Herr Heitzmann smiled. "You mean to play again?"

"No. I want to buy your machine. On behalf of the University."

Herr Heitzmann sat down and looked serious. "I doubt that I could sell it to you. I had hoped to make a good sum in Dresden before selling it there."

"Five hundred kilomarks."

Herr Heitzmann shook his head. "That is a fair proposition," he said, "and I thank you for making it. But I cannot accept."

"Seven hundred and fifty," Professor Baumeister said. "That is my final offer."

"In gold?"

"In a draft on an account the University maintains in Furstenwald—you can present it there for gold the first thing in the morning."

"You must understand," said Herr Heitzmann, "that the machine requires a certain amount of care, or it will not perform properly."

"I am buying it as is," said Professor Baumeister. "As it stands here before us."

"Done, then," said Herr Heitzmann, and he put out his hand.

The board was folded away, and six stout fellows carried the machine into the professor's room for safekeeping, where he remained with it for an hour or more. When he returned to the inn parlor at last, Doctor Eckardt asked if he had been playing chess again.

Professor Baumeister nodded. "Three games."

"Did you win?"

"No, I lost them all. Where is the showman?"

"Gone," said Father Karl, who was sitting near them. "He left as soon as you took the machine to your room."

Doctor Eckardt said, "I thought he planned to stay the night here."

"So did I," said Father Karl. "And I confess I believed the machine would not function without him. I was surprised to hear that our friend the professor had been playing in private."

Just then a small, twisted man, with a large head

crowned with wild black hair, limped into the inn parlor. It was Lame Hans, but no one knew that then. He asked Scheer the innkeeper for a room.

Scheer smiled. "Sitting rooms on the first floor are a hundred marks," he said. He could see by Lame Hans' worn clothes that he could not afford a sitting room.

"Something cheaper."

"My regular rooms are thirty marks. Or I can let you have a garret for ten."

Hans rented a garret room, and ordered a meal of beer, tripe, and kraut. That was the last time anyone except Gretchen noticed Lame Hans that night.

And now I must leave off recounting what I myself saw, and tell many things that rest solely on the testimony of Lame Hans, given to me while he ate his potato soup in his cell. But I believe Lame Hans to be an honest fellow; and as he no longer, as he says, cares much to live, he has no reason to lie.

One thing is certain. Lame Hans and Gretchen the serving girl fell in love that night. Just how it happened I cannot say—I doubt that Lame Hans knows himself. She was sent to prepare the cot in his garret. Doubtless she was tired after drawing beer in the parlor all day, and was happy to sit for a few moments and talk with him. Perhaps she smiled—she was always a girl who smiled a great deal—and laughed at some bitter joke he made. And as for Lame Hans, how many blue eyed girls could ever have smiled at him, with his big head and twisted leg?

In the morning the machine would not play chess.

Professor Baumeister sat before it for a long time, arranging the pieces and making first one opening and then another, and tinkering with the mechanism; but nothing happened.

And then, when the morning was half gone, Lame Hans came into his room. "You paid a great deal of money for this machine," he said, and sat down in the best chair.

"Were you in the inn parlor last night?" asked Professor Baumeister. "Yes, I paid a great deal: seven hundred and fifty kilomarks."

"I was there," said Lame Hans. "You must be a very rich man to be able to afford such a sum."

"It was the University's money," explained Professor Baumeister.

"Ah," said Lame Hans. "Then it will be embarrassing for you if the machine does not play."

"It does play," said the professor. "I played three games with it last night after it was brought here."

"You must learn to make better use of your knights," Lame Hans told him, "and to attack on both sides of the board at once. In the second game you played well until you lost the queen's rook; then you went to pieces."

The professor sat down, and for a moment said nothing. And then: "You are the operator of the machine. I was correct in the beginning; I should have known."

Lame Hans looked out the window.

"How did you move the pieces—by radio? I suppose there must still be radio control equipment in existence somewhere."

"I was inside," Lame Hans said. "I'll show you sometime; it's not important. What will you tell the University?"

"That I was swindled, I suppose. I have some money of my own, and I will try to pay back as much as I can out of that—and I own two houses in Furstenwald that can be sold."

"Do you smoke?" asked Lame Hans, and he took out his short pipe, and a bag of tobacco.

"Only after dinner," said the professor, "and not often then."

"I find it calms my nerves," said Lame Hans. "That is why I suggested it to you. I do not have a second pipe, but I can offer you some of my tobacco, which is very good. You might buy a clay from the innkeeper here."

"No thank you. I fear I must abandon such little pleasures for a long time to come."

"Not necessarily," said Lame Hans. "Go ahead, buy that pipe. This is good Turkish tobacco—would you believe, to look at me, that I know a great deal about tobacco? It has been my only luxury."

"If you are the one who played chess with me last night," Professor Baumeister said, "I would be willing to believe that you know a great deal about anything. You play like the devil himself."

"I know a great deal about more than tobacco. Would you like to get your money back?"

And so it was that that very afternoon (if it can be credited), the mail coach carried away bills printed in large black letters. These said:

IN THE VILLAGE OF ODER SPREE
BEFORE THE INN OF THE GOLDEN APPLES
ON SATURDAY
AT 9:00 O'CLOCK
THE FANTASTIC BRASS CHESSPLAYING
AUTOMATON WILL BE ON DISPLAY
FREE TO EVERYONE
AND WILL PLAY ANY CHALLENGER
AT EVEN ODDS
TO A LIMIT OF DM 2,000,000

Now you will think from what I have told you that Lame Hans was a cocky fellow; but that is not the case, though like many of us who are small of stature he pretended to be self-reliant when he was among men taller than he. The truth is that though he did not show it he was very frightened when he met Herr Heitzmann (as the two of them had arranged earlier that he should) in a certain malodorous tavern near the Schwarzthor in Furstenwald.

"So there you are, my friend," said Herr Heitzmann. "How did it go?"

"Terribly," Lame Hans replied as though he felt nothing. "I was locked up in that brass snuffbox for half the night, and had to play twenty games with that fool of a scholar. And when at last I got out, I couldn't get a ride here and had to walk most of the way on this bad leg of mine. I trust it was comfortable on the cart-seat? The horse didn't give you too much trouble?"

"I'm sorry you've had a poor time of it, but now you can relax. There's nothing more do to until he's convinced the machine is broken and irreparable."

Lame Hans looked at him as though in some surprise. "You didn't see the signs? They are posted everywhere."

"What signs?"

"He's offering to bet two thousand kilomarks that no one can beat the machine."

Herr Heitzmann shrugged. "He will discover that it is inoperative before the contest, and cancel it."

"He could not cancel after the bet was made," said Lame Hans. "Particularly if there were a proviso that if either were unable to play, the bet was forfeited. Some upright citizen would be selected to hold the stakes, naturally."

"I don't suppose he could at that," said Herr Heitzmann, taking a swallow of schnapps from the glass before him. "However, he wouldn't bet *me*—he'd think I knew some way to influence the machine. Still, he's never seen *you.*"

"Just what I've been thinking myself," said Lame Hans, "on my hike."

"It's a little out of your line."

"If you'll put up the cash, I'd be willing to go a little out of my line for my tenth of that kind of money. But what is there to do? I make the bet, find someone to hold the stakes, and stand ready to play on Saturday morning. I could even offer to play him—for a smaller bet— to give him a chance to get some of his own back. That is, if he has anything left after paying off. It would make it seem more sporting."

"You're certain you could beat him?"

"I can beat anybody—you know that. Besides, I beat

him a score of times yesterday; the game you saw was just the first."

Herr Heitzmann ducked under the threatening edge of a tray carried by an overenthusiastic waiter. "All the same," he said, "when he discovers it won't work. . . ."

"I could even spend a bit of time in the machine. That's no problem. It's in a first floor room, with a window that won't lock."

And so Lame Hans left for our village again, this time considerably better dressed and with two thousand kilomarks in his pocket. Herr Heitzmann, with his appearance considerably altered by a plastiskin mask, left also, an hour later, to keep an eye on the two thousand.

"But," the professor said when Lame Hans and he were comfortably ensconced in his sitting room again, with pipes in their mouths and glasses in their hands and a plate of sausage on the table, "But who is going to operate the machine for us? Wouldn't it be easier if you simply didn't appear? Then you would forfeit."

"And Heitzmann would kill me," said Lame Hans.

"He didn't strike me as the type."

"He would hire it done," Hans said positively. "Whenever he got the cash. There are deserters about who are happy enough to do that kind of work for drinking money. For that matter, there are soldiers who aren't deserters who'll do it—men on detached duty of one kind and another. When you've spent all winter slaughtering Russians, one more body doesn't make much difference." He blew a smoke ring, then ran the long stem of his clay pipe through it as though he were driving home a bayonet. "But if I play the machine and lose, he'll only think you figured things out and got somebody to work it, and that I'm not as good as he supposed. Then he won't want anything more to do with me."

"All right then."

"A tobacconist should do well in this village, don't

you think? I had in mind that little shop two doors down from here. When the coaches stop, the passengers will see my sign; there should be many who'll want to fill their pouches."

"Gretchen prefers to stay here, I suppose."

Lame Hans nodded. "It doesn't matter to me. I've been all over, and when you've been all over, it's all the same."

Like everyone else in the village, and for fifty kilometers around, I had seen the professor's posters, and I went to bed Friday night full of pleasant anticipation. Lame Hans has told me that he retired in the same frame of mind, after a couple of glasses of good plum brandy in the inn parlor with the professor. He and the professor had to appear strangers and antagonists in public, as will be readily seen; but this did not prevent them from eating and drinking together while they discussed arrangements for the match, which was to be held—with the permission of Burgermeister Landsteiner—in the village street, where an area for the players had been cordoned off and high benches erected for the spectators.

Hans woke (so he has told me) when it was still dark, thinking that he had heard thunder. Then the noise came again, and he knew it must be the artillery, the big seige guns, firing at the Russians trapped in Kostrzyn. The army had built wood-fired steam tractors to pull those guns—he had seen them in Wriezen—and now the soldiers were talking about putting armor on the tractors and mounting cannon, so the knights of the chessboard would exist in reality once more.

The firing continued, booming across the dry plain, and he went to the window to see if he could make out the flashes, but could not. He put on a thin shirt and a pair of cotton trousers (for though the sun was not yet up it was as hot as if the whole of Brandenburg had been thrust into a furnace) and went into the street to look at the empty shop in which he planned to set up his tobac-

co business. A squadron of *Ritters* galloped through the
village, doubtless on their way to the seige. Lame Hans
shouted, "What do you mean to do? Ride your horses
against the walls?" but they ignored him. Now that the
truce was broken, Von Koblenz's army would soon be
advancing up the Oder valley, Lame Hans thought. The
Russians were said to have been preparing powered
balloons to assist in the defense, and this hot summer
weather, when the air seemed never to stir, would favor
their use. He decided that if he were the Commissar, he
would allow Von Koblenz to reach Glogow, and
then. . . .

But he was not the Commissar. He went back into the
inn and smoked his pipe until Frau Scheer came down
to prepare his breakfast. Then he went to the professor's
room where the machine was kept. Gretchen was already waiting there.

"Now then," Professor Baumeister said, "I understand that the two of you have it all worked out between
you." And Gretchen nodded solemnly, so that her
plump chin looked like a soft little pillow pressed
against her throat.

"It is quite simple," said Lame Hans. "Gretchen does
not know how to play, but I have worked out the moves
for her and drawn them on a sheet of paper, and we have
practiced in my room with a board. We will run through
it once here when she is in the machine; then there will
be nothing more to do."

"Is it a short game? It won't do for her to become
confused."

"She will win in fourteen moves," Lame Hans promised. "But still it is unusual. I don't think anyone has
done it before. You will see in a moment."

To Gretchen, Professor Baumeister said: "You're
sure you won't be mixed up? Everything depends on
you."

The girl shook her head, making her blond braids
dance. "No, Herr Professor." She drew a folded piece of

paper from her bosom. "I have it all here, and as my Hans told you, we have practiced in his room, where no one could see us."

"You aren't afraid?"

"When I am going to marry Hans, and be mistress of a fine shop? Oh, no, Herr Professor—for that I would do much worse things than to hide in this thing that looks like a stove, and play a game."

"We are ready, then," the professor said. "Hans, you still have not explained how it is that a person can hide in there, when the sides can be removed allowing people to look through the machinery. And I confess I still don't understand how it can be done, or how the pieces are moved."

"Here," said Lame Hans, and he pulled out the board as Herr Heitzmann had done in the inn parlor. "Now will you assist me in removing the left side? You should learn the way it comes loose, Professor—someday you may have to do it yourself." (The truth was that he was not strong enough to handle the big brass sheet by himself, and did not wish to be humiliated before Gretchen.)

"I had forgotten how much empty space there is inside," Professor Baumeister said when they had it off. "It looks more impossible than ever."

"It is simple, like all good tricks," Lame Hans told him. "And it is the sign of a good trick that it is the thing that makes it appear difficult that makes it easy. Here is where the chessboard is, you see, when it is folded up. But when it is unfolded, the panel under it swings out on a hinge to support it, and there are sides, so that a triangular space is formed."

The professor nodded and said, "I remember thinking when I played you that it looked like a potato bin, with the chessboard laid over the top."

"Exactly," Lame Hans continued. "The space is not noticeable when the machine is open, because this circuit card is just in front of it. But see here." And he released a little catch at the top of the circuit card, and pivoted it up to show the empty space behind it. "I am in the machine when it is carried in, but when Heitzmann pulls out the board, I lift this and fit myself under it; then when the machine is opened for inspection I am out of view. I can look up through the dark glass of the black squares, and because the pieces are so tall, I can make out their positions. But because it is bright outside, but dim where I am, I cannot be seen."

"I understand," said the professor. "But will Gretchen have enough light in there to read her piece of paper?"

"That was why I wanted to hold the match in the street. With the board in sunshine she will be able to see her paper clearly."

Gretchen was on her knees, looking at the space behind the circuit card. "It is very small in there," she said.

"It is big enough," said Lame Hans. "Do you have the magnet?" And then to the professor: "The pieces are moved by moving a magnet under them. The white pieces are brass, but the black ones are of iron, and the magnet gives them a sliding motion that is very impressive."

"I know," said the professor, remembering that he had felt a twinge of uneasiness whenever the machine had shifted a piece. "Gretchen, see if you can get inside."

The poor girl did the best she could, but encountered the greatest difficulty in wedging herself into the small space under the board. Work in the kitchen of the inn had provided her with many opportunities to snatch a mouthful of pastry or a choice potato dumpling or a half stein of dark beer, and she had availed herself of most of them—with the result that she possessed a lush and blooming figure of the sort that appeals to men like Lame Hans, who having been withered before birth by the isotopes of the old wars are themselves thin and small by nature. But though full breasts like ripe melons, and a rounded comfortable stomach and generous hips, may be pleasant things to look at when the moonlight is streaming through the bedroom window, they are not really well suited to folding up in a little three-cornered space under a chessboard; and in the end poor Gretchen was forced to remove her gown, and her shift as well, before she could cram herself, with much gasping and grunting, into it.

An hour later Willi Schacht the smith's apprentice and five other men carried the machine out into the street and set it in the space that had been cordoned off for the players, and if they noticed the extra weight, they did not complain of it. And there the good people who had come to see the match looked at the machine, and fanned themselves, and said that they were glad they weren't in the army on a day like this—because what must it be to serve one of those big guns, which get hot enough to poach an egg after half a dozen shots, even in ordinary weather? And between moppings and fannings they talked about the machine, and the mysterious Herr Zimmer (that was the name Lame Hans had given) who was going to play it for two hundred gold kilomarks.

Nine chimes sounded from the old clock in the steeple of Father Karl's church, and Herr Zimmer did not appear.

Doctor Eckardt, who had been chosen again to hold the stakes, came forward and whispered for some time with Professor Baumeister. The professor (if the truth were known) was beginning to believe that perhaps Lame Hans had decided that it was best to forfeit after all—though in fact if anyone had looked they would have seen Lame Hans sitting at the bar of the inn at that very moment, having a good nip of plum brandy and then another, while he allowed the suspense to build up as a good showman should.

At last Doctor Eckardt climbed upon a chair and announced: "It is now nearly ten. When the bet was made, it was agreed by both parties that if either failed to appear—or appearing, failed to play—the other should be declared the winner. If the worthy stranger, Herr Zimmer, does not make an appearance before ten minutes past ten, I intend to award the money entrusted to me to our respected acquaintance Professor Baumeister."

There was a murmur of excitement at this, but just when the clock began to strike, Lame Hans called from the door of the inn, "WAIT!" Then hats were thrown into the air, and women stood on toe-tips to see; and fathers lifted their children up as the lame Herr Zimmer made his way down the steps of the inn and took his place in the chair that had been arranged in front of the board.

"Are you ready to begin?" said Doctor Eckardt.

"I am," said Lame Hans, and opened.

The first five moves were made just as they had been rehearsed. But in the sixth, in which Gretchen was to have slid her queen half across the board, the piece stopped a square short.

Any ordinary player would have been dismayed, but Lame Hans was not. He only put his chin on his hand, and contrived (though wishing he had not drunk the brandy) a series of moves within the frame of the fourteen move game, by which he should lose despite the queen's being out of position. He made the first of these moves; and black moved the queen again, this time in a way that was completely different from anything on the paper Hans had given Gretchen. *She was deceiving me when she said she did not know how to play,* he thought to himself. *And now she finds she can't read the paper in there, or perhaps she has decided to surprise me. Naturally she would learn the fundamentals of the game, when it is played in the inn parlor every night.* (But he knew that she had not been deceiving him.) Then he saw that this new move of the queen's was in fact a clever attack, into which he could play and lose.

And then the guns around Kostrzyn, which had been silent since the early hours of the morning, began to boom again. Three times Lame Hans' hand stretched out to touch his king and make the move that would render it quite impossible for him to escape the queen, and three times it drew back. "You have five minutes in which to move," Doctor Eckardt said. "I will tell you when only thirty seconds remain, and count the last five."

The machine was built to play chess, thought Lame Hans. *Long ago, and they were warlocks in those days. Could it be that Gretchen, in kicking about. . .?*

Some motion in the sky made him raise his eyes, looking above the board and over the top of the machine itself. An artillery observation balloon (gray-black, a German balloon then) was outlined against the blue sky. He thought of himself sitting in a dingy little shop full of tobacco all day long, and no one to play chess with—no one he could not checkmate easily.

He moved a pawn, and the black bishop slipped out of the king's row to tighten the net.

If he won, they would have to pay him. Heitzmann would think everything had gone according to plan, and Professor Baumeister, surely, would hire no assassins. He launched his counterattack: the real attack at the left side of the board, with a false one down the center. Professor Baumeister came to stand beside him, and Doctor Eckardt warned him not to distract the player. There had been seven more than fourteen moves—and there was a trap behind the trap.

He took the black queen's knight and lost a pawn. He was sweating in the heat, wiping his brow with his sleeve between moves.

A black rook, squat in its iron sandbags, advanced three squares, and he heard the crowd cheer. "That is mate, Herr Zimmer," Doctor Eckardt announced. He saw the look of relief on Professor Baumeister's face, and knew that his own was blank. Then over the cheering someone shouted: *"Cheat! Cheat!"* Gray-black pillbox police caps were forcing their way through the hats and parasols of the spectators.

"*There is a man in there! There is someone inside!*" It was too clear and too loud—a showman's voice. A tall stranger was standing on the topmost bench waving Heitzmann's sweatstained velvet hat.

A policeman asked: "The machine opens, does it not, Herr Professor? Open it quickly before there is a riot."

Professor Baumeister said, "I don't know how."

"It looks simple enough," declared the other policeman, and he began to unfasten the catches, wrapping his hand in his handkerchief to protect it from the heat of the brass. "Wait!" ordered Professor Baumeister, but neither one waited; the first policeman went to the aid of the other, and together they lifted away one side of the machine and let it fall against the railing. The movable circuit card had not been allowed to swing back into place, and Gretchen's plump, naked legs protruded from the cavity beneath the chessboard. The first policeman seized them by the ankles and pulled her out until her half-open eyes stared at the bright sky. Doctor Eckardt bent over her and flexed her left arm at the elbow. "Rigor is beginning," he said. "She died of the heat, undoubtedly."

Lame Hans threw himself on her body weeping.

Such is the story of Lame Hans. The captain of police in his kindness has allowed me to push the machine to a position which permits Hans to reach the board through the bars of his cell, and he plays chess there all day long, moving first his own white pieces and then the black ones of the machine, and always losing. Sometimes when he is not quick enough to move the black queen I see her begin to rock and to slide herself, and the dials and the console lights to glow with impatience; and then Hans must reach out and take her to her new position at once. Do you not think that this is sad for Lame Hans? I have heard that many who have been twisted by the old wars have these psychokinetic abilities without knowing it; and Professor Baumeister, who is in the cell next to his, says that someday a technology may be founded on them.

UNICORN VARIATION

Roger Zelazny

A bizarrerie of fires, cunabulum of light, it moved with a deft, almost dainty deliberation, phasing into and out of existence like a storm-shot piece of evening; or perhaps the darkness between the flares was more akin to its truest nature—swirl of black ashes assembled in prancing cadence to the lowing note of desert wind down the arroyo behind buildings as empty yet filled as the pages of unread books or stillnesses between the notes of a song.

Gone again. Back again. Again.

Power, you said? Yes. It takes considerable force of identity to manifest before or after one's time. Or both.

As it faded and gained it also advanced, moving through the warm afternoon, its tracks erased by the wind. That is, on those occasions when there were tracks.

A reason. There should always be a reason. Or reasons.

It knew why it was there—but not why it was *there*, in that particular locale.

It anticipated learning this shortly, as it approached the desolation-bound line of the old street. However, it knew that the reason may also come before, or after. Yet again, the pull was there and the force of its being was such that it had to be close to something.

The buildings were worn and decayed and some of them fallen and all of them drafty and dusty and empty. Weeds grew among floorboards. Birds nested upon rafters. The droppings of wild things were everywhere, and it knew them all as they would have known it, were they to meet face to face.

It froze, for there had come the tiniest unanticipated sound from somewhere ahead and to the left. At that moment, it was again phasing into existence and it released its outline which faded as quickly as a rainbow in hell, that but the naked presence remained beyond subtraction.

Invisible, yet existing, strong, it moved again. The clue. The cue. Ahead. A gauche. Beyond the faded word SALOON on weathered board above. Through the swinging doors. (One of them pinned alop.)

Pause and assess.

Bar to the right, dusty. Cracked mirror behind it. Empty bottles. Broken bottles. Brass rail, black, encrusted. Tables to the left and rear. In various states of repair.

Man seated at the best of the lot. His back to the door. Levi's. Hiking boots. Faded blue shirt. Green backpack leaning against the wall to his left.

Before him, on the tabletop, is the faint, painted outline of a chessboard, stained, scratched, almost obliterated.

The drawer in which he had found the chessmen is still partly open.

He could no more have passed up a chess set without working out a problem or replaying one of his better games than he could have gone without breathing, circulating his blood or maintaining a relatively stable body temperature.

It moved nearer, and perhaps there were fresh prints in the dust behind it, but none noted them.

It, too, played chess.

It watched as the man replayed what had perhaps

been his finest game, from the world preliminaries of seven years past. He had blown up after that—surprised to have gotten even as far as he had—for he never could perform well under pressure. But he had always been proud of that one game, and he relived it as all sensitive beings do certain turning points in their lives. For perhaps twenty minutes, no one could have touched him. He had been shining and pure and hard and clear. He had felt like the best.

It took up a position across the board from him and stared. The man completed the game, smiling. Then he set up the board again, rose and fetched a can of beer from his pack. He popped the top.

When he returned, he discovered that White's King's Pawn had been advanced to K4. His brow furrowed. He turned his head, searching the bar, meeting his own puzzled gaze in the grimy mirror. He looked under the table. He took a drink of beer and seated himself.

He reached out and moved his Pawn to K4. A moment later, he saw White's King's Knight rise slowly into the air and drift forward to settle upon KB3. He stared for a long while into the emptiness across the table before he advanced his own Knight to his KB3.

White's Knight moved to take his Pawn. He dismissed the novelty of the situation and moved his Pawn to Q3. He all but forgot the absence of a tangible opponent as the White Knight dropped back to its KB3. He paused to take a sip of beer, but no sooner had he placed the can upon the tabletop than it rose again, passed across the board and was upended. A gurgling noise followed. Then the can fell to the floor, bouncing, ringing with an empty sound.

"I'm sorry," he said, rising and returning to his pack. "I'd have offered you one if I'd thought you were something that might like it."

He opened two more cans, returned with them, placed one near the far edge of the table, one at his own right hand.

"Thank you," came a soft, precise voice from a point beyond it.

The can was raised, tilted slightly, returned to the tabletop.

"My name is Martin," the man said.

"Call me Tlingel," said the other. "I had thought that perhaps your kind was extinct. I am pleased that you at least have survived to afford me this game."

"Huh?" Martin said. "We were all still around the last time that I looked—a couple of days ago."

"No matter. I can take care of that later," Tlingel replied. "I was misled by the appearance of this place."

"Oh. It's a ghost town. I backpack a lot."

"Not important. I am near the proper point in your career as a species. I can feel that much."

"I am afraid that I do not follow you."

"I am not at all certain that you would wish to. I assume that you intend to capture that pawn?"

"Perhaps. Yes, I do wish to. What are you talking about?"

The beer can rose. The invisible entity took another drink.

"Well," said Tlingel, "to put it simply, your—successors—grow anxious. Your place in the scheme of things being such an important one, I had sufficient power to come and check things out."

" 'Successors'? I do not understand."

"Have you seen any griffins recently?"

Martin chuckled.

"I've heard the stories," he said, "seen the photos of the one supposedly shot in the Rockies. A hoax, of course."

"Of course it must seem so. That is the way with mythical beasts."

"You're trying to say that it was real?"

"Certainly. Your world is in bad shape. When the last grizzly bear died recently, the way was opened for the griffins—just as the death of the last aepyornis brought in the yeti, the dodo the Loch Ness creature, the passenger pigeon the sasquatch, the blue whale the kraken, the American eagle the cockatrice—"

"You can't prove it by me."

"Have another drink."

Martin began to reach for the can, halted his hand and stared.

A creature approximately two inches in length, with a human face, a lion-like body and feathered wings was crouched next to the beer can.

"A mini-sphinx," the voice continued. "They came when you killed off the last smallpox virus."

"Are you trying to say that whenever a natural species dies out a mythical one takes its place?" he asked.

"In a word—yes. Now. It was not always so, but you have destroyed the mechanisms of evolution. The balance is now redressed by those others of us, from the morning land—we, who have never truly been endangered. We return, in our time."

"And you—whatever you are, Tlingel—you say that humanity is now endangered?"

"Very much so. But there is nothing that you can do about it, is there? Let us get on with the game."

The sphinx flew off. Martin took a sip of beer and captured the Pawn.

"Who," he asked then, "are to be our successors?"

"Modesty almost forbids," Tlingel replied. "In the case of a species as prominent as your own, it naturally has to be the loveliest, most intelligent, most important of us all."

"And what are you? Is there any way that I can have a look?"

"Well—yes. If I exert myself a trifle."

The beer can rose, was drained, fell to the floor. There followed a series of rapid rattling sounds retreating from the table. The air began to flicker over a large area opposite Martin, darkening within the glowing flamework. The outline continued to brighten, its interior growing jet black. The form moved, prancing about the saloon, multitudes of tiny, cloven hoofprints scoring and cracking the floorboards. With a final, near-blinding flash it came into full view and Martin gasped to behold it.

A black unicorn with mocking, yellow eyes sported before him, rising for a moment onto its hind legs to strike a heraldic pose. The fires flared about it a second longer, then vanished.

Martin had drawn back, raising one hand defensively.

"Regard me!" Tlingel announced. "Ancient symbol of wisdom, valor and beauty, I stand before you!"

"I thought your typical unicorn was white," Martin finally said.

"I am archetypical," Tlingel responded, dropping to all fours, "and possessed of virtues beyond the ordinary."

"Such as?"

"Let us continue our game."

"What about the fate of the human race? You said—"

". . .And save the small talk for later."

"I hardly consider the destruction of humanity to be small talk."

"And if you've any more beer. . ."

"All right," Martin said, retreating to his pack as the creature advanced, its eyes like a pair of pale suns. "There's some lager."

Something had gone out of the game. As Martin sat before the ebon horn on Tlingel's bowed head, like an insect about to be pinned, he realized that his playing was off. He had felt the pressure the moment he had seen the beast—and there was all that talk about an imminent doomsday. Any run-of-the-mill pessimist could say it without troubling him, but coming from a source as peculiar as this. . .

His earlier elation had fled. He was no longer in top form. And Tlingel was good. Very good. Martin found himself wondering whether he could manage a stalemate.

After a time, he saw that he could not and resigned.

The unicorn looked at him and smiled.

"You don't really play badly—for a human," it said.

"I've done a lot better."

"It is no shame to lose to me, mortal. Even among mythical creatures there are very few who can give a unicorn a good game."

"I am pleased that you were not wholly bored," Martin said. "Now will you tell me what you were talking about concerning the destruction of my species?"

"Oh, that," Tlingel replied. "In the morning land where those such as I dwell, I felt the possibility of your passing come like a gentle wind to my nostrils, with the promise of clearing the way for us—"

"How is it supposed to happen?"

Tlingel shrugged, horn writing on the air with a toss of the head.

"I really couldn't say. Premonitions are seldom specific. In fact, that is what I came to discover. I should have been about it already, but you diverted me with beer and good sport."

"Could you be wrong about this?"

"I doubt it. That is the other reason I am here."

"Please explain."

"Are there any beers left?"

"Two, I think."

"Please."

Martin rose and fetched them.

"Damn! The tab broke off this one," he said.

"Place it upon the table and hold it firmly."

"All right."

Tlingel's horn dipped forward quickly, piercing the can's top."

". . .Useful for all sorts of things," Tlingel observed, withdrawing it.

"The other reason you're here. . ." Martin prompted.

"It is just that I am special. I can do things that the others cannot."

"Such as?"

"Find your weak spot and influence events to exploit it, to—hasten matters. To turn the possibility into a probability, and then—"

"*You* are going to destroy us? Personally?"

"That is the wrong way to look at it. It is more like a game of chess. It is as much a matter of exploiting your opponent's weaknesses as of exercising your own strengths. If you had not already laid the groundwork I would be powerless. I can only influence that which already exists."

"So what will it be? World War III? An ecological disaster? A mutated disease?"

"I do not really know yet, so I wish you wouldn't ask me in that fashion. I repeat that at the moment I am only observing. I am only an agent—"

"It doesn't sound that way to me."

Tlingel was silent. Martin began gathering up the chessmen.

"Aren't you going to set up the board again?"

"To amuse my destroyer a little more? No thanks."

"That's hardly the way to look at it—"

"Besides, those are the last beers."

"Oh," Tlingel stared wistfully at the vanishing pieces, then remarked, "I would be willing to play you again without additional refreshment. . ."

"No thanks."

"You are angry."

"Wouldn't you be, if our situations were reversed?"

"You are anthropomorphizing."

"Well?"

"Oh, I suppose I would."

"You could give us a break, you know—at least, let us make our own mistakes."

"You've hardly done that yourself, though, with all the creatures my fellows have succeeded."

Martin reddened.

"Okay. You just scored one. But I don't have to like it."

"You are a good player. I know that. . ."

"Tlingel, if I were capable of playing at my best again, I think I could beat you."

The unicorn snorted two tiny wisps of smoke.

"Not *that* good," Tlingel said.

"I guess you'll never know."

"Do I detect a proposal?"

"Possibly. What's another game worth to you?"

Tlingel made a chuckling noise.

"Let me guess: You are going to say that if you beat me you want my promise not to lay my will upon the weakest link in mankind's existence and shatter it."

"Of course."

"And what do I get for winning?"

"The pleasure of the game. That's what you want, isn't it?"

"The terms sound a little lopsided."

"Not if you are going to win anyway. You keep insisting that you will."

"All right. Set up the board."

"There is something else that you have to know about me first."

"Yes?"

"I don't play well under pressure, and this game is going to be a terrific strain. You want my best game, don't you?"

"Yes, but I'm afraid I've no way of adjusting your own reactions to the play."

"I believe I could do that myself if I had more than the usual amount of time between moves."

"Agreed."

"I mean a lot of time."

"Just what do you have in mind?"

"I'll need time to get my mind off it, to relax, to come back to the positions as if they were only problems. . ."

"You mean to go away from here between moves?"

"Yes."

"All right. How long?"

"I don't know. A few weeks, maybe."

"Take a month. Consult your experts, put your computers onto it. It may make for a slightly more interesting game."

"I really didn't have that in mind."

"Then it's time that you're trying to buy."

"I can't deny that. On the other hand, I will need it."

"In that case, I have some terms. I'd like this place cleaned up, fixed up, more lively. It's a mess. I also want beer on tap."

"Okay. I'll see to that."

"Then I agree. Let's see who goes first."

Martin switched a black and a white pawn from hand to hand beneath the table. He raised his fists then and extended them. Tlingel leaned forward and tapped. The black horn's tip touched Martin's left hand.

"Well, it matches my sleek and glossy hide," the unicorn announced.

Martin smiled, setting up the white for himself, the black pieces for his opponent. As soon as he had finished, he pushed his Pawn to K4.

Tlingel's delicate, ebon hoof moved to advance the Black King's Pawn to K4.

"I take it that you want a month now, to consider your next move?"

Martin did not reply but moved his Knight to KB3. Tlingel immediately moved a Knight to QB3.

Martin took a swallow of beer and then moved his Bishop to N5. The unicorn moved the other Knight to B3. Martin immediately castled and Tlingel moved the Knight to take his Pawn.

"I think we'll make it," Martin said suddenly, "if you'll just let us alone. We do learn from our mistakes, in time."

"Mythical beings do not exactly exist in time. Your world is a special case."

"Don't you people ever make mistakes?"

"Whenever we do they're sort of poetic."

Martin snarled and advanced his Pawn to Q4. Tlingel immediately countered by moving the Knight to Q3.

"I've got to stop," Martin said, standing. "I'm getting mad, and it will affect my game."

"You will be going, then?"

"Yes."

He moved to fetch his pack.

"I will see you here in one month's time?"

"Yes."

"Very well."

The unicorn rose and stamped upon the floor and lights began to play across its dark coat. Suddenly, they blazed and shot outward in all directions like a silent explosion. A wave of blackness followed.

Martin found himself leaning against the wall, shaking. When he lowered his hand from his eyes, he saw that he was alone, save for the knights, the bishops, the kings, the queens, their castles and both the kings' men.

He went away.

Three days later Martin returned in a small truck, with a generator, lumber, windows, power tools, paint, stain, cleaning compounds, wax. He dusted and vacuumed and replaced rotten wood. He installed the windows. He polished the old brass until it shone. He stained and rubbed. He waxed the floors and buffed them. He plugged holes and washed glasses. He hauled all the trash away.

It took him the better part of a week to turn the old place from a wreck back into a saloon in appearance. Then he drove off, returned all of the equipment he had rented and bought a ticket for the Northwest.

The big, damp forest was another of his favorite places for hiking, for thinking. And he was seeking a complete change of scene, a total revision of outlook. Not that his next move did not seem obvious, standard even. Yet, something nagged. . .

He knew that it was more than just the game. Before
that he had been ready to get away again, to walk drow-
sing among shadows, breathing clean air.

Resting, his back against the bulging root of a giant
tree, he withdrew a small chess set from his pack, set it
up on a rock he'd moved into position nearby. A fine,
mist-like rain was settling, but the tree sheltered him, so
far. He reconstructed the opening through Tlingel's
withdrawal of the Knight to Q3. The simplest thing
would be to take the Knight with the Bishop. But he did
not move to do it.

He watched the board for a time, felt his eyelids
drooping, closed them and drowsed. It may only have
been for a few minutes. He was never certain afterwards.

Something aroused him. He did not know what. He
blinked several times and closed his eyes again. Then he
reopened them hurriedly.

In his nodded position, eyes directed downward, his
gaze was fixed upon an enormous pair of hairy, unshod
feet—the largest pair of feet that he had ever beheld.
They stood unmoving before him, pointed toward his
right.

Slowly—very slowly—he raised his eyes. Not very far,
as it turned out. The creature was only about four and
a half feet in height. As it was looking at the chessboard
rather than at him, he took the opportunity to study it.

It was unclothed but very hairy, with a dark brown
pelt, obviously masculine, possessed of low brow ridges,
deep-set eyes that matched its hair, heavy shoulders,
five-fingered hands that sported opposing thumbs.

It turned suddenly and regarded him, flashing a large
number of shining teeth.

"White's pawn should take the pawn," it said in a
soft, nasal voice.

"Huh? Come on," Martin said. "Bishop takes
knight."

"You want to give me black and play it that way? I'll
walk all over you."

Martin glanced again at its feet.

". . .Or give me white and let me take that pawn. I'll still do it."

"Take white," Martin said, straightening. "Let's see if you know what you're talking about." He reached for his pack. "Have a beer?"

"What's a beer?"

"A recreational aid. Wait a minute."

Before they had finished the six-pack, the sasquatch—whose name, he had learned, was Grend—had finished Martin. Grend had quickly entered a ferocious mid-game, backed him into a position of dwindling security and pushed him to the point where he had seen the end and resigned.

"That was one hell of a game," Martin declared, leaning back and considering the ape-like countenance before him.

"Yes, we Bigfeet are pretty good, if I do say it. It's our one big recreation, and we're so damned primitive we don't have much in the way of boards and chessmen. Most of the time, we just play it in our heads. There're not many can come close to us."

"How about unicorns?" Martin asked.

Grend nodded slowly.

"They're about the only ones can really give us a good game. A little dainty, but they're subtle. Awfully sure of themselves, though, I must say. Even when they're wrong. Haven't seen any since we left the morning land, of course. Too bad. Got any more of that beer left?"

"I'm afraid not. But listen, I'll be back this way in a month. I'll bring some more if you'll meet me here and play again."

"Martin, you've got a deal. Sorry. Didn't mean to step on your toes."

He cleaned the saloon again and brought in a keg of beer which he installed under the bar and packed with ice. He moved in some bar stools, chairs and tables which he had obtained at a Goodwill store. He hung red curtains. By then it was evening. He set up the board, ate a light meal, unrolled his sleeping bag behind the bar and camped there that night.

The following day passed quickly. Since Tlingel might show up at any time, he did not leave the vicinity, but took his meals there and sat about working chess problems. When it began to grow dark, he lit a number of oil lamps and candles.

He looked at his watch with increasing frequency. He began to pace. He couldn't have made a mistake. This was the proper day. He—

He heard a chuckle.

Turning about, he saw a black unicorn head floating in the air above the chessboard. As he watched, the rest of Tlingel's body materialized.

"Good evening, Martin." Tlingel turned away from the board. "The place looks a little better. Could use some music. . ."

Martin stepped behind the bar and switched on the transistor radio he had brought along. The sounds of a string quartet filled the air. Tlingel winced.

"Hardly in keeping with the atmosphere of the place."

He changed stations, located a Country & Western show.

"I think not," Tlingel said. "It loses something in transmission."

He turned it off.

"Have we a good supply of beverage?"

Martin drew a gallon stein of beer—the largest mug that he could locate, from a novelty store—and set it upon the bar. He filled a much smaller one for himself. He was determined to get the beast drunk if it were at all possible.

"Ah! Much better than those little cans," said Tlingel, whose muzzle dipped for but a moment. "Very good."

The mug was empty. Martin refilled it.

"Will you move it to the table for me?"

"Certainly."

"Have an interesting month?"

"I suppose I did."

"You've decided upon your next move?"

"Yes."

"Then let's get on with it."

Martin seated himself and captured the Pawn.

"Hm. Interesting."

Tlingel stared at the board for a long while, then raised a cloven hoof which parted in reaching for the piece.

"I'll just take that bishop with this little knight. Now I suppose you'll be wanting another month to make up your mind what to do next."

Tlingel leaned to the side and drained the mug.

"Let me consider it," Martin said, "while I get you a refill."

Martin sat and stared at the board through three more refills. Actually, he was not planning. He was waiting. His response to Grend had been Knight takes Bishop, and he had Grend's next move ready.

"Well?" Tlingel finally said. "What do you think?"

Martin took a small sip of beer.

"Almost ready," he said. "You hold your beer awfully well."

Tlingel laughed.

"A unicorn's horn is a detoxicant. It's possession is a universal remedy. I wait until I reach the warm glow stage, then I use my horn to burn off any excess and keep me right there."

"Oh," said Martin. "Neat trick, that."

". . .If you've had too much, just touch my horn for a moment and I'll put you back in business."

"No, thanks. That's all right. I'll just push this little pawn in front of the queen's rook two steps ahead."

"Really. . ." said Tlingel. "That's interesting. You know, what this place really needs is a piano—rinkytink, funky . . . Think you could manage it?"

"I don't play."

"Too bad."

"I suppose I could hire a piano player."

"No. I do not care to be seen by other humans."

"If he's really good, I suppose he could play blindfolded."

"Never mind."

"I'm sorry."

"You are also ingenious. I am certain that you will figure something out by next time."

Martin nodded.

"Also, didn't these old places used to have sawdust all over the floors?"

"I believe so."

"That would be nice."

"Check."

Tlingel searched the board frantically for a moment.

"Yes. I meant 'yes'. I said 'check'. It means 'yes' sometimes, too."

"Oh. Rather. Well, while we're here. . ."

Tlingel advanced the Pawn to Q3.

Martin stared. That was not what Grend had done. For a moment, he considered continuing on his own from here. He had tried to think of Grend as a coach up until this point. He had forced away the notion of crudely and crassly pitting one of them against the other. Until P-Q3. Then he recalled the game he had lost to the sasquatch.

"I'll draw the line here," he said, "and take my month."

"All right. Let's have another drink before we say good night. Okay?"

"Sure. Why not?"

They sat for a time and Tlingel told him of the morning land, of primeval forests and rolling plains, of high craggy mountains and purple seas, of magic and mythic beasts.

Martin shook his head.

"I can't quite see why you're so anxious to come here," he said, "with a place like that to call home."

Tlingel sighed.

"I suppose you'd call it keeping up with the griffins. It's the thing to do these days. Well. Till next month. . ."

Tlingel rose and turned away.

"I've got complete control now. Watch!"

The unicorn form faded, jerked out of shape, grew white, faded again, was gone, like an afterimage.

Martin moved to the bar and drew himself another mug. It was a shame to waste what was left. In the morning, he wished the unicorn were there again. Or at least the horn.

It was a gray day in the forest and he held an umbrella over the chessboard upon the rock. The droplets fell from the leaves and made dull, plopping noises as they struck the fabric. The board was set up again through Tlingel's P-Q3. Martin wondered whether Grend had remembered, had kept proper track of the days. . .

"Hello," came the nasal voice from somewhere behind him and to the left.

He turned to see Grend moving about the tree, stepping over the massive roots with massive feet.

"You remembered," Grend said. "How good! I trust you also remembered the beer?"

"I've lugged up a whole case. We can set up the bar right here."

"What's a bar?"

"Well, it's a place where people go to drink—in out of the rain—a bit dark, for atmosphere—and they sit up on stools before a big counter, or else at little tables—and they talk to each other—and sometimes there's music— and they drink."

"We're going to have all that here?"

"No. Just the dark and the drinks. Unless you count the rain as music. I was speaking figuratively."

"Oh. It does sound like a very good place to visit, though."

"Yes. If you will hold this umbrella over the board, I'll set up the best equivalent we can have here."

"All right. Say, this looks like a version of that game we played last time."

"It is. I got to wondering what would happen if it had gone this way rather than the way that it went."

"Hmm. Let me see. . ."

Martin removed four six-packs from his pack and opened the first.

"Here you go."

"Thanks."

Grend accepted the beer, squatted, passed the umbrella back to Martin.

"I'm still white?"

"Yeah."

"Pawn to King six."

"Really?"

"Yep."

"About the best thing for me to do would be to take this pawn with this one."

"I'd say. Then I'll just knock off your knight with this one."

"I guess I'll just pull this knight back to K2."

". . .And I'll take this one over to B3. May I have another beer?"

An hour and a quarter later, Martin resigned. The rain had let up and he had folded the umbrella.

"Another game?" Grend asked.

"Yes."

The afternoon wore on. The pressure was off. This one was just for fun. Martin tried wild combinations, seeing ahead with great clarity, as he had that one day. . .

"Stalemate," Grend announced much later. "That was a good one, though. You picked up considerably."

"I was more relaxed. Want another?"

"Maybe in a little while. Tell me more about bars now."

So he did. Finally, "How is all that beer affecting you?" he asked.

"I'm a bit dizzy. But that's all right. I'll still cream you the third game."

And he did.

"Not bad for a human, though. Not bad at all. You coming back next month?"

"Yes."

"Good. You'll bring more beer?"

"So long as my money holds out."

"Oh. Bring some plaster of paris then. I'll make you some nice footprints and you can take casts of them. I understand they're going for quite a bit."

"I'll remember that."

Martin lurched to his feet and collected the chess set.

"Till then."

"Ciao."

Martin dusted and polished again, moved in the player piano and scattered sawdust upon the floor. He installed a fresh keg. He hung some reproductions of period posters and some atrocious old paintings he had located in a junk shop. He placed cuspidors in strategic locations. When he was finished, he seated himself at the bar and opened a bottle of mineral water. He listened to the New Mexico wind moaning as it passed, to grains of sand striking against the windowpanes. He wondered whether the whole world would have that dry, mournful sound to it if Tlingel found a means for doing away with humanity, or—disturbing thought—whether the successors to his own kind might turn things into something resembling the mythical morning land.

This troubled him for a time. Then he went and set up the board through Black's P-Q3. When he turned back to clear the bar he saw a line of cloven hoofprints advancing across the sawdust.

"Good evening, Tlingel," he said. "What is your pleasure?"

Suddenly, the unicorn was there, without preliminary pyrotechnics. It moved to the bar and placed one hoof upon the brass rail.

"The usual."

As Martin drew the beer, Tlingel looked about.

"The place has improved, a bit."

"Glad you think so. Would you care for some music?"

"Yes."

Martin fumbled at the back of the piano, locating the switch for the small, battery-operated computer which controlled the pumping mechanism and substituted its own memory for rolls. The keyboard immediately came to life.

"Very good," Tlingel stated. "Have you found your move?"

"I have."

"Then let us be about it."

He refilled the unicorn's mug and moved it to the table, along with his own.

"Pawn to King six," he said, executing it.

"What?"

"Just that."

"Give me a minute. I want to study this."

"Take your time."

"I'll take the pawn," Tlingel said, after a long pause and another mug.

"Then I'll take this knight."

Later, "Knight to K2," Tlingel said.

"Knight to B3."

An extremely long pause ensued before Tlingel moved the Knight to N3.

The hell with asking Grend, Martin suddenly decided. He'd been through this part any number of times already. He moved his Knight to N5.

"Change the tune on that thing!" Tlingel snapped.

Martin rose and obliged.

"I don't like that one either. Find a better one or shut it off!"

After three more tries, Martin shut it off.

"And get me another beer!"

He refilled their mugs.

"All right."

Tlingel moved the Bishop to K2.

Keeping the unicorn from castling had to be the most important thing at the moment. So Martin moved his Queen to R5. Tlingel made a tiny, strangling noise, and when Martin looked up smoke was curling from the unicorn's nostrils.

"More beer?"

"If you please."

As he returned with it, he saw Tlingel move the Bishop to capture the Knight. There seemed no choice for him at that moment, but he studied the position for a long while anyhow.

Finally, "Bishop takes bishop," he said.

"Of course."

"How's the warm glow?"

Tlingel chuckled.

"You'll see."

The wind rose again, began to howl. The building creaked.

"Okay," Tlingel finally said, and moved the Queen to Q2.

Martin stared. What was he doing? So far, it had gone all right, but— He listened again to the wind and thought of the risk he was taking.

"That's all, folks," he said, leaning back in his chair. "Continued next month."

Tlingel sighed.

"Don't run off. Fetch me another. Let me tell you of my wanderings in your world this past month."

"Looking for weak links?"

"You're lousy with them. How do you stand it?"

"They're harder to strengthen than you might think. Any advice?"

"Get the beer."

They talked until the sky paled in the east, and Martin found himself taking surreptitious notes. His admiration for the unicorn's analytical abilities increased as the evening advanced.

When they finally rose, Tlingel staggered.

"You all right?"

"Forgot to detox, that's all. Just a second. Then I'll be fading."

"Wait!"

"Whazzat?"

"I could use one, too."

"Oh. Grab hold, then."

Tlingel's head descended and Martin took the tip of the horn between his fingertips. Immediately, a delicious, warm sensation flowed through him. He closed his eyes to enjoy it. His head cleared. An ache which had been growing within his frontal sinus vanished. The tiredness went out of his muscles. He opened his eyes again.

"Thank—"

Tlingel had vanished. He held out a handful of air.

"—you."

"Rael here is my friend," Grend stated. "He's a griffin."

"I'd noticed."

Martin nodded at the beaked, golden-winged creature.

"Pleased to meet you, Rael."

"The same," cried the other in a high-pitched voice. "Have you got the beer?"

"Why—uh—yes."

"I've been telling him about beer," Grend explained, half-apologetically. "He can have some of mine. He won't kibitz or anything like that."

"Sure. All right. Any friend of yours. . ."

"The beer!" Rael cried. "Bars!"

"He's not real bright," Grend whispered. "But he's good company. I'd appreciate your humoring him."

Martin opened the first six-pack and passed the griffin and the sasquatch a beer apiece. Rael immediately punctured the can with his beak, chugged it, belched and held out his claw.

"Beer!" he shrieked. "More beer!"

Martin handed him another.

"Say, you're still into that first game, aren't you?" Grend observed, studying the board. "Now, *that* is an interesting position."

Grend drank and studied the board.

"Good thing it's not raining," Martin commented.

"Oh, it will. Just wait a while."

"More beer!" Rael screamed.

Martin passed him another without looking.

"I'll move my pawn to N6," Grend said.

"You're kidding."

"Nope. Then you'll take that pawn with your bishop's pawn. Right?"

"Yes. . ."

Martin reached out and did it.

"Okay. Now I'll just swing this knight to Q5."

Martin took it with the Pawn.

Grend moved his Rook to K1.

"Check," he announced.

"Yes. That *is* the way to go," Martin observed.

Grend chuckled.

"I'm going to win this game another time," he said.

"I wouldn't put it past you."

"More beer?" Rael said softly.

"Sure."

As Martin passed him another, he noticed that the griffin was now leaning against the treetrunk.

After several minutes, Martin pushed his King to B1.

"Yeah, that's what I thought you'd do," Grend said.

"You know something?"

"What?"

"You play a lot like a unicorn."

"Hm."

Grend moved his Rook to R3.

Later, as the rain descended gently about them and Grend beat him again, Martin realized that a prolonged period of silence had prevailed. He glanced over at the griffin. Rael had tucked his head beneath his left wing, balanced upon one leg, leaned heavily against the tree and gone to sleep.

"I told you he wouldn't be much trouble," Grend remarked.

Two games later, the beer was gone, the shadows were lengthening and Rael was stirring.

"See you next month?"

"Yeah."

"You bring any plaster of paris?"

"Yes, I did."

"Come on, then. I know a good place pretty far from here. We don't want people beating about *these* bushes. Let's go make you some money."

"To buy beer?" Rael said, looking out from under his wing.

"Next month," Grend said.

"You ride?"

"I don't think you could carry both of us," said Grend, "and I'm not sure I'd want to right now if you could."

"Bye-bye then," Rael shrieked, and he leaped into the air, crashing into branches and treetrunks, finally breaking through the overhead cover and vanishing.

"There goes a really decent guy," said Grend. "He sees everything and he never forgets. Knows how everything works—in the woods, in the air—even in the water. Generous, too, whenever he has anything."

"Hm," Martin observed.

"Let's make tracks," Grend said.

"Pawn to N6? Really?" Tlingel said. "All right. The Bishop's pawn will just knock off the pawn."

Tlingel's eyes narrowed as Martin moved the Knight to Q5.

"At least this is an interesting game," the unicorn remarked. "Pawn takes Knight."

Martin moved the Rook.

"Check."

"Yes, it is. This next one is going to be a three flagon move. Kindly bring me the first."

Martin thought back as he watched Tlingel drink and ponder. He almost felt guilty for hitting it with a powerhouse like the sasquatch behind its back. He was convinced now that the unicorn was going to lose. In every variation of this game that he'd played with Black against Grend, he'd been beaten. Tlingel was very good, but the sasquatch was a wizard with not much else to do but mental chess. It was unfair. But it was not a matter of personal honor, he kept telling himself. He was playing to protect his species against a supernatural force which might well be able to precipitate World War III by some arcane mind-manipulation or magically induced computer foulup. He didn't dare give the creature a break.

"Flagon number two, please."

He brought it another. He studied it as it studied the board. It was beautiful, he realized for the first time. It was the loveliest living thing he had ever seen. Now that the pressure was on the verge of evaporating and he could regard it without the overlay of fear which had always been there in the past. he could pause to admire it. If something *had* to succeed the human race, he could think of worse choices. . .

"Number three now."

"Coming up."

Tlingel drained it and moved the King to B1.

Martin leaned forward immediately and pushed the Rook to R3.

Tlingel looked up, stared at him.

"Not bad."

Martin wanted to squirm. He was struck by the nobility of the creature. He wanted so badly to play and beat the unicorn on his own, fairly. Not this way.

Tlingel looked back at the board, then almost carelessly moved the Knight to K4.

"Go ahead. Or will it take you another month?"

Martin growled softly, advanced the Rook and captured the Knight.

"Of course."

Tlingel captured the Rook with the Pawn. This was not the way that the last variation with Grend had run. Still. . .

He moved his Rook to KB3. As he did, the wind seemed to commence a peculiar shrieking, above, amid, the ruined buildings.

"Check," he announced.

The hell with it! he decided. I'm good enough to manage my own endgame. Let's play this out.

He watched and waited and finally saw Tlingel move the King to N1.

He moved his Bishop to R6. Tlingel moved the Queen to K2. The shrieking came again, sounding nearer now. Martin took the Pawn with the Bishop.

The unicorn's head came up and it seemed to listen for a moment. Then Tlingel lowered it and captured the Bishop with the King.

Martin moved his Rook to KN3.

"Check."

Tlingel returned the King to B1.

Martin moved the Rook to KB3.

"Check."

Tlingel pushed the King to N2.

Martin moved the Rook back to KN3.

"Check."

Tlingel returned the King to B1, looked up and stared at him, showing teeth.

"Looks as if we've got a drawn game," the unicorn stated. "Care for another one?"

"Yes, but not for the fate of humanity."

"Forget it. I'd given up on that a long time ago. I decided that I wouldn't care to live here after all. I'm a little more discriminating than that.

"Except for this bar." Tlingel turned away as another shriek sounded just beyond the door, followed by strange voices. "What is that?"

"I don't know," Martin answered, rising.

The doors opened and a golden griffin entered.

"Martin!" it cried. "Beer! Beer!"

"Uh—Tlingel, this is Rael, and, and—"

Three more griffins followed him in. Then came Grend, and three others of his own kind.

"—and that one's Grend," Martin said lamely. "I don't know the others."

They all halted when they beheld the unicorn.

"Tlingel," one of the sasquatches said. "I thought you were still in the morning land."

"I still am, in a way. Martin, how is it that you are acquainted with my former countrymen?"

"Well—uh—Grend here is my chess coach."

"Aha! I begin to understand."

"I am not sure that you really do. But let me get everyone a drink first."

Martin turned on the piano and set everyone up.

"How did you find this place?" he asked Grend as he was doing it. "And how did you get here?"

"Well. . ." Grend looked embarrassed. "Rael followed you back."

"Followed a jet?"

"Griffins are supernaturally fast."

"Oh."

"Anyway, he told his relatives and some of my folks

about it. When we saw that the griffins were determined to visit you, we decided that we had better come along to keep them out of trouble. They brought us."

"I—see. Interesting. . ."

"No wonder you played like a unicorn, that one game with all the variations."

"Uh—yes."

Martin turned away, moved to the end of the bar.

"Welcome, all of you," he said. "I have a small announcement. Tlingel, awhile back you had a number of observations concerning possible ecological and urban disasters and lesser dangers. Also, some ideas as to possible safeguards against some of them."

"I recall," said the unicorn.

"I passed them along to a friend of mine in Washington who used to be a member of my old chess club. I told him that the work was not entirely my own."

"I should hope so."

"He has since suggested that I turn whatever group was involved into a think tank. He will then see about paying something for its efforts."

"I didn't come here to save the world," Tlingel said.

"No, but you've been very helpful. And Grend tells me that the griffins, even if their vocabulary is a bit limited, know almost all that there is to know about ecology."

"That is probably true."

"Since they have inherited a part of the Earth, it would be to their benefit as well to help preserve the place. Inasmuch as this many of us are already here, I can save myself some travel and suggest right now that we find a meeting place—say here, once a month—and that you let me have your unique viewpoints. You must know more about how species become extinct than anyone else in the business."

"Of course," said Grend, waving his mug, "but we really should ask the yeti, also. I'll do it, if you'd like. Is that stuff coming out of the big box music?"

"Yes."

"I like it. If we do this think tank thing, you'll make enough to keep this place going?"

"I'll buy the whole town."

Grend conversed in quick gutturals with the griffins, who shrieked back at him.

"You've got a think tank," he said, "and they want more beer."

Martin turned toward Tlingel.

"They were your observations. What do you think?"

"It may be amusing," said the unicorn, "to stop by occasionally." Then, "So much for saving the world. Did you say you wanted another game?"

"I've nothing to lose."

Grend took over the tending of the bar while Tlingel and Martin returned to the table.

He beat the unicorn in thirty-one moves and touched the extended horn.

The piano keys went up and down. Tiny sphinxes buzzed about the bar, drinking the spillage.

THE IMMORTAL GAME

Poul Anderson

The first trumpet sounded far and clear and brazen cold, and Rogard the Bishop stirred to wakefulness with it. Lifting his eyes, he looked through the suddenly rustling, murmuring line of soldiers, out across the broad plain of Cinnabar and the frontier, and over to the realm of LEUKAS.

Away there, across the somehow unreal red-and-black distances of the steppe, he saw sunlight flash on armor and caught the remote wild flutter of lifted banners. *So it is war,* he thought. *So we must fight again.*

Again? He pulled his mind from the frightening dimness of that word. Had they ever fought before?

On his left, Sir Ocher laughed aloud and clanged down the vizard on his gay young face. It gave him a strange, inhuman look, he was suddenly a featureless thing of shining metal and nodding plumes, and the steel echoed in his voice: "Ha, a fight! Praise God, Bishop, for I had begun to fear I would rust here forever."

Slowly, Rogard's mind brought forth wonder. "Were you sitting and thinking—before now?" he asked.

"Why—" Sudden puzzlement in the reckless tones: "I think I was. . . . Was I?" Fear turning into defiance: "Who cares? I've got some LEUKANS to kill!" Ocher reared in his horse till the great metallic wings thundered.

On Rogard's right, Flambard the King stood, tall in crown and robes. He lifted an arm to shade his eyes against the blazing sunlight. "They are sending DIOMES, the royal guardsman, first," he murmured. "A good man." The coolness of his tone was not matched by the other hand, its nervous plucking at his beard.

Rogard turned back, facing over the lines of Cinnabar to the frontier. DIOMES, the LEUKAN King's own soldier, was running. The long spear flashed in his hand, his shield and helmet threw back the relentless light in a furious dazzle, and Rogard thought he could hear the clashing of iron. Then that noise was drowned in the trumpets and drums and yells from the ranks of Cinnabar, and he had only his eyes.

DIOMES leaped two squares before coming to a halt on the frontier. He stopped then, stamping and thrusting against the Barrier which suddenly held him, and cried challenge. A muttering rose among the cuirassed soldiers of Cinnabar, and spears lifted before the flowing banners.

King Flambard's voice was shrill as he leaned forward and touched his own guardsman with his scepter. "Go, Carlon! Go to stop him!"

"Aye, sire," Carlon's stocky form bowed, and then he wheeled about and ran, holding his spear aloft, until he reached the frontier. Now he and DIOMES stood face to face, snarling at each other across the Barrier, and for a sick moment Rogard wondered what those two had done, once in an evil and forgotten year, that there should be such hate between them.

"Let me go, sire!" Ocher's voice rang eerily from the slit-eyed mask of his helmet. The winged horse stamped on the hard red ground, and the long lance swept a flashing arc. "Let me go next."

"No, no, Sir Ocher." It was a woman's voice. "Not yet. There'll be enough for you and me to do, later in this day."

Looking beyond Flambard, the Bishop saw his

Queen, Evyan the Fair, and there was something within
him which stumbled and broke into fire. Very tall and
lovely was the gray-eyed Queen of Cinnabar, where she
stood in armor and looked out at the growing battle.
Her sun-browned young face was coifed in steel, but one
rebellious lock blew forth in the wind, and she brushed
at it with a gauntleted hand while the other drew her
sword snaking from its sheath. "Now may God
strengthen our arms," she said, and her voice was low
and sweet. Rogard drew his cope tighter about him and
turned his mitered head away with a sigh. But there was
a bitter envy in him for Columbard, the Queen's Bishop
of Cinnabar.

Drums thumped from the LEUKAN ranks, and another
soldier ran forth. Rogard sucked his breath hissingly in,
for this man came till he stood on DIOMES' right. And the
newcomer's face was sharp and pale with fear. There
was no Barrier between him and Carlon.

"To his death," muttered Flambard between his
teeth. "They sent that fellow to his death."

Carlon snarled and advanced on the LEUKAN. He had
little choice—if he waited, he would be slain, and his
King had not commanded him to wait. He leaped, his
spear gleamed, and the LEUKAN soldier toppled and lay
emptily sprawled in the black square.

"First blood!" cried Evyan, lifting her sword and
hurling sunbeams from it. "First blood for us!"

Aye, so, thought Rogard bleakly, *But King*
MIKILLATI *had a reason for sacrificing that man. Maybe
we should have let Carlon die. Carlon the bold, Carlon the
strong, Carlon the lover of laughter. Maybe we should
have let him die.*

And now the Barrier was down for Bishop ASATOR of
LEUKAS, and he came gliding down the red squares, high
and cold in his glistening white robes, until he stood on
the frontier. Rogard thought he could see ASATOR's eyes
as they swept over Cinnabar. The LEUKAN Bishop was
poised to rush in with his great mace should Flambard,

for safety, seek to change with Earl Ferric as the Law permitted.

Law?

There was no time to wonder what the Law was, or why it must be obeyed, or what had gone before this moment of battle. Queen Evyan had turned and shouted to the soldier Raddic, guardsman of her own Knight Sir Cupran: "Go! Halt him!" And Raddic cast her his own look of love, and ran, ponderous in his mail, up to the frontier. There he and ASATOR stood, no Barrier between them if either used a flanking move.

Good! Oh, good, my Queen! thought Rogard wildly. For even if ASATOR did not withdraw, but slew Raddic, he would be in Raddic's square, and his threat would be against a wall of spears. *He will retreat, he will retreat—*

Iron roared as ASATOR'S mace crashed through helm and skull and felled Raddic the guardsman.

Evyan screamed, once only. "And I sent him! I sent him!" Then she began to run.

"Lady!" Rogard hurled himself against the Barrier. He could not move, he was chained here in his square, locked and barred by a Law he did not understand, while his lady ran toward death. "O Evyan, Evyan!"

Straight as a flying javelin ran the Queen of Cinnabar. Turning, straining after her, Rogard saw her leap the frontier and come to a halt by the Barrier which marked the left-hand bound of the kingdoms, beyond which lay only dimness to the frightful edge of the world. There she wheeled to face the dismayed ranks of LEUKAS, and her cry drifted back like the shriek of a stooping hawk: "MIKILLATI! Defend yourself!"

The thunder-crack of cheering from Cinnabar drowned all answer, but Rogard saw, at the very limits of his sight, how hastily King MIKILLATI stepped from the line of her attack, into the stronghold of Bishop ASATOR . Now, thought Rogard fiercely, now the white-robed ruler could never seek shelter from one of his Earls. Evyan had stolen his greatest shield.

"Hola, my Queen!" With a sob of laughter, Ocher struck spurs into his horse. Wings threshed, blowing Rogard's cope about him, as the Knight hurtled over the head of his own guardsman and came to rest two squares in front of the Bishop. Rogard fought down his own anger; he had wanted to be the one to follow Evyan. But Ocher was a better choice.

Oh, much better! Rogard gasped as his flittering eyes took in the broad battlefield. In the next leap, Ocher could cut down DIOMES, and then between them he and Evyan could trap MIKILLATI!

Briefly, that puzzlement nagged at the Bishop. Why should men die to catch someone else's King? What was there in the Law that said Kings should strive for mastery of the world and—

"Guard yourself, Queen!" Sir MERKON, King's Knight of LEUKAS, sprang in a move like Ocher's. Rogard's breath rattled in his throat with bitterness, and he thought there must be tears in Evyan's bright eyes. Slowly, then, the Queen withdrew two squares along the edge, until she stood in front of Earl Ferric's guardsman. It was still a good place to attack from, but not what the other had been.

BOAN, guardsman of the LEUKAN Queen DOLORA, moved one square forward, so that he protected great DIOMES from Ocher. Ocher snarled and sprang in front of Evyan, so that he stood between her and the frontier: clearing the way for her, and throwing his own protection over Carlon.

MERKON jumped likewise, landing to face Ocher with the frontier between them. Rogard clenched his mace and vision blurred for him; the LEUKANS were closing in on Evyan.

"Ulfar!" cried the King's Bishop. "Ulfar, can you help her?"

The stout old yeoman who was guardsman of the Queen's Bishop nodded wordlessly and ran one square forward. His spear menaced Bishop ASATOR, who growled at him—no Barrier between those two now!

MERKON of LEUKAS made another soaring leap, landing three squares in front of Rogard. "Guard yourself!" the voice belled from his faceless helmet. "Guard yourself, O Queen!"

No time now to let Ulfar slay ASATOR. Evyan's great eyes looked wildly about her; then, with swift decision, she stepped between MERKON and Ocher. Oh, a lovely move! Out of the fury in his breast, Rogard laughed.

The guardsman of the LEUKAN King's Knight clanked two squares ahead, lifting his spear against Ocher. It must have taken boldness thus to stand before Evyan herself; but the Queen of Cinnabar saw that if she cut him down, the Queen of LEUKAS could slay her. "Get free, Ocher!" she cried. "Get away!" Ocher cursed and leaped from danger, landing in front of Rogard's guardsman.

The King's Bishop bit his lip and tried to halt the trembling in his limbs. How the sun blazed! Its light was a cataract of dry white fire over the barren red and black squares. It hung immobile, enormous in the vague sky, and men gasped in their armor. The noise of bugles and iron, hoofs and wings and stamping feet, was loud under the small wind that blew across the world. There had never been anything but this meaningless war, there would never be aught else, and when Rogard tried to think beyond the moment when the fight had begun, or the moment when it would end, there was only an abyss of darkness.

Earl RAFAEON of LEUKAS took one ponderous step toward his King, a towering figure of iron readying for combat. Evyan whooped. "Ulfar!" she yelled. "Ulfar, your chance!"

Columbard's guardsman laughed aloud. Raising his spear, he stepped over into the square held by ASATOR. The white-robed Bishop lifted his mace, futile and feeble, and then he rolled in the dust at Ulfar's feet. The men of Cinnabar howled and clanged sword on shield.

Rogard held aloof from triumph. ASATOR, he thought grimly, had been expendable anyway. King MIKILLATI had something else in mind.

It was like a blow when he saw Earl RAFAEON'S guardsman run forward two squares and shout to Evyan to guard herself. Raging, the Queen of Cinnabar withdrew a square to her rearward. Rogard saw sickly how unprotected King Flambard was now, the soldiers scattered over the field and the hosts of LEUKAS marshaling. But Queen DOLORA, he thought with a wild clutching of hope, Queen DOLORA, her tall cold beauty was just as open to a strong attack.

The soldier who had driven Evyan back took a leap across the frontier. "Guard yourself, O Queen!" he cried again. He was a small, hard-bitten, unkempt warrior in dusty helm and corselet. Evyan cursed, a bouncing soldierly oath, and moved one square forward to put a Barrier between her and him. He grinned impudently in his beard.

It is ill for us, it is a bootless and evil day. Rogard tried once more to get out of his square and go to Evyan's aid, but his will would not carry him. The Barrier held, invisible and uncrossable, and the Law held, the cruel and senseless Law which said a man must stand by and watch his lady be slain, and he railed at the bitterness of it and lapsed into a gray waiting.

Trumpets lifted brazen throats, drums boomed, and Queen DOLORA of LEUKAS stalked forth into battle. She came high and white and icily fair, her face chiseled and immobile in its haughtiness under the crowned helmet, and stood two squares in front of her husband, looming over Carlon. Behind her, her own Bishop SORKAS poised in his stronghold, hefting his mace in armored hands. Carlon of Cinnabar spat at DOLORA's feet, and she looked at him from cool blue eyes and then looked away. The hot dry wind did not ruffle her long pale hair; she was like a statue, standing there and waiting.

"Ocher," said Evyan softly, "out of my way."

"I like not retreat, my lady," he answered in a thin tone.

"Nor I," said Evyan. "But I must have an escape route open. We will fight again."

Slowly, Ocher withdrew, back to his own home. Evyan chuckled once, and a wry grin twisted her young face.

Rogard was looking at her so tautly that he did not see what was happening until a great shout of iron slammed his head around. Then he saw Bishop SORKAS, standing in Carlon's square with a bloodied mace in his hands, and Carlon lay dead at his feet.

Carlon, your hands are empty, life has slipped from them and there is an unending darkness risen in you who loved the world. Goodnight, my Carlon, goodnight.

"Madame—" Bishop SORKAS spoke quietly, bowing a little, and there was a smile on his crafty face. "I regret, madame, that—ah—"

"Yes. I must leave you." Evyan shook her head, as if she had been struck, and moved a square backwards and sideways. Then, turning, she threw the glance of an eagle down the black squares to LEUKAS' Earl ARACLES. He looked away nervously, as if he would crouch behind the three soldiers who warded him. Evyan drew a deep breath sobbing into her lungs.

Sir THEUTAS, DOLORA's Knight, sprang from his stronghold, to place himself between Evyan and the Earl. Rogard wondered dully if he meant to kill Ulfar the soldier; he could do it now. Ulfar looked at the Knight who sat crouched, and hefted his spear and waited for his own weird.

"Rogard!"

The Bishop leaped, and for a moment there was fire-streaked darkness before his eyes.

"Rogard, to me! To me, and help sweep them from the world!"

Evyan's voice.

She stood in her scarred and dinted armor, holding

her sword aloft, and on that smitten field she was laughing with a new-born hope. Rogard could not shout his reply. There were no words. But he raised his mace and ran.

The black squares slid beneath his feet, footfalls pounding, jarring his teeth, muscles stretching with a resurgent glory and all the world singing. At the frontier, he stopped, knowing it was Evyan's will though he could not have said how he knew. Then he faced about, and with clearing eyes looked back over that field of iron and ruin. Save for one soldier, Cinnabar was now cleared of LEUKAN forces, Evyan was safe, a counterblow was readying like the first whistle of hurricane. Before him were the proud banners of LEUKAS—now to throw them into the dust! Now to ride with Evyan into the home of MIKILLATI!

"Go to it, sir," rumbled Ulfar, standing on the Bishop's right and looking boldly at the white Knight who could slay him. "Give 'em hell from us."

Wings beat in the sky, and THEUTAS soared down to land on Rogards' left. In the hot light, the blued metal of his armor was like running water. His horse snorted, curveting and flapping its wings; he sat it easily, the lance swaying in his grasp, the blank helmet turned to Flambard. One more such leap, reckoned Rogard wildly, and he would be able to assail the King of Cinnabar. Or—no—a single spring from here and he would spit Evyan on his lance.

And there is a Barrier between us!

"Watch yourself, Queen!" The arrogant LEUKAN voice boomed hollow out of the steel mask.

"Indeed I will, Sir Knight!" There was only laughter in Evyan's tone. Lightly, then, she sped up the row of black squares. She brushed by Rogard, smiling at him as she ran, and he tried to smile back but his face was stiffened. Evyan, Evyan, she was plunging alone into her enemy's homeland!

Iron belled and clamored. The white guardsman in

her path toppled and sank at her feet. One fist lifted strengthlessly, and a dying shrillness was in the dust: "Curse you, curse you, MIKILLATI, curse you for a stupid fool, leaving me here to be slain—no, no, no—"

Evyan bestrode the body and laughed again in the very face of Earl ARACLES. He cowered back, licking his lips—he could not move against her, but she could annihilate him in one more step. Beside Rogard, Ulfar whooped, and the trumpets of Cinnabar howled in the rear.

Now the great attack was launched! Rogard cast a fleeting glance at Bishop SORKAS. The lean white-coped form was gliding forth, mace swinging loose in one hand, and there was a little sleepy smile on the pale face. No dismay—? SORKAS halted, facing Rogard, and smiled a little wider, skinning his teeth without humor. "You can kill me if you wish," he said softly. "But do you?"

For a moment Rogard wavered. To smash that head—!

"Rogard! Rogard, to me!"

Evyan's cry jerked the King's Bishop around. He saw now what her plan was, and it dazzled him so that he forgot all else. LEUKAS *is ours!*

Swiftly he ran. DIOMES and BOAN howled at him as he went between them, brushing impotent spears against the Barriers. He passed Queen DOLORA, and her lovely face was as if cast in steel, and her eyes followed him as he charged over the plain of LEUKAS. Then there was no time for thinking, Earl RAFAEON loomed before him, and he jumped the last boundary into the enemy's heartland.

The Earl lifted a meaningless ax. The Law read death for him, and Rogard brushed aside the feeble stroke. The blow of his mace shocked in his own body, slamming his jaws together. RAFAEON crumpled, falling slowly, his armor loud as he struck the ground. Briefly, his fingers clawed at the iron-hard black earth, and then he lay still.

They have slain Raddic and Carlon—we have three

guardsmen, a Bishop, and an Earl—Now we need only be butchers! Evyan, Evyan, warrior Queen, this is your victory!

DIOMES of LEUKAS roared and jumped across the frontier. Futile, futile, he was doomed to darkness. Evyan's lithe form moved up against ARACLES, her sword flamed and the Earl crashed at her feet. Her voice was another leaping brand: "Defend yourself, King!"

Turning, Rogard grew aware that MIKILLATI himself had been right beside him. There was a Barrier between the two men—but MIKILLATI had to retreat from Evyan, and he took one step foreward and sideways. Peering into his face, Rogard felt a sudden coldness. There was no defeat there, it was craft and knowledge and an unbending steel will—*what was LEUKAS planning?*

Evyan tossed her head, and the wind fluttered the lock of hair like a rebel banner. "We have them, Rogard!" she cried.

Far and faint, through the noise and confusion of battle, Cinnabar's bugles sounded the command of her King. Peering into the haze, Rogard saw that Flambard was taking precautions. Sir THEUTAS was still a menace, where he stood beside SORKAS. Sir Cupran of Cinnabar flew heavily over to land in front of the Queen's Earl's guardsman, covering the route THEUTAS must follow to endanger Flambard.

Wise, but—Rogard looked again at MIKILLATI's chill white face, and it was as if a breath of cold blew through him. Suddenly he wondered why they fought. For victory, yes, for mastery over the world—but when the battle had been won, what then?

He couldn't think past that moment. His mind recoiled in horror he could not name. In that instant he knew icily that this was not the first war in the world, there had been others before, and there would be others again. *Victory is death.*

But Evyan, glorious Evyan, she could not die. She would reign over all the world and—

Steel blazed in Cinnabar. MERKON of LEUKAS came surging forth, one tigerish leap which brought him down on Ocher's guardsman. The soldier screamed, once, as he fell under the trampling, tearing hoofs, but it was lost in the shout of the LEUKAN Knight: "Defend yourself, Flambard! Defend yourself!"

Rogard gasped. It was like a blow in the belly. He had stood triumphant over the world, and now all in one swoop it was brought toppling about him. THEUTAS shook his lance, SORKAS his mace, DIOMES raised a bull's bellow—somehow, incredibly somehow, the warriors of LEUKAS had entered Cinnabar and were thundering at the King's own citadel.

"No, no—" Looking down the long empty row of squares, Rogard saw that Evyan was weeping. He wanted to run to her, hold her close and shield her against the falling world, but the Barriers were around him. He could not stir from his square, he could only watch.

Flambard cursed lividly and retreated into his Queen's home. His men gave a shout and clashed their arms—there was still a chance!

No, not while the Law bound men, thought Rogard, not while the Barriers held. Victory was ashen, and victory and defeat alike were darkness.

Beyond her thinly smiling husband, Queen DOLORA swept forward. Evyan cried out as the tall white woman halted before Rogard's terrified guardsman, turned to face Flambard where he crouched, and called to him: "Defend yourself, King!"

"No—no—you fool!" Rogard reached out, trying to break the Barrier, clawing at MIKILLATI. "Can't you see, none of us can win, it's death for us all if the war ends. Call her back!"

MIKILLATI ignored him. He seemed to be waiting.

And Ocher of Cinnabar raised a huge shout of laughter. It belled over the plain, dancing joyous mirth, and men lifted weary heads and turned to the young

Knight where he sat in his own stronghold, for there was
youth and triumph and glory in his laughing. Swiftly,
then, a blur of steel, he sprang, and his winged horse
rushed out of the sky on DOLORA herself. She turned to
meet him, lifting her sword, and he knocked it from her
hand and stabbed with his own lance. Slowly, too
haughty to scream, the white Queen sank under his
horse's hoofs.

And MIKILLATI smiled.

*"I see," nodded the visitor. "Individual computers,
each controlling its own robot piece by a tight beam,
and all the computers on a given side linked to form a
sort of group-mind constrained to obey the rules of
chess and make the best possible moves. Very nice. And
it's a pretty cute notion of yours, making the robots
look like medieval armies." His glance studied the tiny
figures where they moved on the oversized board under
one glaring floodlight.*

*"Oh, that's pure frippery," said the scientist. "This
is really a serious research project in multiple
computer-linkages. By letting them play game after
game, I'm getting some valuable data."*

*"It's a lovely set-up," said the visitor admiringly.
"Do you realize that in this particular contest the two
sides are reproducing one of the great classic games?"*

"Why, no. Is that a fact?"

*"Yes. It was a match between Anderssen and
Kieseritsky, back in—I forget the year, but it was quite
some time ago. Chess books often refer to it as the Immortal Game. . . . So your computers must share many
of the properties of a human brain."*

*"Well, they're complex things, all right," admitted
the scientist. "Not all their characteristics are known
yet. Sometimes my chessmen surprise even me."*

*"Hm." The visitor stooped over the board. "Notice
how they're jumping around inside their squares, waving their arms, batting at each other with their weap-*

*ons?" He paused, then murmured slowly: "I wonder—
I wonder if your computers may not have consciousness. If they might not have—minds."*

"Don't get fantastic," snorted the scientist.

*"But how do you know?" persisted the visitor.
"Look, your feedback arrangement is closely
analogous to a human nervous system. How do you
know that your individual computers, even if they are
constrained by the group linkage, don't have individual
personalities? How do you know that their electronic
senses don't interpret the game as, oh, as an interplay
of free will and necessity; how do you know they don't
receive the data of the moves as their own equivalent of
blood, sweat, and tears?" He shuddered a little.*

*"Nonsense," grunted the scientist. "They're only ro-
bots. Now—Hey! Look there! Look at that move!"*

Bishop SORKAS took one step ahead, into the black
square adjoining Flambard's. He bowed and smiled.
"The war is ended," he said.

Slowly, very slowly, Flambard looked about him.
SORKAS, MERKON, THEUTAS, they were crouched to leap
on him wherever he turned; his own men raged helpless
against the Barriers; there was no place for him to go.

He bowed his head. "I surrender." he whispered.

Rogard looked across the red and black to Evyan.
Their eyes met, and they stretched out their arms to each
other.

*"Checkmate," said the scientist. "That game's
over."*

*He crossed the room to the switchboard and turned
off the computers.*

MIDNIGHT BY THE MORPHY WATCH

Fritz Leiber

Being World's Chess Champion (crowned or un-crowned), puts a more deadly and maddening strain on a man even than being President of the United States. We have a prime example enthroned right now. For more than ten years the present champion was clearly the greatest chess player in the world, but during that time he exhibited such willful and seemingly self-destructive behavior—refusing to enter crucial tournaments, quitting them for crankish reasons while holding a commanding lead, entertaining what many called a paranoid delusion that the whole world was plotting to keep him from reaching the top—that many informed experts wrote him off as a contender for the highest honors. Even his staunchest supporters experienced agonizing doubts—until he finally silenced his foes and supremely satisfied his friends by decisively winning the crucial and ultimate match on a fantastic polar island.

Even minor players bitten by the world's-championship bug—or the fantasy of it—experience a bit of that terrible strain, occasionally in very strange and even eerie fashion. . .

* * *

Stirf Ritter-Rebil was indulging in one of his numerous creative avocations—wandering at random through his beloved downtown San Francisco with its sometimes dizzily slanting sidewalks, its elusive narrow courts and alleys, and its kaleidescope of ever-changing store and restaurant-fronts amongst the ones that persist as landmarks. To divert his gaze there were interesting almond and black faces among the paler ones. There was the dangerous surge of traffic threatening to invade the humpy sidewalks.

The sky was a careless silvery gray, like an expensive whore's mink coat covering bizarre garb or nakedness. There were even wisps of fog, that Bay Area benizon. There were bankers and hippies, con men and corporation men, queers of all varieties, beggars and sports, murderers and saints (at least in Ritter's freewheeling imagination). And there were certainly alluring girls aplenty in an astounding variety of packages—and pretty girls are the essential spice in any really tasty ragout of people. In fact there may well have been Martians and time travelers.

Ritter's ramble had taken on an even more dreamlike, whimsical and unpredictable quality than usual—with an unflagging anticipation of mystery, surprise, and erotic or diamond-studded adventure around the very next corner.

He frequently thought of himself by his middle name, Ritter, because he was a sporadically ardent chess player now in the midst of a sporad. In German "Ritter" means "knight," yet Germans do not call a knight a Ritter, but a springer, or jumper (for its crookedly hopping move), a matter for inexhaustible philological, historical, and socioracial speculation. Ritter was also a deeply devoted student of the history of chess, both in its serious and anecdotal aspects.

He was a tall, white-haired man, rather thin, saved from the look of mere age by ravaged handsomeness, an altogether youthful though worldly and sympathetically

cynical curiosity in his gaze (when he wasn't day-
dreaming), and a definitely though unobtrusively theatrical carriage.

He was more daydreamingly lost than usual on this
particular ramble, though vividly aware of all sorts of
floating, freakish, beautiful and grotesque novelties
about him. Later he recollected that he must have been
fairly near Portsmouth Square and not terribly far from
the intersection of California and Montgomery. At all
events, he was fascinated looking into the display window of a secondhand store he'd never recalled seeing
before. It must be a new place, for he knew all the stores
in the area, yet it had the dust and dinginess of an *old*
place—its owner must have moved in without re-
furbishing the premises or even cleaning them up. And
it had a delightful range of items for sale, from genuine
antiques to mod facsimiles of same. He noted in his first
scanning glance, and with growing delight, a Civil War
saber, a standard promotional replica of the starship *En-
terprise*, a brand-new deck of tarots, an authentic
shrunken head like a black globule of detritus from a
giant's nostril, some fancy roach-clips, a silver
lusterware creamer, a Sony tape recorder, a last year's
whiskey jug in the form of a cable car, a scatter of Gene
McCarthy and Nixon buttons, a single brass Lucas
"King of the Road" headlamp from a Silver Ghost
Rolls Royce, an electric toothbrush, a 1920's radio, a
last month's copy of the *Phoenix*, and three dime-a-
dozen plastic chess sets.

And then, suddenly, all these were wiped from his
mind. Unnoticed were the distant foghorns, the com-
plaining prowl of slowed traffic, the shards of human
speech behind him mosaicked with the singsong chatter
of Chinatown, the reflection in the plate glass of a girl in
a grandmother dress selling flowers, and of opening umbrellas as drops of rain began to sprinkle from the mist.
For every atom of Stirf Ritter-Rebil's awareness was

burningly concentrated on a small figure seeking anonymity among the randomly set-out chessmen of one of the plastic sets. It was a squat, tarnished silver chess pawn in the form of a barbarian warrior. Ritter knew it was a chess pawn—and what's more, he knew to what fabulous historic set it belonged, because he had seen one of its mates in a rare police photograph given him by a Portuguese chess-playing acquaintance. He knew that he had quite without warning arrived at a once-in-a-lifetime experience.

Heart pounding but face a suave mask, he drifted into the store's interior. In situations like this it was all-essential not to let the seller know what you were interested in or even that you were interested at all.

The shadowy interior of the place lived up to its display window. There was the same piquant clutter of dusty memorables and among them several glass cases housing presumably choicer items, behind one of which stood a gaunt yet stocky elderly man whom Ritter sensed was the proprietor, but pretended not even to notice.

But his mind was so concentrated on the tarnished silver pawn he *must* possess that it was a stupefying surprise when his automatically flitting gaze stopped at a second even greater once-in-a-lifetime item in the glass case behind which the proprietor stood. It was a dingy, old-fashioned gold pocket watch with the hours not in Roman numerals as they should have been in so venerable a timepiece, but in the form of dull gold and silver chess pieces as depicted in game-diagrams. Attached to the watch by a bit of thread was a slim, hexagonal gold key.

Ritter's mind almost froze with excitement. Here was the big brother of the skulking barbarian pawn. Here, its true value almost certainly unknown to its owner, was one of the supreme rarities of the world of chess-memorabilia. Here was no less than the gold watch Paul Morphy, meteorically short-reigned King of American chess, had been given by an adoring public in New York City on May 25, 1859, after the triumphal tour of London and Paris which had proven him to be perhaps the greatest chess genius of all time.

Ritter veered as if by lazy chance toward the case, his eyes resolutely fixed on a dull silver ankh at the opposite end from the chess watch.

He paused like a sleepwalker across from the proprietor after what seemed like a suitable interval and—hoping the pounding of his heart wasn't audible—made a desultory inquiry about the ankh. The proprietor replied in as casual a fashion, though getting the item out for his inspection.

Ritter brooded over the silver love-cross for a bit, then shook his head and idly asked about another item and still another, working his insidious way toward the Morphy watch.

The proprietor responded to his queries in a low, bored voice, though in each case dutifully getting the item out to show Ritter. He was a very old and completely bald man with a craggy Baltic cast to his features. He vaguely reminded Ritter of someone.

Finally Ritter was asking about an old silver railroad watch next to the one he still refused to look at directly.

Then he shifted to another old watch with a complicated face with tiny windows showing the month and the phases of the moon, on the other side of the one that was keeping his heart a-pound.

His gambit worked. The proprietor at last dragged out the Morphy watch, saying softly, "Here is an odd old piece that might interest you. The case is solid gold. It threatens to catch your interest, does it not?"

Ritter at last permitted himself a second devouring glance. It confirmed the first. Beyond shadow of a doubt this was the genuine relic that had haunted his thoughts for two thirds of a lifetime.

What he said was "It's odd, all right. What are those funny little figures it has in place of hours?"

"Chessmen," the other explained. "See, that's a King at six o'clock, a pawn at five, a Bishop at four, a Knight at three, a Rook at two, a Queen at one, another King at midnight, and then repeat, eleven to seven, around the dial."

"Why midnight rather than noon?" Ritter asked stupidly. He knew why.

The proprietor's wrinkled fingernail indicated a small window just above the center of the face. In it showed the letters P.M. "That's another rare feature," he explained. "I've handled very few watches that knew the difference between night and day."

"Oh, and I suppose those squares on which the chessmen are placed and which go around the dial in two and a half circles make a sort of checkerboard?"

"Chessboard," the other corrected. "Incidentally, there are exactly 64 squares, the right number."

Ritter nodded. "I suppose you're asking a fortune for it," he remarked, as if making conversation.

The other shrugged. "Only a thousand dollars."

Ritter's heart skipped a beat. He had more than ten times that in his bank account. A trifle, considering the stake.

But he bargained for the sake of appearances. At one point he argued, "But the watch doesn't run, I suppose."

"But it still has its hands," the old Balt with the hauntingly familiar face countered. "And it still has its works, as you can tell by the weight. They could be repaired, I imagine. A French movement. See, there's the hexagonal winding-key still with it."

A price of seven hundred dollars was finally agreed on. He paid out the fifty dollars he always carried with him and wrote a check for the remainder. After a call to his bank, it was accepted.

The watch was packed in a small box in a nest of fluffy cotton. Ritter put it in a pocket of his jacket and buttoned the flap.

He felt dazed. The Morphy watch, the watch Paul Morphy had kept his whole short life, despite his growing hatred of chess, the watch he had willed to his French admirer and favorite opponent Jules Arnous de Riviere, the watch that had then mysteriously disappeared, the watch of watches—was his!

He felt both weightless and dizzy as he moved toward the street, which blurred a little.

As he was leaving he noticed in the window something he'd forgotten—he wrote a check for fifty dollars for the silver barbarian pawn without bargaining.

He was in the street, feeling glorious and very tired. Faces and umbrellas were alike blurs. Rain pattered on his face unnoticed, but there came a stab of anxiety.

He held still and very carefully used his left hand to transfer the heavy little box—and the pawn in a twist of paper—to his trouser pocket, where he kept his left hand closed around them. Then he felt secure.

He flagged down a cab and gave his home address.

The passing scene began to come unblurred. He recognized Rimini's Italian Restaurant where his own chess game was now having a little renaissance after five years of foregoing tournament chess because he knew he was too old for it. A chess-smitten young cook there, indulged by the owner, had organized a tourney. The entrants were mostly young people. A tall, moody girl he thought of as the Czarina, who played a remarkable game, and a likeable, loudmouthed young Jewish lawyer he thought of as Rasputin, who played almost as good a game and talked a better one, both stood out. On impulse Ritter had entered the tournament because it was such a trifling one that it didn't really break his rule against playing serious chess. And, his old skills reviving nicely, he had done well enough to have a firm grip on third place, right behind Rasputin and the Czarina.

But now that he had the Morphy watch. . .

Why the devil should he think that having the Morphy watch should improve his chess game? he asked himself sharply. It was as silly as faith in the power of the relics of saints.

In his hand inside his left pocket the watch box vibrated eagerly, as if it contained a big live insect, a golden bee or beetle. But that, of course, was his imagination.

Stirf Ritter-Rebil (a proper name, he always felt, for a chess player, since they specialize in weird ones, from Euwe to Znosko-Borovsky, from Noteboom to Dus-Chotimirski) lived in a one-room and bath, five blocks west of Union Square and packed with files, books and also paintings wherever the wall space allowed, of his dead wife and parents, and of his son. Now that he was older, he liked living with clues to all of his life in view. There was a fine view of the Pacific and the Golden Gate and their fogs to the west, over a sea of roofs. On the orderly cluttered tables were two fine chess sets with positions set up.

Ritter cleared a space beside one of them and set in its center the box and packet. After a brief pause—as if for propitiatory prayer, he told himself sardonically—he gingerly took out the Morphy watch and centered it for inspection with the unwrapped silver pawn behind it.

Then, wiping and adjusting his glasses and from time to time employing a large magnifying glass, he examined both treasures exhaustively.

The outer edge of the dial was circled with a ring or wheel of 24 squares, 12 pale and 12 dark alternating. On the pale squares were the figures of chessmen indicating the hours, placed in the order the old Balt had described. The Black pieces went from midnight to five and were of silver set with tiny emeralds or bright jade, as his magnifying glass confirmed. The White pieces went from six to eleven and were of gold set with minute rubies or amythysts. He recalled that descriptions of the watch always mentioned the figures as being colored.

Inside that came a second circle of 24 pale and dark squares.

Finally, inside *that*, there was a two-thirds circle of 16

squares below the center of the dial.

In the corresponding space above the center was the little window showing PM.

The hands on the dial were stopped at 11:57—three minutes to midnight.

With a paperknife he carefully pried open the hinged back of the watch, on which were floridly engraved the initials PM—which he suddenly realized also stood for Paul Morphy.

On the inner golden back covering the works was engraved "France H&H"—the old Balt was right again—while scratched in very tiny—he used his magnifier once more—were a half dozen sets of numbers, most of the sevens having the French slash. Pawnbrokers' marks. Had Arnous de Riviere pawned the treasure? Or later European owners? Oh well, chess players were an impecunious lot. There was also a hole by which the watch could be wound with its hexagonal key. He carefully wound it but of course nothing happened.

He closed the back and brooded on the dial. The 64 squares—24 plus 24 plus 16—made a fantastic circular board. One of the many variants of chess he had played once or twice was cylindrical.

"*Les echecs fantasques,*" he quoted. "It's a cynical madman's allegory with its doddering monarch, vampire queen, gangster knights, double-faced bishops, ramming rooks and inane pawns, whose supreme ambition is to change their sex and share the dodderer's bed."

With a sigh of regret he tore his gaze away from the watch and took up the pawn behind it. Here was a grim little fighter, he thought, bringing the tarnished silver figure close to his glasses. Naked long-sword clasped against his chest, point down, iron skullcap low on forehead, face merciless as Death's. What did the golden legionaires look like?

Then Ritter's expression grew grim too, as he decided to do something he'd had in mind ever since glimpsing the barbarian pawn in the window. Making a long arm, he slid out a file drawer and after flipping a few tabs drew out a folder marked "Death of Alekhine." The light was getting bad. He switched on a big desk lamp against the night.

Soon he was studying a singularly empty photograph. It was of an unoccupied old armchair with a peg-in chess set open on one of the flat wooden arms. Behind the chess set stood a tiny figure. Bringing the magnifying glass once more into play, he confirmed what he had expected: that it was a precise mate to the barbarian pawn he had bought today.

He glanced through another item from the folder—an old letter on onionskin paper in a foreign script with cedillas under half the "C's" and tildas over half the "A's."

It was from his Portuguese friend, explaining that the photo was a reproduction of one in the Lisbon police files.

The photo was of the chair in which Alexander Alekhine had been found dead of a heart attack on the top floor of a cheap Lisbon rooming house in 1946.

Alekhine had won the World's Chess Championship from Capablanca in 1927. He had held the world's record for the greatest number of games played simultaneously and blindfolded—32. In 1946 he was preparing for an official match with the Russian champion Botvinnik, although he had played chess for the Axis in World War II. Though at times close to psychosis, he was considered the profoundest and most brilliant attacking player who had ever lived.

Had he also, Ritter asked himself, been one of the players to own the Morphy silver-and-gold chess set and the Morphy watch?

He reached for another file folder labeled "Death of Steinitz." This time he found a brownish daguerreotype showing an empty, narrow, old-fashioned hospital bed with a chessboard and set on a small table beside it. Among the chess pieces, Ritter's magnifier located another one of the unmistakable barbarian pawns.

Wilhelm Steinitz, called the Father of Modern Chess, who had held the world's championship for 28 years, until his defeat by Emmanuel Lasker in 1894. Steinitz, who had had two psychotic episodes and been hospitalized for them in the last years of his life, during the second of which he had believed he could move the chess pieces by electricity and challenged God to a match, offering God the odds of Pawn and Move. It was after the second episode that the daguerreotype had been taken which Ritter had acquired many years ago from the aged Emmanuel Lasker.

Ritter leaned back wearily from the table, took off his glasses and knuckled his tired eyes. It was later than he'd imagined.

He thought about Paul Morphy retiring from chess at the age of 21 after beating every important player in the world and issuing a challenge, never accepted, to take on any master at the odds of Pawn and Move. After that contemptuous gesture in 1859 he had brooded for 25 years, mostly a recluse in his family home in New Orleans, emerging only fastidiously dressed and be-caped for an afternoon promenade and regular attendance at the opera. He suffered paranoid episodes during which he believed his relatives were trying to steal his fortune and, of all things, his clothes. And he never spoke of chess or played it, except for an occasional game with his friend Maurian at the odds of Knight and Move.

Twenty-five years of brooding in solitude without the solace of playing chess, but with the Morphy chess set and the Morphy watch in the same room, testimonials to his world mastery.

Ritter wondered if those circumstances—with Morphy constantly thinking of chess, he felt sure—were not ideal for the transmission of the vibrations of thought and feeling into inanimate objects, in this case the golden Morphy set and watch.

Material objects intangibly vibrating with 25 years of

the greatest chess thought and then by strange chance (chance alone?) falling into the hands of two other periodically psychotic chess champions, as the photographs of the pawns hinted.

An absurd fancy, Ritter told himself. And yet one to the pursuit of which he had devoted no small part of his life.

And now the richly vibrant objects were in *his* hands. What would be the effect of that on *his* game?

But to speculate in that direction was doubly absurd.

A wave of tiredness went through him. It was close to midnight.

He heated a small supper for himself, consumed it, drew the heavy window drapes tight, and undressed.

He turned back the cover of the big couch next to the table, switched off the light, and inserted himself into bed.

It was Ritter's trick to put himself to sleep by playing through a chess opening in his thoughts. Like any talented player, he could readily contest one blindfold game, though he could not quite visualize the entire board and often had to count moves square by square, especially with the Bishops. He selected Breyer's Gambit, an old favorite of his.

He made a half dozen moves. Then suddenly the board was brightly illuminated in his mind, as if a light had been turned on there. He had to stare around to assure himself that the room was still dark as pitch. There was only the bright board inside his head.

His sense of awe was lost in luxuriant delight. He moved the mental pieces rapidly, yet saw deep into the possibilities of each position.

Far in the background he heard a church clock on Franklin boom out the dozen strokes of midnight. After a short while he announced mate in five by White. Black studied the position for perhaps a minute, then resigned.

Lying flat on his back he took several deep breaths. Never before had he played such a brilliant blindfold game—or game with sight even. That it was a game with himself didn't seem to matter—his personality had split neatly into two players.

He studied the final position for a last time, returned the pieces to their starting positions in his head, and rested a bit before beginning another game.

It was then he heard the ticking, a nervous sound five times as fast as the distant clock had knelled. He lifted his wristwatch to his ear. Yes, it was ticking rapidly too, but this was another ticking, louder.

He sat up silently in bed, leaned over the table, switched on the light.

The Morphy watch. That was where the louder ticks were coming from. The hands stood at twelve ten and the small window showed AM.

For a long while he held that position—mute, motionless, aghast, wondering, fearing, doubting, dreaming dreams no mortal ever dared to dream before.

Let's see, Edgar Allan Poe had died when Morphy was 12 years old and beating his uncle, Ernest Morphy, then chess king of New Orleans.

It seemed impossible that a stopped watch with works well over one hundred years old should begin to run. Doubly impossible that it should begin to run at approximately the right time—his wrist watch and the Morphy watch were no more than a minute apart.

Yet the works might be in better shape than either he or the old Balt had guessed; watches did capriciously start and stop running. Coincidences were only coincidences.

Yet he felt profoundly uneasy. He pinched himself and went through the other childish tests.

He said aloud, "I am Stirf Ritter-Rebil, an old man who lives in San Francisco and plays chess, and who yesterday discovered an unusual curio. But really, everything is perfectly normal. . ."

Nevertheless, he suddenly got the feeling of "A man-

eating lion is aprowl." It was the childish form terror
still took for him on rare occasions. For a minute or so
everything seemed *too* still, despite the ticking. The stirring of the heavy drapes at the window gave him a
shiver, and the walls seemed thin, their protective power
nil.

Gradually the sense of a killer lion moving outside
them faded and his nerves calmed.

He switched off the light, the bright mental board returned, and the ticking became reassuring rather than
otherwise. He began another game with himself, playing
for Black the Classical Defense to the Ruy Lopez, another of his favorites.

This game proceeded as brilliantly and vividly as the
first. There was the sense of a slim, man-shaped glow
standing beside the bright board in the mental dark. After a while the shape grew amorphous and less bright,
then split into three. However, it bothered him little, and
when he at last announced mate in three for Black, he
felt great satisfaction and profound fatigue.

Next day he was in exceptionally good spirits. Sunlight banished all night's terrors as he went about his
ordinary business and writing chores. From time to time
he reassured himself that he could still visualize a mental
chessboard very clearly, and he thought now and again
about the historical chess mystery he was in the midst of
solving. The ticking of the Morphy watch carried an exciting, eager note. Toward the end of the afternoon he
realized he was keenly anticipating visiting Rimini's to
show off his new-found skill.

He got out an old gold watch chain and fob, snapped
it to the Morphy watch, which he carefully wound
again, pocketed them securely in his vest, and set out for
Rimini's. It was a grand day—cool, brightly sunlit and
a little windy. His steps were brisk. He wasn't thinking
of all the strange happenings but of *chess*. It's been said
that a man can lose his wife one day and forget her that
night, playing *chess*.

Rimini's was a good, dark, garlic-smelling restaurant

with an annex devoted to drinks, substantial free pasta appetizers and, for the nonce, chess. As he drifted into the long L-shaped room, Ritter became pleasantly aware of the row of boards, chessmen, and the intent, mostly young, faces bent above them.

Then Rasputin was grinning at him calculatedly and yapping at him cheerfully. They were due to play their tournament game. They checked out a set and were soon at it. Beside them the Czarina also contested a crucial game, her moody face askew almost as if her neck were broken, her bent wrists near her chin, her long fingers pointing rapidly at her pieces as she calculated combinations, like a sorceress putting a spell on them.

Ritter was aware of her, but only peripherally. For last night's bright mental board had returned, only now it was superimposed on the actual board before him. Complex combinations sprang to mind effortlessly. He beat Rasputin like a child. The Czarina caught the win from the corner of her eye and growled faintly in approval. She was winning her own game; Ritter beating Rasputin bumped her into first place. Rasputin was silent for once.

A youngish man with a black mustache was sharply inspecting Ritter's win. He was the California state champion, Martinez, who had recently played a simultaneous at Rimini's, winning fifteen games, losing none, drawing only with the Czarina. He now suggested a casual game to Ritter, who nodded somewhat abstractedly.

They contested two very hairy games—a Sicilian Defense by Martinez in which Ritter advanced all his pawns in front of his castled King in a wild-looking attack, and a Ruy Lopez by Martinez that Ritter answered with the Classical Defense, going to great lengths to preserve his powerful King's Bishop. The mental board stayed superimposed, and it almost seemed to Ritter that there was a small faint halo over the piece he must next move or capture. To his mild astonishment he won both games.

A small group of chess-playing onlookers had gath-

ered around their board. Martinez was looking at him
speculatively, as if to ask, "Now just where did you
spring from, old man, with your power game? I don't
recall ever hearing of you."

Ritter's contentment would have been complete, except that among the kibitzers, toward the back, there
was a slim young man whose face was always shadowed
when Ritter glimpsed it. Ritter saw him in three different places, though never in movement and never for
more than an instant. Somehow he seemed one onlooker
too many. This disturbed Ritter obscurely, and his face
had a thoughtful, abstracted expression when he finally
quit Rimini's for the faintly drizzling evening streets. After a block he looked around, but so far as he could tell,
he wasn't being followed. This time he walked the whole
way to his apartment, passing several landmarks of
Dashiell Hammett, Sam Spade, and *The Maltese Falcon*.

Gradually, under the benizon of the foggy droplets,
his mood changed to one of exaltation. He had just now
played some beautiful chess, he was in the midst of an
amazing historic chess mystery he'd always yearned to
penetrate, and somehow the Morphy watch was working *for* him—he could actually hear its muffled ticking in
the street, coming up from his waist to his ear.

Tonight his room was a most welcome retreat, *his*
place, like an extension of his mind. He fed himself.
Then he reviewed, with a Sherlock Holmes smile, what
he found himself calling "The Curious Case of the
Morphy Timepiece." He wished he had a Dr. Watson to
hear him expound. First, the appearance of the watch
after Morphy returned to New York on the *Persia* in
1859. Over paranoid years Morphy had imbued it with
psychic energy and vast chessic wisdom. Or else—mark
this, Doctor—he had set up the conditions whereby subsequent owners of the watch would *think* he had done
such, for the supernatural is not our balliwick, Watson.
Next (after de Riviere) great Steinitz had come into
possession of it and challenged God and died mad.

Then, after a gap, paranoid Alekhine had owned it and devised diabolically brilliant, hyper-Morphian strategies of attack, and died all alone after a thousand treacheries in a miserable Lisbon flat with a peg-in chess set and the telltale barbarian pawn next to his corpse. Finally after a haitus of almost thirty years (where had the watch and set been then? Who'd had their custody? Who was the old Balt?) the timepiece and a pawn had come into his own possession. A unique case, Doctor. There isn't even a parallel in Prague in 1863.

The nighted fog pressed against the windowpane and now and again a little rain pattered. San Francisco was a London City and had its own resident great detective. One of Dashiell Hammett's hobbies had been chess, even though there was no record of Spade having played the game.

From time to time Ritter studied the Morphy watch as it glowed and ticked on the table space he'd cleared. PM once more, he noted. The time: White Queen, ruby glittering, past Black King, microscopically emerald studded—I mean five minutes past midnight, Doctor. The witching hour, as the superstitiously-minded would have it.

But to bed, to bed, Watson. We have much to do tomorrow—and, paradoxically, tonight.

Seriously, Ritter was glad when the golden glow winked out on the watch face, though the strident ticking kept on, and he wriggled himself into his couch-bed and arranged himself for thought. The mental board flashed on once more and he began to play. First he reviewed all the best games he'd ever played in his life—there weren't very many—discovering variations he'd never dreamed of before. Then he played through all his favorite games in the history of chess, from MacDonnell-La Bourdonnais to Fischer-Spasski, not forgetting Steinitz-Zukertort and Alekhine-Bogolyubov. They were richer masterpieces than ever before—the mental board saw very deep. Finally he split his mind again and challenged himself to an eight-game blindfold match, Black against White. Against all expectation, Black won with three wins, two losses, and three draws.

But the night was not all imaginative and ratiocinative delight. Twice there came periods of eerie silence, which the ticking of the watch in the dark made only more complete, and two spells of the man-eating lion a-prowl that raised his hair at the roots. Once again there loomed the slim, faint, man-shaped glow beside the mental board and he wouldn't go away. Worse, he was joined by two other man-shaped glows, one short and stocky, with a limp, the other fairly tall, stocky too, and restless. These inner intruders bothered Ritter increasingly—who were they? And wasn't there beginning to be a faint fourth? He recalled the slim young elusive watcher with shadowed face of his games with Martinez and wondered if there was a connection.

Disturbing stuff—and most disturbing of all, the apprehension that his mind might be racked apart and fragmented abroad with all its machine-gun thinking, that it already extended by chessic veins from one chess-playing planet to another, to the ends of the universe.

He was profoundly glad when toward the end of his self-match, his brain began to dull and slow. His last memory was of an attempt to invent a game to be played on the circular board on the watch dial. He thought he was succeeding as his mind at last went spiraling off into unconsciousness.

Next day he awoke restless, scratchy, and eager—and with the feeling that the three or four dim figures had stood around his couch all night vibrating like strobe lights to the rhythm of the Morphy watch.

Coffee heightened his alert nervousness. He rapidly dressed, snapped the Morphy watch to its chain and fob, pocketed the silver pawn, and went out to hunt down the store where he'd purchased the two items.

In a sense he never found it, though he tramped and minutely scanned Montgomery, Kearny, Grant, Stock-

ton, Clay, Sacramento, California, Pine, Bush, and all
the rest.

What he did find at long last was a store window with
a grotesque pattern of dust on it that he was certain was
identical with that on the window through which he had
first glimpsed the barbarian Pawn day before yesterday.

Only now the display space behind the window was
empty and the whole store too, except for a tall, lanky
Black with a fabulous Afro hair-do, sweeping up.

Ritter struck up a conversation with the man as he
worked, and slowly winning his confidence, discovered
that he was one of three partners opening a store there
that would be stocked solely with African imports.

Finally, after the Black had fetched a great steaming
pail of soapy water and a long-handled roller mop and
begun to efface forever the map of dust by which Ritter
had identified the place, the man at last grew confidential.

"Yeah," he said, "there *was* a queer old character had
a second-hand store here until yesterday that had every
crazy thing you could dig for sale, some junk, some real
fancy. Then he cleared everything out into two big
trucks in a great rush, with me breathing down his neck
every minute because he'd been supposed to do it the
day before.

"Oh, but he was a fabulous cat, though," the Black
went on with a reminiscent grin as he sloshed away the
last peninsulas and archipelagos of the dust map. "One
time he said to me. 'Excuse me while I rest,' and—you're
not going to believe this—he went into a corner and
stood on his head. I'm telling you he did, man. I'd like
to bust a gut. I thought he'd have a stroke—and he did
get a bit lavender in the face—but after three minutes
exact—I timed him—he flipped back onto his feet neat
as you could ask and went on with his work twice as fast
as before, supervising his carriers out of their skulls.
Wow, that was an event."

Ritter departed without comment. He had got the

final clue he'd been seeking to the identity of the old Balt and likewise the fourth and most shadowy form that had begun to haunt his mental chessboard.

Casually standing on his head, saying "It threatens to catch your interest"—why, it had to be Aaron Nimzovich, most hyper-eccentric player of them all and Father of Hypermodern Chess, who had been Alekhine's most dangerous but ever-evaded challenger. Why, the old Balt had even looked exactly like an aged Nimzovich—hence Ritter's constant sense of a facial familiarity. Of course, Nimzovich had supposedly died in the 1930's in his home city of Riga in the U.S.S.R., but what were life and breath to the forces with which Ritter was now embroiled?

It seemed to him that there were four dim figures stalking him relentlessly as lions right now in the Chinatown crowds, while despite the noise he could hear and feel the ticking of the Morphy watch at his waist.

He fled to the Danish Kitchen at the St. Francis Hotel and consumed cup on cup of good coffee and two orders of Eggs Benedict, and had his mental chessboard flashing on and off in his mind like a strobe light, and wondered if he shouldn't hurl the Morphy watch into the Bay to be rid of the influence racking his mind apart and destroying his sense of reality.

But then with the approach of evening, the urge toward *chess* gripped him more and more imperiously and he headed once again for Rimini's.

Rasputin and the Czarina were there and also Martinez again, and with the last a distinguished silver-haired man whom Martinez introduced as the South American international master, Pontebello, suggesting that he and Ritter have a quick game.

The board glowed again with the superimposed mental one, the halos were there once more, and Ritter won as if against a tyro.

At that, chess fever seized him entirely and he suggested he immediately play four simultaneous blindfold games with the two masters and the Czarina and Rasputin, Pontebello acting also as referee.

There were incredulous looks aplenty at that, but he *had* won those two games from Martinez and now the one from Pontebello, so arrangements were quickly made. Ritter insisting on an actual blindfold. All the other players crowded around to observe.

The simul began. There were now four mental boards glowing in Ritter's mind. It did not matter—*now*—that there were four dim forms with them, one by each. Ritter played with a practiced brilliance, combinations bubbled, he called out his moves crisply and unerringly. And so he beat the Czarina and Rasputin quickly. Pontebello took a little longer, and he drew with Martinez by perpetual check.

There was silence as he took off the blindfold to scan a circle of astonished faces and four shadowed ones behind them. He felt the joy of absolute chess mastery. The only sound he heard was the ticking, thunderous to him, of the Morphy watch.

Pontebello was first to speak. To Ritter, "Do you realize, master, what you've just done?" To Martinez, "Have you the scores of all four games?" To Ritter again, "Excuse me, but you look pale, as if you've just seen a ghost." "Four," Ritter corrected quietly. "Those of Morphy, Steinitz, Alekhine, and Nimzovich."

"Under the circumstances, most appropriate," commented Pontebello, while Ritter sought out again the four shadowed faces in the background. They were still there, though they had shifted their positions and withdrawn a little into the varied darknesses of Rimini's.

Amid talk of scheduling another blindfold exhibition and writing a multiple-signed letter describing tonight's simul to the U.S. Chess Federation—not to mention Pontebello's searching queries as to Ritter's chess career —he tore himself away and made for home through the dark streets, certain that four shadowy figures stalked behind him. The call of the mental *chess* in his own room was not to be denied.

Ritter forgot no moment of that night, for he did not sleep at all. The glowing board in his mind was an unquenchable beacon, and all-demanding mandala. He replayed all the important games of history, finding new moves. He contested two matches with himself, then one each with Morphy, Steinitz, Alekhine and Nimzovich, winning the first two, drawing the third, and losing the last by a half point. Nimzovich was the only one to speak, saying, "I am both dead and alive, as I'm sure you know. Please don't smoke, or threaten to."

He stacked eight mental boards and played two games of three-dimensional chess. Black winning both. He traveled to the ends of the universe, finding chess everywhere he went, and contesting a long game, more complex than 3-D chess, on which the fate of the universe depended. He drew it.

And all through the long night the four were with him in the room and the man-eating lion stared in through the window with black-and-white checkered mask and silver mane. While the Morphy watch ticked like a death-march drum. All figures vanished when the dawn came creeping, though the mental board stayed bright and busy into full daylight and showed no signs of vanishing ever. Ritter felt overpoweringly tired, his mind racked to atoms, on the verge of death.

But he knew what he had to do. He got a small box and packed into it, in cotton wool, the silver barbarian Pawn, the old photograph and daguerrotype, and a piece of paper on which he scribbled only:

Morphy, 1859-1884
de Riviere, 1884-?
Steinitz, ?-1900
Alekhine, ?-1946
Nimzovich, 1946-now
Ritter-Rebil, 3 days

Then he packed the watch in the box too, it stopped ticking, its hands were still at last, and in Ritter's mind the mental board winked out.

He took one last devouring gaze at the grotesque, glittering dial. Then he shut the box, wrapped and sealed and corded it, boldly wrote on it in black ink "Chess Champion of the World" and added the proper address.

He took it to the post office on Van Ness and sent it off by registered mail. Then he went home and slept like the dead.

Ritter never received a response. But he never got the box back either. Sometimes he wonders if the subsequent strange events in the Champion's life might have had anything to do with the gift.

And on even rarer occasions he wonders what would have happened if he had faced the challenge of death and let his mind be racked to bits, if that was what was to happen.

But on the whole he is content. Questions from Martinez and the others he has put off with purposefully vague remarks.

He still plays chess at Rimini's. Once he won another game from Martinez, when the latter was contesting a simul against twenty-three players.

UNSOUND VARIATIONS

George R.R. Martin

After they swung off the Interstate, the road became a narrow two-lane that wound a tortuous path through the mountains in a series of switchbacks, each steeper than the last. Peaks rose all around them, pine-covered and crowned by snow and ice, while swift cold waterfalls flashed by, barely seen, on either side. The sky was a bright and brilliant blue. It was exhilarating scenery, but it did nothing to lighten Peter's mood. He concentrated blindly on the road, losing himself in the mindless reflexes of driving.

As the mountains grew higher, the radio reception grew poorer, stations fading in and out with every twist in the road, until at last they could get nothing at all. Kathy went from one end of the band to the other, searching, and then back again. Finally she snapped off the radio in disgust. "I guess you'll just have to talk to me," she said.

Peter didn't need to look at her to hear the sharpness in her tone, the bitter edge of sarcasm that had long ago replaced fondness in her voice. She was looking for an argument, he knew. She was angry about the radio, and she resented him dragging her on this trip, and most of all she resented being married to him. At times, when he was feeling very sorry for himself, he did not even blame her. He had not turned out to be much of a bargain as a husband; a failed writer, failed journalist, failing businessman, depressed and depressing. He was still a lively sparring partner, however. Perhaps that was why she tried to provoke fights so often. After all the blood had been let, one or both of them would start crying, and then they would usually make love, and life would be pleasant for an hour or two. It was about all they had left.

Not today, though. Peter lacked the energy, and his mind was on other things. "What do you want to talk about?" he asked her. He kept his tone amicable and his eyes on the road.

"Tell me about these clowns we're going to visit," she said.

"I did. They were my teammates on the chess team, back when I was at Northwestern."

"Since when is chess a team sport anyway?" Kathy said. "What'd you do, vote on each move?"

"No. In chess, a team match is really a bunch of individual matches. Usually four or five boards, at least in college play. There's no consultation or anything. The team that wins the most individual games wins the match point. The way it works—"

"I get it," she said sharply. "I may not be a chessplayer, but I'm not stupid. So you and these other three were the Northwestern team?"

"Yes and no," Peter said. The Toyota was straining; it wasn't used to grades this steep, and it hadn't been adjusted for altitude before they took off from Chicago. He drove carefully. They were up high enough now to come across icy patches, and snow drifting across the road.

"Yes and no," Kathy said sarcastically. "What does that mean?"

"Northwestern had a big chess club back then. We played in a lot of tournaments—local, state, national. Sometimes we fielded more than one team, so the line-up was a bit different every tournament. It depended on who could play and who couldn't, who had a midterm, who'd played in the last match—lots of things. We four were Northwestern's B team in the North American Intercollegiate Team Championships, ten years ago this week. Northwestern hosted that tournament, and I ran it, as well as playing."

"What do you mean *B team?*"

Peter cleared his throat and eased the Toyota around a sharp curve, gravel rattling against the underside of the car as one wheel brushed the shoulder. "A school wasn't limited to just one team," he said. "If you had the money and a lot of people who wanted to play, you could enter several. Your best four players would make up your A team, the real contender. The second four would be the B team, and so on." He paused briefly, and continued with a faint note of pride in his voice. "The nationals at Northwestern were the biggest ever held, up to that time, although of course that record has since been broken. We set a second record, though, that still stands. Since the tournament was on our home grounds, we had lots of players on hand. We entered six teams. No other school has ever had more than four in the nationals, before or after." The record still brought a smile to his face. Maybe it wasn't much of a record, but it was the only one he had, and it was *his*. Some people lived and died without ever setting a record of any kind, he reflected silently. Maybe he ought to tell Kathy to put his on his tombstone: HERE LIES PETER K. NORTEN. HE FIELDED SIX TEAMS. He chuckled.

"What's so funny?"

"Nothing."

She didn't pursue it. "So you ran this tournament, you say?"

"I was the club president and the chairman of the local committee. I didn't direct, but I put together the bid that brought the nationals to Evanston, made all the preliminary arrangements. And I organized all six of our teams, decided who would play on each one, appointed the team captains. But during the tournament itself I was only the captain of the B team.''

She laughed. "So you were a big deal on the second-string. It figures. The story of our life.''

Peter bit back a sharp reply, and said nothing. The Toyota swerved around another hairpin, and a vast Colorado mountain panorama opened up in front of them. It left him strangely unmoved.

After a while Kathy said, ''When did you stop playing chess?''

"I sort of gave it up after college. Not a conscious decision, really. I just kind of drifted out of it. I haven't played a game of tournament chess in almost nine years. I'm probably pretty rusty by now. But back then I was fairly good.''

"How good is fairly good?''

"I was rated as a Class A player, like everyone else on our B team.''

"What does that mean?''

"It means my USCF rating was substantially higher than that of the vast majority of tournament chess players in the country,'' he said. "And the tournament players are generally much better than the unrated woodpushers you encounter in bars and coffee houses. The ratings went all the way down to Class E. Above Class A you had Experts, and Masters, and Senior Masters at the top, but there weren't many of them.''

"Three classes above you?''

"Yes.''

"So you might say, at your very best, you were a fourth-class chess player.''

At that Peter did look over at her. She was leaning back in her seat, a faint smirk on her face. "Bitch,'' he said. He was suddenly angry.

"Keep your eyes on the road!'' Kathy snapped.

He wrenched the car around the next turn hard as he could, and pressed down on the gas. She hated it when he drove fast. "I don't know why the hell I try to talk to you," he said.

"My husband, the big deal," she said. She laughed. "A fourth-class chess player playing on the junior varsity team. And a fifth-rate driver, too."

"Shut up," Peter said furiously. "You don't know what the hell you're talking about. Maybe we were only the B team, but we were good. We finished better than anyone had any right to expect, only a half-point behind Northwestern A. And we almost scored one of the biggest upsets in history."

"Do tell."

Peter hesitated, already regretting his words. The memory was important to him, almost as important as his silly little record. *He* knew what it meant, how close they had come. But she'd never understand, it would only be another failure for her to laugh at. He should never have mentioned it.

"Well?" she prodded. "What about this great upset, dear? Tell me."

It was too late, Peter realized. She'd never let him drop it now. She'd needle him and needle him until he told her. He sighed and said, "It was ten years ago this week. The nationals were always held between Christmas and New Year's, when everyone was on break. An eight-round team tournament, two rounds a day. All of our teams did moderately well. Our A team finished seventh overall."

"You were on the B team, sweetie."

Peter grimaced. "Yes. And we were doing best of all, up to a point. Scored a couple nice upsets late in the tournament. It put us in a strange position. Going into the last round, the University of Chicago was in first place, alone, with a 6-1 match record. They'd beaten our team, among their other victims, and they were defending national champions. Behind them were three other schools at 5½-1½. Berkeley, the University of Massachusetts, and—I don't know, someone else, it doesn't matter. What mattered was that all three of those teams had already played U of C. Then you had a whole bunch of teams at 5-2, including both Northwestern A and B. One of the 5-2 teams had to be paired up against Chicago in the final round. By some freak, it turned out to be us. Everyone thought that cinched the tournament for them.

"It was really a mismatch. They were the defending champions, and they had an awesome team. Three Masters and an Expert, if I recall. They outrated us by hundreds of points on every board. It should have been easy. It wasn't.

"It was never easy between U. of C. and Northwestern. All through my college years, we were the two big midwestern chess powers, and we were arch-rivals. The Chicago captain, Hal Winslow, became a good friend of mine, but I gave him a lot of headaches. Chicago *always* had a stronger team than we did, but we gave them fits nonetheless. We met in the Chicago Intercollegiate League, in state tournaments, in regional tournaments, and several times in the nationals. Chicago won most of those, but not all. We took the city championship away from them once, and racked up a couple other big upsets too. And that year, in the nationals, we came *this* close"—he held up two fingers, barely apart—"to the biggest upset of all." He put his hand back on the wheel, and scowled.

"Go on," she said. "I'm breathless to know what comes next."

Peter ignored the sarcasm. "An hour into the match, we had half the tournament gathered around our tables, watching. Everyone could see that Chicago was in trouble. We clearly had superior positions on two boards, and we were even on the other two.

"It got better. I was playing Hal Winslow on third board. We had a dull, even position, and we agreed to a draw. And on fourth board, E.C. gradually got outplayed and finally resigned in a dead lost position."

"E.C.?"

"Edward Colin Stuart. We all called him E.C. Quite a character. You'll meet him up at Bunnish's place."

"He lost?"

"Yes."

"This doesn't sound like such a thrilling upset to me," she said dryly. "Though maybe by your standards, it's a triumph."

"E.C. lost," Peter said, "but by that time, Delmario had clearly busted his man on board two. The guy dragged it out, but finally we got the point, which tied the score at 1½-1½, with one game in progress. And we were winning that one. It was incredible. Bruce Bunnish was our first board. A real turkey, but a half-decent player. He was another A player, but he had a trick memory. Photographic. Knew every opening backwards and forwards. He was playing Chicago's big man." Peter smiled wryly. "In more ways than one. A Master name of Robinson Vesselere. Damn strong chessplayer, but he must have weighed four hundred pounds. He'd sit there absolutely immobile as you played him, his hands folded on top of his stomach, little eyes squinting at the board. And he'd crush you. He should have crushed Bunnish easily. Hell, he was rated four hundred points higher. But that wasn't what had gone down. With that trick memory of his, Bunnish had somehow outplayed Vesselere in an obscure variation of the Sicilian. He was swarming all over him. An incredible attack. The position was as complicated as anything I'd ever seen, very sharp and tactical. Vesselere was counterattacking on the queenside, and he had some pressure, but nothing like the threats Bunnish had on the kingside. It was a won game. We were all sure of that."

"So you almost won the championship?"

"No," Peter said. "No, it wasn't that. If we'd won the match, we would have tied Chicago and a few others teams at 6-2, but the championship would have gone to someone else, some team with 6½ match points.

Berkeley maybe, or Mass. It was just the upset itself we wanted. It would have been *incredible*. They were the best college chess team in the country. We weren't even the best at our school. If we had beaten them, it would have caused a sensation. And we came so close."

"What happened?"

"Bunnish blew it," Peter said sourly. "There was a critical position. Bunnish had a sac. A sacrifice, you know? A double piece sac. Very sharp, but it would have busted up Vesselere's kingside and driven his king out into the open. But Bunnish was too timid for that. Instead he kept looking at Vesselere's queenside attack, and finally he made some feebly defensive move. Vesselere shifted another piece to the queenside, and Bunnish defended again. Instead of following up his advantage, he made a whole series of cautious little adjustments to the position, and before long his attack had dissipated. After that, of course, Vesselere overwhelmed him." Even now, after ten years, Peter felt the disappointment building inside him as he spoke. "We lost the match 2½-1½, and Chicago won another national championship. Afterwards, even Vesselere admitted that he was busted if Brucie had played knight takes pawn at the critical point. *Damn.*"

"You lost. That's what this amounts to. You lost."

"We came close."

"Close only counts in horseshoes and grenades," Kathy said. "You lost. Even then you were a loser, dear. I wish I'd known."

"*Bunnish* lost, damn it," Peter said. "It was just like him. He had a Class A rating, and that trick memory, but as a team player he was worthless. You don't know how many matches he blew for us. When the pressure was on, we could always count on Bunnish to fold. But that time was the worst, that game against Vesselere. I could have killed him. He was an arrogant asshole, too."

Kathy laughed. "Isn't this arrogant asshole the one

we are now speeding to visit?"

"It's been ten years. Maybe he's changed. Even if he hasn't, well, he's a multimillionaire asshole now. Electronics. Besides, I want to see E.C. and Steve again, and Bunnish said they'd be there."

"Delightful," said Kathy. "Well, rush on, then. I wouldn't want to miss this. It might be my only opportunity to spend four days with an asshole millionaire and three losers."

Peter said nothing, but he pressed down on the accelerator, and the Toyota plunged down the mountain road, faster and faster, rattling as it picked up speed. Down and down, he thought, down and down. Just like my goddamned life.

Four miles up Bunnish's private road, they finally came within sight of the house. Peter, who still dreamed of buying his own house after a decade of living in cheap apartments, took one look and knew he was gazing at a three million dollar piece of property. There were three levels, all blending into the mountainside so well you hardly noticed them, built of natural wood and native stone and tinted glass. A huge solar greenhouse was the most conspicuous feature. Beneath the house, a four-car garage was sunk right into the mountain itself.

Peter pulled into the last empty spot, between a brand new silver Cadillac Seville that was obviously Bunnish's, and an ancient rusted VW Beetle that was obviously not. As he pulled the key from the ignition, the garage doors shut automatically behind them, blocking out daylight and the gorgeous mountain vistas. The door closed with a resounding metallic clang.

"Someone knows we're here," Kathy observed.

"Get the suitcases," Peter snapped.

To the rear of the garage they found the elevator, and Peter jabbed the topmost of the two buttons. When the elevator doors opened again, it was on a huge living room. Peter stepped out and stared at a wilderness of potted plants beneath a vaulting skylight, at thick brown carpets, fine wood panelling, bookcases packed with leather-bound volumes, a large fireplace, and Edward Colin Stuart, who rose from a leather-clad armchair across the room when the elevator arrived.

"E.C.," Peter said, setting down his suitcase. He smiled.

"Hello, Peter," E.C. said, coming toward them quickly. They shook hands.

"You haven't changed a goddamned bit in ten years," Peter said. It was true. E.C. was still slender and compact, with a bushy head of sandy blond hair and a magnificent handlebar mustache. He was wearing jeans and a tapered purple shirt, with a black vest, and he seemed just as he had a decade ago: brisk, trim, efficient. "Not a damn bit," Peter repeated.

"More's the pity," E.C. said. "One is supposed to change, I believe." His blue eyes were as unreadable as ever. He turned to Kathy, and said, "I'm E.C. Stuart."

"Oh, pardon," Peter said. "This is my wife, Kathy."

"Delighted," she said, taking his hand and smiling at him.

"Where's Steve?" Peter asked. "I saw his VW down in the garage. Gave me a start. How long has he been driving that thing now? Fifteen years?"

"Not quite," E.C. said. "He's around somewhere, probably having a drink." His mouth shifted subtly when he said it, telling Peter a good deal more than his words did.

"And Bunnish?"

"Brucie has not yet made his appearance. I think he was waiting for you to arrive. You probably want to settle in to your rooms."

"How do we find them, if our host is missing?" Kathy asked dryly.

"Ah," said E.C., "you haven't been acquainted with the wonders of Bunnishland yet. Look." He pointed to the fireplace.

Peter would have sworn that there had been a painting above the mantle when they had entered, some sort of surreal landscape. Now there was a large rectangular screen, with words on it, vivid red against black. WELCOME, PETER. WELCOME, KATHY, YOUR SUITE IS ON THE SECOND LEVEL, FIRST DOOR. PLEASE MAKE YOURSELF COMFORTABLE.

Peter turned. "How. . .?"

"No doubt triggered by the elevator," E.C. said. "I was greeted the same way. Brucie is an electronics genius, remember. The house is full of gadgets and toys. I've explored a bit." He shrugged. "Why don't you two unpack and then wander back? I won't go anywhere."

They found their rooms easily enough. The huge, tiled bath featured an outside patio with a hot tub, and the suite had its own sitting room and fireplace. Above it was an abstract painting, but when Kathy closed the room door it faded away and was replaced by another message: I HOPE YOU FIND THIS SATISFACTORY.

"Cute guy, this host of ours," Kathy said, sitting on the edge of the bed. "Those TV screens or whatever they are better not be two-way. I don't intend to put on any show for any electronic voyeur."

Peter frowned. "Wouldn't surprise me if the house *was* bugged. Bunnish was always a strange sort."

"How strange?"

"He was hard to like," Peter said. "Boastful, always bragging about how good he was as a chessplayer, how smart he was, that sort of thing. No one really believed him. His grades were good, I guess, but the rest of the time he seemed close to dense. E.C. has a wicked way with hoaxes and practical jokes, and Bunnish was his favorite victim. I don't know how many laughs we had at his expense. Bunnish was kind of a goon in person, too. Pudgy, round-faced with big cheeks like some kind of chipmunk, wore his hair in a crew cut. He was in ROTC. I've never seen anyone who looked more ridiculous in a uniform. He never dated.''

"Gay?"

"No, not hardly. Asexual is closer to it." Peter looked around the room and shook his head. "I can't imagine how Bunnish made it this big. Him of all people." He sighed, opened his suitcase, and started to unpack. "I might have believed it of Delmario," he continued. "Steve and Bunnish were both in Tech, but Steve always seemed much brighter. We all thought he was a real whiz-kid. Bunnish just seemed like an arrogant mediocrity."

"Fooled you," Kathy said. She smiled sweetly. "Of course, he's not the only one to fool you, is he? Though perhaps he was the first."

"Enough," Peter said, hanging the last of his shirts in the closet. "Come on, let's get back downstairs. I want to talk to E.C."

They had no sooner stepped out of their suite when a voice hailed them. "*Pete?*"

Peter turned, and the big man standing in the doorway down the hall smiled a blurry smile at him. "Don't you recognize me, Pete?"

"Steve?" Peter said wonderingly.

"Sure, hey, who'd you think?" He stepped out of his own room, a bit unsteadily, and closed the door behind him. "This must be the wife, eh? Am I right?"

"Yes," Peter said. "Kathy, this is Steve Delmario. Steve, Kathy." Delmario came over and pumped her hand enthusiastically, after clapping Peter roundly on the back. Peter found himself staring. If E.C. had scarcely changed at all in the past ten years, Steve had made up for it. Peter would never have recognized his old teammate on the street.

The old Steve Delmario had lived for chess and electronics. He was a fierce competitor, and he loved to tinker things together, but he was frustratingly uninterested in anything outside his narrow passions. He had been a tall, gaunt youth with incredibly intense eyes held captive behind coke-bottle lenses in heavy black frames. His black hair had always been either ruffled and unkempt or—when he treated himself to one of his do-it-yourself haircuts—grotesquely butchered. He was equally careless about his clothing, most of which was Salvation Army chic minus the chic: baggy brown pants with cuffs, ten-year-old shirts with frayed collars, a zippered and shapeless grey sweater he wore everywhere. Once E.C. had observed that Steve Delmario looked like the last man left alive on earth after a nuclear holocaust, and for almost a semester thereafter the whole club had called Delmario, "the last man on earth." He took it with good humor. For all his quirks, Delmario had been well-liked.

The years had been cruel to him, however. The coke-bottle glasses in the black frames were the same, and the clothes were equally haphazard—shabby brown cords, a short-sleeved white shirt with three felt-tip pens in the pocket, a faded sweater-vest with every button buttoned, scuffed hush puppies—but the rest had all changed. Steve had gained about fifty pounds, and he had a bloated, puffy look about him. He was almost entirely bald, nothing left of the wild black hair but a few sickly strands around his ears. And his eyes had lost their feverish intensity, and were filled instead with a fuzziness that Peter found terribly disturbing. Most shocking of all was the smell of alcohol on his breath. E.C. had hinted at it, but Peter still found it difficult to accept. In college, Steve Delmario had never touched anything but an infrequent beer.

"It is good to see you again," Peter said, though he was no longer quite sure that was true. "Shall we go downstairs? E.C. is waiting."

Delmario nodded. "Sure, sure, let's do it." He clapped Peter on the back again. "Have you seen Bunnish yet? Damn, this is some place he's got, isn't it? You seen those message screens? Clever, real clever. Never would have figured Bunnish to go as far as this, not our old Funny Bunny, eh?" He chuckled. "I've looked at some of his patents over the years, you know. Real ingenious. Real fine work. And from *Bunnish*. I guess you just never know, do you?"

The living room was awash with classical music when they descended the spiral stair. Peter didn't recognize the composition; his own tastes had always run to rock. But classical music had been one of E.C.'s passions, and he was sitting in an armchair now, eyes closed, listening.

"Drinks," Delmario was saying. "I'll fix us all some drinks. You folks must be thirsty. Bunny's got a wet bar right behind the stair here. What do you want?"

"What are the choices?" Kathy asked.

"Well, he's got anything you could think of," said Delmario.

"A Beefeater martini, then," she said. "Very dry."

Delmario nodded. "Pete?"

"Oh," said Peter. He shrugged. "A beer, I guess."

Delmario went behind the stair to fix up their drinks, and Kathy arched her eyebrows at him. "Such refined tastes," she said. "A *beer!*"

Peter ignored her and went over to sit beside E.C. Stuart. "How the hell did you find the stereo?" he asked. "I don't see it anywhere." The music seemed to be coming right out of the walls.

E.C. opened his eyes, gave a quirkish little smile, and brushed one end of his mustache with a finger. "The message screen blabbed the secret to me," he said. "The controls are built into the wall back over there," nodding, "and the whole system is concealed. It's voice activated, too. Computerized. I *told* it what album I wanted to hear."

"Impressive," Peter admitted. He scratched his head. "Didn't Steve put together a voice-activated stereo back in college?"

"Your beer," Delmario said. He was standing over them, holding out a cold bottle of Heineken. Peter took it, and Delmario—with a drink in hand—seated himself

on the ornate tiled coffee table. "I had a system," he
said. "Real crude, though. Remember, you guys used to
kid me about it."

"You bought a good cartridge, as I recall," E.C. said,
"but you had it held by a tone-arm you made out of a
bent coathanger."

"It worked," Delmario protested. "It was voice-activated too, like you said, but real primitive. Just on and
off, that's all, and you had to speak real loud. I figured
I could improve on it after I got out of school, but I
never did." He shrugged. "Nothing like this. This is real
sophisticated."

"I've noticed," E.C. said. He craned up his head
slightly and said, in a very loud clear voice, "I've had
enough music now, thank you." The silence that followed was briefly startling. Peter couldn't think of a
thing to say.

Finally E.C. turned to him and said, all seriously,
"How did Bunnish get you here, Peter?"

Peter was puzzled. "Get me here? He just invited us.
What do you mean?"

"He paid Steve's way, you know," E.C. said. "As for
me, I turned down this invitation. Brucie was never one
of my favorite people, you know that. He pulled strings
to change my mind. I'm with an ad agency in New York.
He dangled a big account in front of them, and I was
told to come here or lose my job. Interesting, eh?"

Kathy had been sitting on the sofa, sipping her
martini and looking bored. "It sounds as though this
reunion is important to him," she observed.

E.C. stood up. "Come here," he said. "I want to show
you something." The rest of them rose obediently, and
followed him across the room. In a shadowy corner surrounded by bookcases, a chessboard had been set up,
with a game in progress. The board was made of squares
of light and dark wood, painstakingly inlaid into a
gorgeous Victorian table. The pieces were ivory and
onyx. "Take a look at that," E.C. said.

"That's a beautiful set," Peter said admiringly. He reached down to lift the Black queen for a closer inspection, and grunted in surprise. The piece wouldn't move.

"Tug away," E.C. said. "It won't do you any good. I've tried. The pieces are glued into position. Every one of them."

Steve Delmario moved around the board, his eyes blinking behind his thick glasses. He set his drink on the table and sank into the chair behind the White pieces. "The position," he said, his voice a bit blurry with drink. "I know it."

E.C. Stuart smiled thinly and brushed his mustache. "Peter," he said, nodding toward the chessboard. "Take a good look."

Peter stared, and all of a sudden it came clear to him, the position on the board became as familiar as his own features in a mirror. "The game," he said. "From the nationals. This is the critical position from Bunnish's game with Vesselere."

E.C. nodded. "I thought so. I wasn't sure."

"Oh, *I'm* sure," Delmario said loudly. "How the hell could I *not* be sure? This is right where Bunny blew it, remember? He played king to knight one, instead of the sac. Cost us the match. Me, I was sitting right next to him, playing the best damned game of chess I ever played. Beat a Master, and what good did it do? Not a damn bit of good, thanks to Bunnish." He looked at the board and glowered. "Knight takes pawn, that's all he's got to play, busts Vesselere wide open. Check, check, check, check, got to be a mate there somewhere."

"You were never able to find it, though, Delmario," Bruce Bunnish said from behind them.

None of them had heard him enter. Peter started like a burglar surprised while copping the family silver.

Their host stood in the doorway a few yards distant. Bunnish had changed, too. He had lost weight since college, and his body looked hard and fit now, though he still had the big round cheeks that Peter remembered.

His crew cut had grown out into a healthy head of brown hair, carefully styled and blow-dried. He wore large, tinted glasses and expensive clothes. But he was still Bunnish. His voice was loud and grating, just as Peter remembered it.

Bunnish strolled over to the chessboard almost casually. "You analyzed that position for weeks afterward, Delmario," he said. "You never found the mate."

Delmario stood up. "I found a dozen mates," he said.

"Yes," Bunnish said, "but none of them were forced. Vesselere was a Master. He wouldn't have played into any of your so-called mating lines."

Delmario frowned and took a drink. He was going to say something else—Peter could see him fumbling for the words—but E.C. stood up and took away his chance. "Bruce," he said, holding out his hand. "Good to see you again. How long has it been?"

Bunnish turned and smiled superciliously. "Is that another of your jokes, E.C.? You know how long it has been, and I know how long it has been, so why do you ask? Norten knows, and Delmario knows. Maybe you're asking for Mrs. Norten." He looked at Kathy. "Do you know how long it has been?"

She laughed. "I've heard."

"Ah," said Bunnish. He swung back to face E.C. "Then we all know, so it must be another of your jokes, and I'm not going to answer. Do you remember how you used to phone me at three in the morning, and ask me what time it was? Then I'd tell you, and you'd ask me what I was doing calling you at that hour?"

E.C. frowned and lowered his hand.

"Well," said Bunnish, into the awkward silence that followed, "no sense standing here around this stupid chessboard. Why don't we all go sit down by the fireplace, and talk." He gestured. "Please."

But when they were seated, the silence fell again. Peter took a swallow of beer and realized that he was more than just ill-at-ease. A palpable tension hung in the air.

"Nice place you've got here, Bruce," he said, hoping to lighten the atmosphere.

Bunnish looked around smugly. "I know," he said. "I've done awfully well, you know. Awfully well. You wouldn't believe how much money I have. I hardly know what to do with it all." He smiled broadly and fatuously. "And how about you, my friend? Here I am boasting once again, when I ought to be listening to all of you recount your own triumphs." Bunnish looked at Peter. "You first, Norten. You're the captain, after all. How have you done?"

"All right," Peter said, uncomfortably. "I've done fine. I own a bookstore."

"A *bookstore!* How wonderful! I recall that you always wanted to be in publishing, though I rather thought you'd be writing books instead of selling them. Whatever happened to those novels you were going to write, Peter? Your literary career?"

Peter's mouth was very dry. "I . . . things change, Bruce. I haven't had much time for writing." It sounded so feeble, Peter thought. All at once, he was desperately wishing he was elsewhere.

"No time for writing," echoed Bunnish. "A pity, Norten. You had such promise."

"He's still promising," Kathy put in sharply. "You ought to hear him promise. He's been promising as long as I've known him. He never writes, but he does promise."

Bunnish laughed. "Your wife is very witty," he said to Peter. "She's almost as funny as E.C. was, back in college. You must enjoy being married to her a great deal. I recall how fond you were of E.C.'s little jokes." He looked at E.C. "Are you still a funny man, Stuart?"

E.C. looked annoyed. "I'm hysterical," he said, in a flat voice.

"Good," said Bunnish. He turned to Kathy and said, "I don't know if Peter has told you all the stories about old E.C., but he really played some amazing pranks.

Hilarious man, that's our E.C. Stuart. Once, when our class team had won the city championship, he had a girl-friend of his call up Peter and pretend to be an AP reporter. She interviewed him for an hour before he caught on."

Kathy laughed. "Peter is sometimes a bit slow," she said.

"Oh, that was nothing. Normally I was the one E.C. liked to play tricks on. I didn't go out much, you know. Deathly afraid of girls. But E.C. had a hundred girl-friends, all of them gorgeous. One time he took pity on me and offered to fix me up on a blind date. I accepted eagerly, and when the girl arrived on the corner where we were supposed to meet, she was wearing dark glasses and carrying a cane. Tapping. You know."

Steve Delmario guffawed, tried to stifle his laughter, and nearly choked on his drink. "Sorry," he wheezed, "sorry."

Bunnish waved casually. "Oh, go ahead, laugh. It *was* funny. The girl wasn't really blind, you know, she was a drama student who was rehearsing a part in a play. But it took me all night to find that out. I was such a fool. And that was only one joke. There were hundreds of others."

E.C. looked somber. "That was a long time ago. We were kids. It's all behind us now, Bruce."

"Bruce?" Bunnish sounded surprised. "Why, Stuart, that's the first time you've ever called me *Bruce*. You *have* changed. You were the one who started calling me Brucie. God, how I hated that name! Brucie, Brucie, Brucie, I *loathed* it. How many times did I ask you to call me Bruce? How many times? Why, I don't recall. I do recall, though, that after three years you finally came up to me at one meeting and said that you'd thought it over, and now you agreed that I was right, that Brucie was not an appropriate name for a Class A chessplayer, a twenty-year old, an officer in ROTC. Your exact words. I remember the whole speech, E.C. It took me so by surprise that I didn't know what to say, so I said, '*Good, it's about time!*' And then you grinned, and said that Brucie was out, that you'd never call me Brucie again. From now on, you said, you'd call me *Bunny*.''

Kathy laughed, and Delmario choked down an explosive outburst, but Peter only felt cold all over. Bunnish's smile was genial enough, but his tone was pure iced venom as he recounted the incident. E.C. did not look amused either. Peter took a swallow of his beer, casting about for some ploy to get the conversation onto a different track. "Do any of you still play?" he heard himself blurt out.

They all looked at him. Delmario seemed almost befuddled. "Play?" he said. He blinked down at his empty glass.

"Help yourself to a refill," Bunnish told him. "You know where it is." He smiled at Peter as Delmario moved off to the bar. "You mean chess, of course."

"Chess," Peter said. "You remember chess. Odd little pastime played with black and white pieces and lots of two-faced clocks." He looked around. "Don't tell me we've *all* given it up?"

E.C. shrugged. "I'm too busy. I haven't played a rated game since college."

Delmario had returned, ice cubes clinking softly in a tumbler full of bourbon. "I played a little after college," he said, "but not for the last five years." He sat down heavily, and stared into the cold fireplace. "Those were my bad years. Wife left me, I lost a couple jobs. Bunny here was way ahead of me. Every goddamn idea I came up with, he had a patent on it already. Got so I was useless. That was when I started to drink." He smiled, and took a sip. "Yeah," he said. "Just then. And I stopped playing chess. It all comes out, you know, it all comes out over the board. I was losing, losing lots. To all these *fish*, god, I tell you, I couldn't take it. Rating went down to Class B." Delmario took another drink, and looked at Peter. "You need something to play good chess, you know what I'm saying? A kind of . . . hell, I don't know . . . a kind of arrogance. Self-confidence. It's all wrapped up with ego, that kind of stuff, and I didn't have it any more, whatever it was. I used to have it, but I lost it all. I had bad luck, and I looked around one day and it was gone, and my chess was gone with it. So I quit." He lifted the tumbler to his lips, hesitated, and drained it all. Then he smiled for them. "Quit," he repeated. "Gave it up. Chucked it away. Bailed out." He chuckled, and stood up, and went off to the bar again.

"I play," Bunnish said forcefully. "I'm a Master now."

Delmario stopped in midstride, and fixed Bunnish with such a look of total loathing that it could have killed. Peter saw that Steve's hand was shaking.

"I'm very happy for you, Bruce," E.C. Stuart said. "Please do enjoy your Mastership, and your money, and Bunnishland." He stood and straightened his vest, frowning. "Meanwhile, I'm going to be going."

"Going?" said Bunnish. "Really, E.C., so soon? Must you?"

"Bunnish," E.C. said, "you can spend the next four days playing your little ego games with Steve and Peter, if you like, but I'm afraid I am not amused. You always were a pimple-brain, and I have better things to do with my life than to sit here and watch you squeeze out ten-year-old pus. Am I making myself clear?"

"Oh, perfectly," Bunnish said.

"Good," said E.C. He looked at the others. "Kathy, it was nice meeting you. I'm sorry it wasn't under better circumstances. Peter, Steve, if either of you comes to New York in the near future, I hope you'll look me up. I'm in the book.

"E.C., don't you. . ." Peter began, but he knew it was useless. Even in the old days, E.C. Stuart was headstrong. You could never talk him into or out of anything.

"Goodbye," he said, interrupting Peter. He went

briskly to the elevator, and they watched the wood-panelled doors close on him.

"He'll be back," Bunnish said after the elevator had gone.

"I don't think so," Peter replied.

Bunnish got up, smiling broadly. Deep dimples appeared in his large, round cheeks. "Oh, but he will, Norten. You see, it's my turn to play the little jokes now, and E.C. will soon find that out."

"What?" Delmario said.

"Don't you fret about it, you'll understand soon enough," Bunnish said. "Meanwhile, please do excuse me. I have to see about dinner. You all must be ravenous. I'm making dinner myself, you know. I sent my servants away, so we could have a nice private reunion." He looked at his watch, a heavy gold Swiss. "Let's all meet in the dining room in, say, an hour. Everything should be ready by then. We can talk some more. About life. About chess." He smiled, and left.

Kathy was smiling too. "Well," she said to Peter after Bunnish had left the room, "this is all vastly more entertaining than I would have imagined. I feel as if I just walked into a Harold Pinter play."

"Who's that?" Delmario asked, resuming his seat.

Peter ignored him. "I don't like any of this," he said. "What the hell did Bunnish mean about playing a joke on us?"

He didn't have to wait long for an answer. While Kathy went to fix herself another martini, they heard the elevator again, and turned expectantly toward the doors. E.C. stepped out frowning. "Where is he?" he said in a hard voice.

"He went to cook dinner," Peter said. "What is it? He said something about a joke. . ."

"Those garage doors won't open," E.C. said. "I can't get my car out. There's no place to go without it. We must be fifty miles from the nearest civilization."

"I'll go down and ram out with my VW," Delmario

said helpfully. "Like in the movies."

"Don't be absurd," E.C. said. "That door is stainless steel. There's no way you're going to batter it down." He scowled and brushed back one end of his mustache. "Battering down Brucie, however, is a much more viable proposition. Where the hell is the kitchen?"

Peter sighed. "I wouldn't if I were you, E.C.," he said. "From the way he's been acting, he'd just love a chance to clap you in jail. If you touch him, it's assault, you know that."

"Phone the police," Kathy suggested.

Peter looked around. "Now that you mention it, I don't see a phone anywhere in this room. Do you?" Silence. "There was no phone in our suite, either, that I recall."

"Hey!" Delmario said. "That's right, Pete, you're right."

E.C. sat down. "He appears to have us checkmated," he said.

"The exact word," said Peter. "Bunnish is playing some kind of game with us. He said so himself. A joke."

"Ha ha," said E.C. "What do you suggest we do, then? Laugh?"

Peter shrugged. "Eat dinner, talk, have our reunion, find out what the hell Bunnish wants with us."

"Win the game, guys, that's what we do," Delmario said.

E.C. stared at him. "What the hell does that mean?"

Delmario sipped his bourbon and grinned. "Peter said Bunny was playing some kind of game with us, right? OK, fine. Let's play. Let's beat him at this goddamned game, whatever the hell it is." He chuckled. "Hell, guys, this is the Funny Bunny we're playing. Maybe he is a Master, I don't give a good goddamn, he'll still find a way to blow it in the end. You know how it was. Bunnish *always* lost the big games. He'll lose this one, too."

"I wonder," said Peter. "I wonder."

* * *

Peter brought another bottle of Heineken back to the suite with him, and sat in a deck chair on the patio drinking it while Kathy tried out the hot tub.

"This is nice," she said from the tub. "Relaxing. Sensuous, even. Why don't you come on in?"

"No, thanks," Peter said.

"We ought to get one of these."

"Right. We could put it in our living room. The people in the apartment downstairs would love it." He took a swallow of beer and shook his head.

"What are you thinking about?" Kathy asked.

Peter smiled grimly. "Chess, believe it or not."

"Oh? Do tell."

"Life is a lot like chess," he said.

She laughed. "Really? I'd never noticed, somehow."

Peter refused to let her needling get to him. "All a matter of choices. Every move you face choices, and every choice leads to different variations. It branches and then branches again, and sometimes the variation you pick isn't as good as it looked, isn't sound at all. But you don't know that until your game is over."

"I hope you'll repeat this when I'm out of the tub," Kathy said. "I want to write it all down for posterity."

"I remember, back in college, how many possibilities life seemed to hold. Variations. I knew, of course, that I'd only live one of my fantasy lives, but for a few years there, I had them all, all the branches, all the variations. One day I could dream of being a novelist, one day I would be a journalist covering Washington, the next— oh, I don't know, a politician, a teacher, whatever. My dream lives. Full of dream wealth and dream women. All the things I was going to do, all the places I was going to live. They were mutually exclusive, of course, but since I didn't have any of them, in a sense I had them all. Like when you sit down at a chessboard to begin a game, and you don't know what the opening will be. Maybe it will be a Sicilian, or a French, or a Ruy Lopez.

They all co-exist, all the variations, until you start making the moves. You always dream of winning, no matter what line you choose, but the variations are still . . . different." He drank some more beer. "Once the game begins, the possibilities narrow and narrow and narrow, the other variations fade, and you're left with what you've got—a position half of your own making, and half chance, as embodied by that stranger across the board. Maybe you've got a good game, or maybe you're in trouble, but in any case there's just that one position to work from. The might-have-beens are gone."

Kathy climbed out of the hot tub and began towelling herself off. Steam rose from the water, and moved gently around her. Peter found himself looking at her almost with tenderness, something he had not felt in a long time. Then she spoke, and ruined it. "You missed your calling," she said, rubbing briskly with the towel. "You should have taken up poster-writing. You have a knack for poster profundity. You know, like, "*I am not in this world to live up to your expect—*' "

"Enough," Peter said. "How much blood do you have to draw, damn it?"

Kathy stopped and looked at him. She frowned. "You're really down, aren't you?" she said.

Peter stared off at the mountains, and did not bother to reply.

The concern left her voice as quickly as it had come. "Another depression, huh? Drink another beer, why don't you? Feel sorry for yourself some more. By midnight you'll have worked yourself up to a good crying jag. Go on."

"I keep thinking of that match," Peter said.

"Match?"

"In the nationals," he said. "Against Chicago. It's weird, but I keep having this funny feeling, like . . . like it was right there that it all started to go bad. We had a chance to do something big, something special. But it slipped away from us, and nothing has been right since.

A losing variation, Kathy. We picked a losing variation, and we've been losing ever since. All of us."

Kathy sat down on the edge of the tub. "All of you?"

Peter nodded. "Look at us. I failed as a novelist, failed as a journalist, and now I've got a failing bookstore. Not to mention a bitch wife. Steve is a drunk who couldn't even get together enough money to pay his way out here. E.C. is an aging account executive with an indifferent track record, going nowhere. Losers. You said it, in the car."

She smiled. "Ah, but what about our host? Bunnish lost bigger than any of you, and he seems to have won everything since."

"Hmmmm," said Peter. He sipped thoughtfully at his beer. "I wonder. Oh, he's rich enough, I'll give you that. But he's got a chessboard in his living room with the pieces glued into position, so he can stare every day at the place he went wrong in a game played ten years ago. That doesn't sound like a winner to me."

She stood up, and shook loose her hair. It was long and auburn and it fell around her shoulders gorgeously, and Peter remembered the sweet lady he had married eight years ago, when he was a bright young writer working hard on his first novel. He smiled. "You look nice," he said.

Kathy seemed startled. "You *are* feeling morose," she said. "Are you sure you don't have a fever?"

"No fever. Just a memory, and a lot of regrets."

"Ah," she said. She walked back toward their bedroom, and snapped the towel at him in passing. "C'mon, captain. Your team is going to be waiting, and all this heavy philosophy has given me quite an appetite."

The food was fine, but the dinner was awful.

They ate thick slabs of rare prime rib, with big baked potatoes and lots of fresh vegetables. The wine looked expensive and tasted wonderful. Afterwards, they had their choice of three desserts, plus fresh-ground coffee and several delicious liqueurs. Yet the meal was strained and unpleasant, Peter thought. Steve Delmario was in pretty bad shape even before he came to the table, and while he was there he drank wine as if it were water, getting louder and fuzzier in the process. E.C. Stuart was coldly quiet, his fury barely held in check behind an icy, aloof demeanor. And Bunnish thwarted every one of Peter's attempts to move conversation to safe neutral ground. His genial expansiveness was a poor mask for gloating, and he insisted on opening old wounds from their college years. Every time Peter recounted an anecdote that was amusing or harmless, Bunnish smiled and countered with one that stank of hurt and rejection.

Finally, over coffee, E.C. could stand no more of it. "Pus," he said loudly, interrupting Bunnish. It was about the third word he'd permitted himself the entire meal. "Pus and more pus. Bunnish, what's the point? You've brought us here. You've got us trapped here, with you. Why? So you can prove that we treated you shabbily back in college? Is that the idea? If so, fine. You've made your point. You were treated shabbily. I am ashamed, I am guilty. Mea culpa, mea culpa, mea maxima culpa. Now let's end it. It's over."

"Over?" said Bunnish, smiling. "Perhaps it is. But you've changed, E.C. Back when I was the butt of your jokes, you'd recount them for weeks. *Over* wasn't so final then, was it? And what about my game with Vesselere in the nationals? When that was over, did we forget it? Oh, no, we did not. That game was played in December, you'll recall. I heard about it until I graduated in May. At every meeting. That game was *never* over for me. Delmario liked to show me a different checkmate every time I saw him. Our dear captain refrained from playing me in any league matches for the rest of the year. And you, E.C., you liked to greet me with, 'Say, Bunny, lost any big ones lately?' You even reprinted that game in the club newsletter, and mailed it in to *Chess Life*. No doubt all this seems like ancient history to you. I have this trick memory, though. I can't forget things quite so easily. I remember it all. I remember the way Vesselere sat there, with his hands folded on his stomach, never moving, staring at me out of those itty bitty eyes of his. I remember the way he moved his pieces, very carefully, very daintily, lifting each one between thumb and forefinger. I remember wandering into the halls between moves, to get a drink of water, and seeing Norten over by the wall charts, talking to Mavora from the A team. You know what he was saying? He was gesturing with his hands, all worked up, and he was telling him, *He's going to blow it, damn it, he's going to blow it!* Isn't that right, Peter? And Les looked over at me as I passed, and said, *Lose this one and your ass is grass, Bunny!* He was another endearing soul. I remember all the people who kept coming to look at my game. I remember Norten standing in the corner with Hal Winslow, the two mighty captains, talking heatedly. Winslow was all rumpled and needed a shave and he had his clipboard, and he was trying to figure out who'd finish where if we won, or tied, or lost. I remember how it felt when I tipped over my king, too. I remember the way Delmario started kicking the wall, the way E.C. shrugged and glanced up at the ceiling, and the way Peter came over and just said *Bunnish!* and shook his head. You see? My trick memory is as tricky as ever, and I haven't forgotten a thing. And especially I haven't forgotten that game. I can recite all the moves to you right now, if you'd like."

"Shit," said Steve Delmario. "Only one important move to recite, Bunny. Knight takes pawn, that's the move you ought to recite. The sac, the winning sac, the one you didn't play. I forget what kind of feeble thing you did instead."

Bunnish smiled. "My move was king to knight one," he said. "To protect my rook pawn. I'd castled long, and Vesselere was threatening to snatch it."

"Pawn, shmawn," said Delmario. "You had him busted. The sac would have gutted that whale like nobody's goddamned business. What a laugh that would have been. The bunny rabbit beating the whale. Old Hal Winslow would have been so shocked he would have dropped his clipboard. But you blew it, guarding some diddlysquat little pawn. You blew it."

"So you told me," said Bunnish. "And told me, and told me."

"Look," Peter said, "I don't see the sense in rehashing all of this. Steve is drunk, Bruce. You can see that. He doesn't know what he's saying."

"He knows exactly what he's saying, Norten," Bunnish replied. He smiled thinly and removed his glasses. Peter was startled by his eyes. The hatred there was almost tangible, and there was something else as well, something old and bitter and somehow *trapped*. The eyes passed lightly over Kathy, who was sitting quietly amidst all the old hostility, and touched Steve Delmario, Peter Norten, and E.C. Stuart each in turn, with vast loathing and vast amusement.

"Enough," Peter said, almost pleadingly.

"*NO!*" said Delmario. The drink had made him belligerent. "It's not enough, it'll never be enough, goddamn it. Get out a set, Bunny! I dare you! We'll analyze it right now, go over the whole thing again, I'll show you how you pissed it all away." He pulled himself to his feet.

"I have a better idea," said Bunnish. "Sit down, Delmario."

Delmario blinked uncertainly, and then fell back into his chair.

"Good," said Bunnish. "We'll get to my idea in a moment, but first I'm going to tell you all a story. As Archie Bunker once said, revenge is the best way to get even. But it isn't revenge unless the victim knows. So I'm going to tell you. I'm going to tell you exactly how I've ruined your lives."

"Oh, come off it!" E.C. said.

"You never did like stories, E.C.," Bunnish said. "Know why? Because when someone tells a story, they become the center of attention. And *you* always needed to be the center of attention, wherever you were. Now you're not the center of anything, though. How does it feel to be insignificant?"

E.C. gave a disgusted shake of his head and poured himself more coffee. "Go on, Bunnish," he said. "Tell your story. You have a captive audience."

"I do, don't I?" Bunnish smiled. "All right. It all begins with that game. Me and Vesselere. I did *not* blow that game. It was never won."

Delmario made a rude noise.

"I know," Bunnish continued, unperturbed, "now, but I did not know then. I thought that you were right. I'd thrown it all away, I thought. It ate at me. For years and years, more years than you would believe. Every night I went to sleep replaying that game in my head. That game blighted my entire life. It became an obsession. I wanted only one thing—another chance. I wanted to go back, somehow, to choose another line, to make different moves, to come out a winner. I'd picked the wrong variation, that was all. I knew that if I had another chance, I'd do better. For more than fifty years, I worked toward that end, and that end alone."

Peter swallowed a mouthful of cold coffee hastily and said, "What? Fifty years? You mean five, don't you?"

"Fifty," Bunnish repeated.

"You are insane," said E.C.

"No," said Bunnish. "I am a genius. Have you ever heard of time travel, any of you?"

"It doesn't exist," said Peter. "The paradoxes. . ."

Bunnish waved him quiet. "You're right and you're wrong, Norten. It exists, but only in a sort of limited fashion. Yet that is enough. I won't bore you with mathematics none of you can understand. Analogy is easier. Time is said to be the fourth dimension, but it differs from the other three in one conspicuous way—our consciousness moves along it. From past to present only, alas. Time itself does not flow, no more than, say, width can flow. Our minds flicker from one instant of time to the next. This analogy was my starting point. I reasoned that if consciousness can move in one direction, it can move in the other direction as well. It took me fifty years to work out the details, however, and make what I call a *flashback* possible.

"That was in my first life, gentlemen, a life of failure and ridicule and poverty. I tended my obsession and did what I had to so as to keep myself fed. And I hated you, each of you, for every moment of those fifty years. My bitterness was inflamed as I watched each of you succeed, while I struggled and failed. I met Norten once, twenty years after college, at an autographing party. You were so patronizing. It was then that I determined to ruin you, all of you.

"And I did. What is there to say? I perfected my device at the age of seventy-one. There is no way to move matter through time, but *mind*, mind is a different issue. My device would send my mind back to any point in my own lifetime that I chose, superimpose my consciousness with all of its memories on the consciousness of my earlier self. I could take nothing with me, of course." Bunnish smiled and tapped his temple significantly. "But I still had my photographic memory. It was more than enough. I memorized things I would need to know in my new life, and I flashed back to my youth. I was given another chance, a chance to make some different moves in the game of life. I did."

Steve Delmario blinked. "Your body," he said blurrily. "What happened to your body, huh?"

"An interesting question. The kick of the flashback kills the would-be time-traveller. The body, that is. The timeline itself goes on, however. At least my equations indicate that it should. I've never been around to witness it. Meanwhile, changes in the past create a new, variant timeline."

"Oh, alternate tracks," Delmario said. He nodded.

"Yeah."

Kathy laughed. "I can't believe I'm sitting here listening to all this," she said. "And that *he*"—she pointed to Delmario—"is taking it seriously."

E.C. Stuart had been looking idly at the ceiling, with a disdainful, faintly tolerant smile on his face. Now he straightened. "I agree," he said to Kathy. "I am not so gullible as you were, Bruce," he told Bunnish, "and if you are trying to get some laughs by having us swallow this crock of shit, it isn't going to work."

Bunnish turned to Peter. "Captain, what's your vote?"

"Well," said Peter carefully, "all this is a little hard to credit, Bruce. You spoke of the game becoming an obsession with you, and I think that's true. I think you ought to be talking to a professional about this, not to us."

"A professional what?" Bunnish said.

Peter fidgeted uncomfortably. You know, a shrink or a counselor."

Bunnish chuckled. "Failure hasn't made you any less patronizing," he said. "You were just as bad in the bookstore, in that line where you turned out to be a successful novelist."

Peter sighed. "Bruce, can't you see how pathetic these delusions of yours are? I mean, you've obviously been quite a success, and none of us have done as well, but even that wasn't enough for you, so you've constructed all these elaborate fantasies about how *you* have been the one behind our various failures. Vicarious, imaginary revenge."

"Neither vicarious nor imaginary, Norten," Bunnish snapped. "I can tell you exactly how I did it."

"Let him tell his stories, Peter," E.C. said. "Then maybe he'll let us out of this funny farm."

"Why thank you, E.C.," Bunnish said. He looked around the table with smug satisfaction, like a man about to live out a dream he has cherished for a long, long time. Finally he fastened on Steve Delmario. "I'll start with you," he said, "because in fact, I *did* start with you. You were easy to destroy, Delmario, because you were always so limited. In the original timeline, you were as wealthy as I am in this one. While I spent my life perfecting my flashback device, you made fast fortunes in the wide world out there. Electronic games at first, later more basic stuff, home computers, that sort of thing. You were born for that, and you were the best in the business, inspired and ingenious.

"When I flashed back, I simply took your place. Before using my device, I studied all your early little games, your cleverest ideas, the basic patents that came later and made you so rich. And I memorized all of them, along with the dates on which you'd come up with each and every one. Back in the past, armed with all this foreknowledge, it was child's play to beat you to the punch. Again and again. In those early years, Delmario, didn't it ever strike you as strange the way I anticipated every one of your small brainstorms? I'm living *your* life, Delmario."

Delmario's hand had begun to tremble as he listened. His face looked dead. "God damn you," he said. "God *damn* you."

"Don't let him get to you, Steve," E.C. put in. "He's just making this up to see us squirm. It's all too absurd for words."

"But it's *true,*" Delmario wailed, looking from E.C. to Bunnish and then, helplessly, at Peter. Behind the thick lenses his eyes seemed wild. "Peter, what he said— all my ideas—he was always ahead of me, he, he, I *told* you, he—"

"Yes," Peter said firmly, "and you told Bruce too, when we were talking earlier. Now he's just using your fears against you."

Delmario opened his mouth, but no words came out.

"Have another drink," Bunnish suggested.

Delmario stared at Bunnish as if he were about to leap up and strangle him. Peter tensed himself to intervene. But then, instead, Delmario reached out for a half-empty wine bottle, and filled his glass sloppily.

"This is contemptible, Bruce," E.C. said.

Bunnish turned to face him. "Delmario's ruin was easy and dramatic," he said. "You were more difficult, Stuart. He had nothing to live for but his work, you see, and when I took that away from him, he just collapsed. I only had to anticipate him a half-dozen times before all of his belief in himself was gone, and he did the rest himself. But you, E.C., you had more resources."

"Go on with the fairy tale, Bunnish," E.C. said in a put-upon tone.

"Delmario's ideas had made me rich," Bunnish said. "I used the money against you. Your fall was less satisfying and less resounding than Delmario's. He went from the heights to the pits. You were only a moderate success to begin with, and I had to settle for turning you into a moderate failure. But I managed. I pulled strings behind the scenes to lose you a number of large accounts. When you were with Foote, Cone I made sure another agency hired away a copywriter named Allerd, just before he came up with a campaign that would have rebounded to your credit. And remember when you left that position to take a better-paying slot at a brand new agency? Remember how quickly that agency folded, leaving you without an income? That was me. I've given your career twenty or thirty little shoves like that. Haven't you ever wondered at how infallibly wrong most of your professional moves have been, Stuart? At your bad luck?"

"No," said E.C. "I'm doing well enough, thank you."

Bunnish smiled. "I played one other little joke on you, too. You can thank me for that case of herpes you picked up last year. The lady who gave it to you was well paid. I had to search for her for a good number of years until I found the right combination—an out-of-work actress who was young and gorgeous and precisely your type, yet sufficiently desperate to do just about anything, and gifted with an incurable venereal disease as well. How did you like her, Stuart? It's your fault, you know. I just put her in your path, you did the rest yourself. And I thought it was so fitting, after my blind date and all."

E.C.'s expression did not change. "If you think this is going to break me down or make me believe you, you're way off base. All this proves is that you've had me investigated, and managed to dig up some dirt on my life."

"Oh," said Bunnish. "Always so skeptical, Stuart. Scared that if you believe, you'll wind up looking foolish. Tsk." He turned toward Peter. "And you, Norten. You. Our fearless leader. You were the most difficult of all."

Peter met Bunnish's eyes and said nothing.

"I read your novel, you know," Bunnish said casually.

"I've never published a novel."

"Oh, but you have! In the original timeline, that is. Quite a success too. The critics loved it, and it even appeared briefly on the bottom of the *Times* bestseller list."

Peter was not amused. "This is so obvious and pathetic," he said.

"It was called *Beasts in a Cage,* I believe," Bunnish said.

Peter had been sitting and listening with contempt, humoring a sick, sad man. Now, suddenly, he sat upright as if slapped.

He heard Kathy suck in her breath. "My god," she said.

E.C. seemed puzzled. "Peter? What is it? You look. . ."

"No one knows about that book," Peter said. "How the hell did you find out? My old agent, you must have gotten the title from him. Yes. That's it, isn't it?"

"No," said Bunnish, smiling complacently.

"You're lying!"

"Peter, what is it?" said E.C. "Why are you so upset?"

Peter looked at him. "My book," he said. "I . . .
Beasts in a Cage was. . ."

"There was such a book?"

"Yes," Peter said. He swallowed nervously, feeling
confused and angry. "Yes, there was. I . . . after college.
My first novel." He gave a nervous laugh. "I thought it
would be the first. I had . . . had a lot of hopes. It was
ambitious. A serious book, but I thought it had com-
mercial possibilities as well. The circus. It was about the
circus, you know how I was always fascinated by the
circus. A metaphor for life, I thought, a kind of life, but
very colorful too, and dying, a dying institution. I
thought I could write the great circus novel. After college, I travelled with Ringling Brothers' Blue Show for a
year, doing research. I was a butcher, I . . . that's what
they call the vendors in the stands, you see. A year of
research, and I took two years to write the novel. The
central character was a boy who worked with the big
cats. I finally finished it and sent it off to my agent, and
less than three weeks after I'd gotten it into the mail, I,
I. . ." He couldn't finish.

But E.C. understood. He frowned. "That circus
bestseller? What was the title?"

"*Blue Show*," Peter said, the words bitter in his
mouth. "By Donald Hastings Sullivan, some old hack
who'd written fifty gothics and a dozen formula
westerns, all under pen names. Such a book, from such
a writer. No one could believe it. E.C., *I* couldn't believe
it. It was *my* book, under a different title. Oh, it wasn't
word-for-word. *Beasts in a Cage* was a lot better written.
But the story, the background, the incidents, even a few
of the character names . . . it was frightening. My agent
never marketed my book. He said it was too much like
Blue Show to be publishable, that no one would touch it.
And even if I did get it published, he warned me, I would
be labelled derivative at best, and a plagiarist at worst.
It looked like a ripoff, he said. Three years of my life,
and he called it a ripoff. We had words. He fired me, and

I couldn't get another agent to take me on. I never wrote another book. The first one had taken too much out of me." Peter turned to Bunnish. "I destroyed my manuscript, burned every copy. No one knew about that book except my agent, me, and Kathy. How did you find out?"

"I told you," said Bunnish. "I read it."

"*You damned liar!*" Peter said. He scooped up a glass in a white rage, and flung it down the table at Bunnish's smiling face, wanting to obliterate that complacent grin, to see it dissolve into blood and ruin. But Bunnish ducked and the glass shattered against a wall.

"Easy, Peter," E.C. said. Delmario was blinking in owlish stupidity, lost in an alcoholic haze. Kathy was gripping the edge of the table. Her knuckles had gone white.

"Methinks our captain doth protest too much," Bunnish said, his dimples showing. "You know I'm telling the truth, Norten. I read your novel. I can recite the whole plot to prove it." He shrugged. "In fact, I did recite the whole plot. To Donald Hastings Sullivan, who wrote *Blue Show* while in my employ. I would have done it myself, but I had no aptitude for writing. Sully was glad for the chance. He got a handsome flat fee and we split the royalties, which were considerable.

"You son of a bitch," Peter said, but he said it without force. He felt his rage ebbing away, leaving behind it only a terrible sickly feeling, the certainty of defeat. He felt cheated and helpless and, all of a sudden, he realized that he believed Bunnish, believed every word of his preposterous story. "It's true, isn't it?" he said. "It is really true. You did it to me. You. You stole my words, my dreams, all of it."

Bunnish said nothing.

"And the rest of it," Peter said, "the other failures, those were all you too, weren't they? After *Blue Show,* when I went into journalism . . . that big story that evaporated on me, all my sources suddenly denying everything or vanishing, so it looked like I'd made it all up. The assignments that evaporated, all those lawsuits, plagiarism, invasion of privacy, libel, every time I turned around I was being sued. Two years, and they just about ran me out of the profession. But it wasn't bad luck, was it? It was you. You stole my *life*."

"You ought to be complimented, Norten. I had to break you twice. The first time I managed to kill your literary career with *Blue Show*, but then while my back was turned you managed to become a terribly popular journalist. Prize-winning, well known, all of it, and by then it was too late to do anything. I had to flash back once more to get you, do everything all over."

"I ought to kill you, Bunnish," Peter heard himself say.

E.C. shook his head. "Peter," he said, in the tone of a man explaining something to a high-grade moron, "this is all an elaborate hoax. Don't take Bunny seriously."

Peter stared at his old teammate. "No, E.C. It's true. It's all true. Stop worrying about being the butt of a joke, and think about it. It makes sense. It explains everything that has happened to us."

E.C. Stuart made a disgusted noise, frowned, and fingered the end of his mustache.

"Listen to your captain, Stuart," Bunnish said.

Peter turned back to him. "Why? That's what I want to know. *Why?* Because we played jokes on you? Kidded you? Maybe we were rotten, I don't know, it didn't seem to be so terrible at the time. You brought a lot of it on yourself. But whatever we might have done to you, we never deserved this. We were your teammates, your friends."

Bunnish's smile curdled, and the dimples disappeared. "You were *never* my friends."

Steve Delmario nodded vigorously at that. "You're no friend of mine, Funny Bunny, I tell you that. Know what you are? A *wimp*. You were always a goddamn wimp, that's why nobody ever liked you, you were just a damn wimp loser with a crewcut. Hell, you think you were the only one ever got kidded? What about me, the ol' last man on earth, huh, what about that? What about the jokes E.C. played on Pete, on Les, on all the others?" He took a drink. "Bringing us here like this, that's another damn wimp thing to do. You're the same Bunny you always were. Wasn't enough to *do* something, you had to brag about it, let everybody know. And if somethin' went wrong, was never your fault, was it? You only lost 'cause the room was too noisy, or the lighting was bad, whatever." Delmario stood up. "You make me sick. Well, you screwed up all our lives maybe, and now you told us about it. Good for you. You had your damn wimp fun. Now let us out of here."

"I second that motion," said E.C.

"Why, I wouldn't think of it," Bunnish replied. "Not just yet. We haven't played any chess yet. A few games for old times' sake."

Delmario blinked, and moved slightly as he stood holding the back of his chair. "The *game*," he said, suddenly reminded of his challenge to Bunnish of a few minutes ago. "We were goin' to play over the game."

Bunnish folded his hands neatly in front of him on the table. "We can do better than that," he said. "I am a very fair man, you see. None of you ever gave me a chance, but I'll give one to you, to each of you. I've stolen your lives. Wasn't that what you said, Norten? Well, *friends,* I'll give you a shot at winning those lives back. We'll play a little chess. We'll replay the game, from the critical position. I'll take Vesselere's side and you can have mine. The three of you can consult, if you like, or I'll play you one by one. I don't care. All you have to do is beat me. Win the game you say I should have won, and I'll let you go, and give you anything you like. Money, property, a job, whatever."

"Go t' hell, wimp," Delmario said. "I'm not interested in your damn money."

Bunnish picked up his glasses from the table and donned them, smiling widely. "Or," he said, "if you prefer, you can win a chance to use my flashback device. You can go back then, anticipate me, do it all over, live the lives you were destined to live before I dealt myself in. Just think of it. It's the best opportunity you'll ever have, any of you, and I'm making it so *easy*. All you have to do is win a won game."

"Winning a won game is one of the hardest things in chess," Peter said sullenly. But even as he said it, his mind was racing, excitement stirring deep in his gut. It was a chance, he thought, a chance to reshape the ruins of his life, to make it come out right. To obliterate the wrong turnings, to taste the wine of success instead of the wormwood of failure, to avoid the mockery that his marriage to Kathy had become. Dead hopes rose like ghosts to dance again in the graveyard of his dreams. He had to take the shot, he knew. He *had* to.

Steve Delmario was there before him. "I can win that goddamned game," he boomed drunkenly. "I could win it with my eyes shut. You're on, Bunny. Get out a set, damn you!"

Bunnish laughed and stood up, putting his big hands flat on the tabletop and using them to push himself to his feet. "Oh no, Delmario. You're not going to have the excuse of being drunk when you lose. I'm going to crush you when you are cold stone sober. Tomorrow. I'll play you tomorrow."

Delmario blinked furiously. "Tomorrow," he echoed.

Later, when they were alone in their room, Kathy turned on him. "Peter," she said, "let's get out of here. Tonight. Now."

Peter was sitting before the fire. He had found a small chess set in the top drawer of his bedside table, and had set up the critical position from Vesselere-Bunnish to study it. He scowled at the distraction and said, "Get out? How the hell do you propose we do that, with our car locked up in that garage?"

"There's got to be a phone here somewhere. We could search, find it, call for help. Or just walk."

"It's December, and we're in the mountains miles from anywhere. We try to walk out of here and we could freeze to death. No." He turned his attention back to the chessboard and tried to concentrate.

"*Peter*," she said angrily.

He looked up again. "What?" he snapped. "Can't you see I'm busy?"

"We have to do *something*. This whole scene is insane. Bunnish needs to be locked up."

"He was telling the truth," Peter said.

Kathy's expression softened, and for an instant there was something like sorrow on her face. "I know," she said softly.

"You know," Peter mimicked savagely. "You know, do you? Well, do you know how it *feels?* That bastard is going to pay. He's responsible for every rotten thing that has happened to me. For all I know, he's probably responsible for *you*."

Kathy's lips moved only slightly, and her eyes moved not at all, but suddenly the sorrow and sympathy were gone from her face, and instead Peter saw familiar pity, well-honed contempt. "He's just going to crush you again," she said coldly. "He wants you to lust after this chance, because he intends to deny it to you. He's going to beat you, Peter. How are you going to like that? How are you going to live with it, afterwards?"

Peter looked down at the chesspieces. "That's what he intends, yeah. But he's a moron. This is a *won* position. It's only a matter of finding the winning line, the right variation. And we've got three shots at it. Steve goes first. If he loses, E.C. and I will be able to learn from his mistakes. I won't lose. I've lost everything else, maybe, but not this. This time I'm going to be a winner. You'll see."

"I'll see, all right," Kathy said. "You pitiful bastard."

Peter ignored her, and moved a piece. Knight takes pawn.

Kathy remained in the suite the next morning. "Go play your damn games if you like," she told Peter. "I'm going to soak in the hot tub, and read. I want no part of this."

"Suit yourself," Peter said. He slammed the door behind him, and thought once again what a bitch he'd married.

Downstairs, in the huge living room, Bunnish was setting up the board. The set he'd chosen was not ornate and expensive like the one in the corner, with its pieces glued into place. Sets like that looked good for decorative purposes, but were useless in serious play. Instead Bunnish had shifted a plain wooden table to the center of the room, and fetched out a standard tournament set: a vinyl board in green and white that he unrolled carefully, a well-worn set of Drueke pieces of standard Staunton design, cast in black and white plastic with lead weights in the bases, beneath the felt, to give them a nice heft. He placed each piece into position from memory, without once looking at the game frozen on the expensive inlaid board across the room. Then he began to set a double-faced chess clock. "Can't play without the clock, you know," he said, smiling. "I'll set it exactly the same as it stood that day in Evanston."

When everything was finished, Bunnish surveyed the board with satisfaction and seated himself behind Vesselere's Black pieces. "Ready?" he asked.

Steve Delmario sat down opposite him, looking pale and terribly hung-over. He was holding a big tumbler full of orange juice, and behind his thick glasses his eyes moved nervously. "Yeah," he said. "Go on."

Bunnish pushed the button that started Delmario's clock.

Very quickly, Delmario reached out, played knight takes pawn—the pieces clicked together softly as he made the capture—and used the pawn he'd taken to punch the clock, stopping his own timer and starting Bunnish's.

"The sac," said Bunnish. "What a surprise." He took the knight.

Delmario played bishop takes pawn, saccing another piece. Bunnish was forced to capture with his king. He seemed unperturbed. He was smiling faintly, his dimples faint creases in his big cheeks, his eyes clear and sharp and cheerful behind his tinted eyeglasses.

Steve Delmario was leaning forward over the board, his dark eyes sweeping back and forth over the position, back and forth, over and over again as if doublechecking that everything was really where he thought it was. He crossed and uncrossed his legs. Peter, standing just behind him, could almost feel the tension beating off Delmario in waves, twisting him. Even E.C. Stuart, seated a few feet distant in a big comfortable armchair, was staring at the game intently. The clock ticked softly. Delmario lifted his hand to move his queen, but hesitated with his fingers poised above it. His hand trembled.

"What's the matter, Steve?" Bunnish asked. He steepled his hands just beneath his chin, and smiled when Delmario looked up at him. "You hesitate. Don't you know? He who hesitates is lost. Uncertain, all of a sudden? Surely that can't be. You were always so certain before. How many mates did you show me? How many?"

Delmario blinked, frowned. "I'm going to show you one more, Bunny," he said furiously. His fingers closed on his queen, shifted it across the board. "Check."

"Ah," said Bunnish. Peter studied the position. The double sac had cleared away the pawns in front of the Black king, and the queen check permitted no retreat. Bunnish marched his king up a square, toward the center of the board, toward the waiting White army. Surely he was lost now. His own defenders were all over on the queenside, and the enemy was all around him. But Bunnish did not seem worried.

Delmario's clock was ticking as he examined the position. He sipped his juice, shifted restlessly in his seat. Bunnish yawned, and grinned tauntingly. "You were the winner that day, Delmario. Beat a Master. The only winner. Can't you find the win now? Where are all those mates, eh?"

"There's so many I don't know which one to go with, Bunny," Steve said. "Now shut up, damn you. I'm trying to think."

"Oh," said Bunnish. "Pardon."

Delmario consumed ten minutes on his clock before he reached out and moved his remaining knight. "Check."

Bunnish advanced his king again.

Delmario licked his lips, slid his queen forward a square. "Check."

Bunnish's king went sideways, toward the safety of the queenside.

Delmario flicked a pawn forward. "Check."

Bunnish had to take. He removed the offending pawn with his king, smiling complacently.

With the file open, Delmario could bring his rooks into play. He shifted one over. "Check."

Bunnish's harried king moved again.

Now Delmario moved the rook forward, sliding it right up the file to confront the enemy king face to face. "Check!" he said loudly.

Peter sucked in his breath sharply, without meaning to. The rook was hanging! Bunnish could just snatch it off. He stared at the position over Delmario's shoulder. Bunnish could take the rook with his king, all right, but then the other rook came over, the king had to go back, then if the queen shifted just one square . . . yes . . . too many mate threats in that variation. Black had lots of resources, but they all ended in disaster. But if Bunnish took with his knight instead of his king, he left that square unguarded . . . hmmm . . . queen check, king up, bishop comes in . . . no, mate was even quicker that way.

Delmario drained his orange juice and set the empty tumbler down with self-satisfied firmness.

Bunnish moved his king diagonally forward. The only possible move, Peter thought. Delmario leaned forward. Behind him, Peter leaned forward too. The White pieces were swarming around Black's isolated king now, but how to tighten the mating net? Steve had three different checks, Peter thought. No, four, he could do that too. He watched and analyzed in silence. The rook check was no good, the king just retreated, and further checks simply drove him to safety. The bishop? No, Bunnish could trade off, take with his rook—he was two pieces up, after all. Several subvariations branched off from the two queen checks. Peter was still trying to figure out where they led, when Delmario reached out suddenly, grabbed a pawn from in front of his king, and moved it up two squares. He slammed it down solidly, and slapped the clock. Then he sat back and crossed his arms. "Your move, Bunny," he said.

Peter studied the board. Delmario's last move didn't give check, but the pawn advance cut off an important escape square. Now that threatened rook check was no longer innocuous. Instead of being chased back to safety, the Black king got mated in three. Of course, Bunnish had a tempo now, it was his move, he could bring up a defender. His queen now, could . . . no, then queen check, king back, rook check, and the Black queen fell . . . bishop maybe . . . no, check there and mate in one, unstoppable. The longer Peter looked at the position, the fewer defensive resources he saw for Black. Bunnish could delay the loss, but he couldn't stop it. He was smashed!

Bunnish did not look smashed. Very calmly he picked up a knight and moved it to queen's knight six. "Check," he said quietly.

Delmario stared. Peter stared. E.C. Stuart got up out

of his chair and drifted closer, his finger brushing back
his mustache as he considered the game. The check was
only a time-waster, Peter thought. Delmario could capture the knight with either of two pawns, or he could
simply move his king. Except . . . Peter scowled . . . if
White took with the bishop pawn, queen came up with
check, king moved to the second, queen takes rook
pawn with check, king . . . no, that was no good. White
got mated by force. The other way seemed to bring on
the mate even faster, after the queen checked from the
eighth rank.

Delmario moved his king up.

Bunnish slid a bishop out along a diagonal. "Check."

There was only one move. Steve moved his king forward again. He was being harassed, but his mating net
was still intact, once the checks had run their course.

Bunnish flicked his knight backward, with another
check.

Delmario was blinking and twisting his legs beneath
the table. Peter saw that if he brought his king back,
Bunnish had a forced series of checks leading to mate
. . . but the Black knight hung now, to both rook and
queen, and . . . Delmario captured it with the rook.

Bunnish grabbed White's advanced pawn with his
queen, removing the cornerstone of the mating net. Now
Delmario could play queen takes queen, but then he lost
his queen to a fork, and after the trade-offs that followed he'd be hopelessly busted. Instead he retreated his
king.

Bunnish made a tsking noise and captured the White
knight with his queen, again daring Delmario to take it.
With knight and pawn both gone, Delmario's mating
threats had all dissipated, and if White snatched that
Black queen, there was a check, a pin, take, take, take,
and . . . Peter gritted his teeth together . . . and White
would suddenly be in the end-game down a piece, hopelessly lost. No. There had to be something better. The
position still had a lot of play in it. Peter stared, and
analyzed.

Steve Delmario stared too, while his clock ticked. The clock was one of those fancy jobs, with a move counter. It showed that he had to make seven more moves to reach time control. He had just under fifteen minutes remaining. Some time pressure, but nothing serious.

Except that Delmario sat and sat, eyes flicking back and forth across the board, blinking. He took off his thick glasses and cleaned them methodically on his shirt-tail. When he slid them back on, the position had not changed. He stared at the Black king fixedly, as if he were willing it to fall. Finally he started to get up. "I need a drink," he said.

"I'll get it," Peter snapped. "Sit down. You've only got eight minutes left."

"Yeah," Delmario said. He sat down again. Peter went to the bar and made him a screwdriver. Steve drained half of it in a gulp, never taking his eyes from the chessboard.

Peter happened to glance at E.C. Stuart. E.C. shook his head and cast his eyes up toward the ceiling. Not a word was spoken, but Peter heard the message: *forget it.*

Steve Delmario sat there, growing more and more agitated. With three minutes remaining on his clock, he reached out his hand, thought better of it, and pulled back. He shifted in his seat, gathered his legs up under him, leaned closer to the board, his nose a bare couple inches above the chessmen. His clock ticked.

He was still staring at the board when Bunnish smiled and said, "Your flag is down, Delmario."

Delmario looked up, blinking. His mouth hung open. "Time," he said urgently. "I just need time to find the win, got to be here someplace, got to, all those checks. . ."

Bunnish rose. "You're out of time, Delmario. Doesn't matter anyway. You're dead lost."

"NO! No I'm not, damn you, there's a win. . ."

Peter put a hand on Steve's shoulder. "Steve, take it easy," he said. "I'm sorry. Bruce is right. You're busted here."

"No," Delmario insisted. "I *know* there's a winning combo, I just got to . . . got to . . . only. . ." His right hand, out over the board, began to shake, and he knocked over his own king.

Bunnish showed his dimples. "Listen to your captain, winner-boy," he said. Then he looked away from Delmario, to where E.C. stood scowling. "You're next, Stuart. Tomorrow. Same time, same place."

"And if I don't care to play?" E.C. said disdainfully.

Bunnish shrugged. "Suit yourself," he said. "I'll be here, and the game will be here. I'll start your clock on time. You can lose over the board or lose by forfeit. You lose either way."

"And me?" Peter said.

"Why, captain," said Bunnish. "I'm saving *you* for last."

Steve Delmario was a wreck. He refused to leave the chessboard except to mix himself fresh drinks. For the rest of the morning and most of the afternoon he remained glued to his seat, drinking like a fish and flicking the chess pieces around like a man possessed, playing and replaying the game. Delmario wolfed down a couple sandwiches that Peter made up for him around lunchtime, but there was no talking to him, no calming him. Peter tried. In an hour or so, Delmario would be passed out from the booze he was downing in such alarming quantities.

Finally he and E.C. left Delmario alone, and went upstairs to his suite. Peter knocked on the door. "You decent, Kathy? E.C. is with me."

She opened the door. She had on jeans and a t-shirt. "Decent as I ever get," she said. "Come on in. How did the great game come out?"

"Delmario lost," Peter said. "It was a close thing, though. I thought we had him for a moment."

Kathy snorted.

"So what now?" E.C. said.

"You going to play tomorrow?"

E.C. shrugged. "Might as well. I've got nothing to lose."

"Good," Peter said. "You can beat him. Steve almost won, and we both know the shape he's in. We've got to analyze, figure out where he went wrong."

E.C. fingered his mustache. He looked cool and thoughtful. "That pawn move," he suggested. "The one that didn't give check. It left White open for that counterattack."

"It also set up the mating net," Peter said. He looked over his shoulder, saw Kathy standing with her arms crossed. "Could you get the chessboard from the bedroom?" he asked her. When she left, Peter turned back to E.C. "I think Steve was already lost by the time he made that pawn move. That was his only good shot —lots of threats there. Everything else just petered out after a few checks. He went wrong before that, I think."

"All those checks," E.C. said. "One too many, maybe?"

"Exactly," said Peter. "Instead of driving him into a checkmate, Steve drove him into safety. You've got to vary somewhere in there."

"Agreed."

Kathy arrived with the chess set and placed it on the low table between them. As Peter swiftly set up the critical position, she folded her legs beneath her and sat on the floor. But she grew bored very quickly when they began to analyze, and it wasn't long before she got to her feet again with a disgusted noise. "Both of you are crazy," she said. "I'm going to get something to eat."

"Bring us back something, will you?" Peter asked. "And a couple of beers?" But he hardly noticed it when she placed the tray beside them.

They stayed at it well into the night. Kathy was the only one who went down to dine with Bunnish. When she returned, she said, "That man is *disgusting*," so emphatically that it actually distracted Peter from the game. But only for an instant.

"Here, try this," E.C. said, moving a knight, and Peter looked back quickly.

"I see you decided to play, Stuart," Bunnish said the next morning.

E.C., looking trim and fresh, his sandy hair carefully combed and brushed, a steaming mug of black coffee in hand, nodded briskly. "You're as sharp as ever, Brucie."

Bunnish chuckled.

"One point, however," E.C. said, holding up a finger. "I still don't believe your cock-and-bull story about time-travel. We'll play this out, alright, but we'll play for money, not for one of your flashbacks. Understood?"

"You jokers are such suspicious types," Bunnish said. He sighed. "Anything you say, of course. You want money. Fine."

"One million dollars."

Bunnish smiled broadly. "Small change," he said. "But I agree. Beat me, and you'll leave here with one million. You'll take a check, I hope?"

"A certified check." E.C. turned to Peter. "You're my witness," he said, and Peter nodded. The three of them were alone this morning. Kathy was firm in her disinterest, and Delmario was in his room sleeping off his binge.

"Ready?" Bunnish asked.

"Go on."

Bunnish started the clock. E.C. reached out and played the sacrifice. Knight takes pawn. His motions were crisp and economical. Bunnish captured, and E.C. played the bishop sac without a second's hesitation. Bunnish captured again, pushed the clock.

E.C. Stuart brushed back his mustache, reached down, and moved a pawn. No check.

"Ah," Bunnish said. "An improvement. You have something up your sleeve, don't you? Of course you do. E.C. Stuart always has something up his sleeve. The hilarious, unpredictable E.C. Stuart. Such a joker. So imaginative."

"Play chess, Brucie," snapped E.C.

"Of course." Peter drifted closer to the board while Bunnish studied the position. They had gone over and over the game last night, and had finally decided that the queen check that Delmario had played following the double sac was unsound. There were several other checks in the position, all tempting, but after hours of analysis he and E.C. had discarded those as well. Each of them offered plenty of traps and checkmates should Black err, but each of them seemed to fail against correct play, and they had to assume Bunnish would play correctly.

E.C.'s pawn move was a more promising line. Subtler. Sounder. It opened lines for White's pieces, and interposed another barrier between Black's king and the safety of the queenside. Suddenly White had threats everywhere. Bunnish had serious troubles to chew on now.

He did not chew on them nearly as long as Peter would have expected. After studying the position for a bare couple minutes, he picked up his queen and snatched off White's queen rook pawn, which was undefended. Bunnish cupped the pawn in his hand, yawned, and slouched back in his chair, looking lazy and unperturbed.

E.C. Stuart permitted himself a brief scowl as he looked over the position. Peter felt uneasy as well. That move ought to have disturbed Bunnish more than it had, he thought. White had so many threats . . . last night they had analyzed the possibilities exhaustively, playing and replaying every variation and subvariation until they were sure that they had found the win. Peter had gone to sleep feeling almost jubilant. Bunnish had a dozen feasible defenses to their pawn thrust. They'd had no way of knowing which one he would choose, so they had satisfied themselves that each and every one ultimately ended in failure.

Only now Bunnish had fooled them. He hadn't played

any of the likely defenses. He had just ignored E.C.'s mating threats, and gone pawn-snatching as blithely as the rankest patzer. Had they missed something? While E.C. considered the best reply, Peter drew up a chair to the side of the board so he could analyze in comfort.

There was nothing, he thought, nothing. Bunnish had a check next move, if he wanted it, by pushing his queen to the eighth rank. But it was meaningless. E.C. hadn't weakened his queenside the way Steve had yesterday, in his haste to find a mate. If Bunnish checked, all Stuart had to do was move his king up to queen two. Then the Black queen would be under attack by a rook, and forced to retreat or grab another worthless pawn. Meanwhile Bunnish would be getting checkmated in the middle of the board. The more Peter went over the variations, the more convinced he became that there was no way Bunnish could possibly work up the kind of counterattack he had used to smash Steve Delmario.

E.C., after a long and cautious appraisal of the board, seemed to reach the same conclusion. He reached out coolly and moved his knight, hemming in Bunnish's lonely king once and for all. Now he threatened a queen check that would lead to mate in one. Bunnish could capture the dominating knight, but then E.C. just recaptured with a rook, and checkmate followed soon thereafter, no matter how Bunnish might wriggle on the hook.

Bunnish smiled across the board at his opponent, and lazily shoved his queen forward a square to the last rank. "Check," he said.

E.C. brushed back his moustache, shrugged, and played his king up. He punched the clock with a flourish. "You're lost," he said flatly.

Peter was inclined to agree. That last check had accomplished nothing; in fact, it seemed to have worsened Black's plight. The mate threats were still there, as unstoppable as ever, and now Black's queen was under attack as well. He could pull it back, of course, but not in time to help with the defense. Bunnish ought to be frantic and miserable.

Instead his smile was so broad that his fat cheeks were threatening to crack in two. "Lost?" he said. "Ah, Stuart, this time the joke is on you!" He giggled like a teen-age girl, and brought his queen down the rank to grab off White's rook. "Check!"

Peter Norten had not played a game of tournament chess in a long, long time, but he still remembered the way it had felt when an opponent suddenly made an unexpected move that changed the whole complexion of a game: the brief initial confusion, the *what is that?* feeling, followed by panic when you realized the strength of the unanticipated move, and then the awful swelling gloom that built and built as you followed through one losing variation after another in your head. There was no worse moment in the game of chess.

That was how Peter felt now.

They had missed it totally. Bunnish was giving up his queen for a rook, normally an unthinkable sacrifice, but not in this position. E.C. *had* to take the offered queen. But if he captured with his king, Peter saw with sudden awful clarity, Black had a combination that won the farm, which meant he had to use the other rook, pulling it off its crucial defense of the central knight . . . and then . . . oh, *shit!*

E.C. tried to find another alternative for more than fifteen minutes, but there was no alternative to be found. He played rook takes queen. Bunnish quickly seized his own rook and captured the knight that had moved so menacingly into position only two moves before. With ruthless precision, Bunnish then forced the trade-off of one piece after another, simplifying every danger off the board. All of a sudden they were in the endgame. E.C. had a queen and five pawns; Bunnish had a rook, two bishops, a knight, and four pawns, and—ironically—his once-imperiled king now occupied a powerful position in the center of the board.

Play went on for hours, as E.C. gamely gave check after check with his rogue queen, fighting to pick up a loose piece or perhaps draw by repetition. But Bunnish was too skilled for such desperation tactics. It was only a matter of technique.

Finally E.C. tipped over his king.

"I thought we looked at every possible defense," Peter said numbly.

"Why, captain," said Bunnish cheerfully. "Every attempt to defend loses. The defending pieces block off escape routes or get in the way. Why should I help mate myself? I'd rather let you try to do that."

"I *will* do that," Peter promised angrily. "Tomorrow."

Bunnish rubbed his hands together. "I can scarcely wait!"

That night the post-mortem was held in E.C.'s suite; Kathy—who had greeted their glum news with an "I told you so" and a contemptuous smile—had insisted that she didn't want them staying up half the night over a chessboard in *her* presence. She told Peter he was behaving like a child, and they had angry words before he stormed out.

Steve Delmario was going over the morning's loss with E.C. when Peter joined them. Delmario's eyes looked awfully bloodshot, but otherwise he appeared sober, if haggard. He was drinking coffee. "How does it look?" Peter asked when he pulled up a seat.

"Bad," E.C. said.

Delmario nodded. "Hell, worse'n bad, it's starting to look like that damn sac is unsound after all. I can't believe it, I just can't, it all looks so promising, got to be something there. *Got* to. But I'm damned if I can find it."

E.C. added, "The surprise he pulled today is a threat in a number of variations. Don't forget, we gave up two pieces to get to this position. Unfortunately, that means that Brucie can easily afford to give some of that material back to get out of the fix. He still comes out ahead, and wins the endgame. We've found a few improvements on my play this morning—"

"That knight doesn't have to drop," interjected Delmario.

". . .but nothing convincing," E.C. concluded.

"You ever think," Delmario said, "that maybe the Funny Bunny was *right?* That maybe the sac don't work, maybe the game was never won at all?" His voice had a note of glum disbelief in it.

"There's one thing wrong with that," Peter said.

"Oh?"

"Ten years ago, after Bunnish had blown the game and the match, Robinson Vesselere *admitted* that he had been lost."

E.C. looked thoughtful. "That's true. I'd forgotten that."

"Vesselere was almost a Senior Master. He had to know what he was talking about. The win is there. I mean to find it."

Delmario clapped his hands together and whooped gleefully. "Well yes, Pete, you're right! Let's go!"

"At last the prodigal spouse returns," Kathy said pointedly when Peter came in. "Do you have any idea what time it is?"

She was seated in a chair by the fireplace, though the fire had burned down to ashes and embers. She wore a dark robe, and the end of the cigarette she was smoking was a bright point in the darkness. Peter had come in smiling, but now he frowned. Kathy had once been a heavy smoker, but she'd given it up years ago. Now she only lit a cigarette when she was very upset. When she lit up, it usually meant they were headed for a vicious row.

"It's late," Peter said. "I don't know how late. What does it matter?" He'd spent most of the night with E.C. and Steve, but it had been worth it. They'd found what they had been looking for. Peter had returned tired but elated, expecting to find his wife asleep. He was in no mood for grief. "Never mind about the time," he said to her, trying to placate. "We've *got* it, Kath."

She crushed out her cigarette methodically. "Got what? Some new move you think is going to defeat our psychopathic host? Don't you understand that I don't give a damn about this stupid game of yours? Don't you listen to a thing I say? I've been waiting up half the night, Peter. It's almost three in the morning. I want to talk."

"Yeah?" Peter snapped. Her tone had gotten his back up. "Did you ever think that maybe I didn't want to listen? Well, think it. I have a big game tomorrow. I need my sleep. I can't afford to stay up till dawn screaming at you. Understand? Why the hell are you so hot to talk anyway? What could you possibly have to say that I haven't heard before, huh?"

Kathy laughed nastily. "I could tell you a few things about your old friend Bunnish that you haven't heard before."

"I doubt it."

"Do you? Well, did you know that he's been trying to get me into bed for the past two days?"

She said it tauntingly, throwing it at him. Peter felt as if he had been struck. "*What?*"

"Sit down," she snapped, "and listen."

Numbly, he did as she bid him. "Did you?" he asked, staring at her silhouette in the darkness, the vaguely ominous shape that was his wife.

"*Did I?* Sleep with him, you mean? Jesus, Peter, how can you ask that? Do you loathe me that much? I'd sooner sleep with a roach. That's what he reminds me of anyway." She gave a rueful chuckle. "He isn't exactly a sophisticated seducer, either. He actually offered me money."

"Why are you telling me this?"

"To knock some goddamned sense into you! Can't

you see that Bunnish is trying to destroy you, all of you, any way he can? He didn't want me. He just wanted to get at you. And you, you and your moron teammates, are playing right into his hands. You're becoming as obsessed with that idiot chess game as *he* is." She leaned forward. Dimly, Peter could make out the lines of her face. "Peter," she said almost imploringly, "don't play him. He's going to beat you, love, just like he beat the others."

"I don't think so, *love*," Peter said from between clenched teeth. The endearment became an epithet as he hurled it back to her. "Why the hell are you always so ready to predict defeat for me, huh? Can't you ever be supportive, not even for a goddamned minute? If you won't help, why don't you just bug off? I've had all I can stand of you, damn it. Always belittling me, mocking. You've never believed in me. I don't know why the hell you married me, if all you wanted to do was make my life a hell. *Just leave me alone!*"

For a long moment after Peter's outburst there was silence. Sitting there in the darkned room, he could almost feel her rage building—any instant now he expected to hear her start screaming. Then he would scream back, and she would get up and break something, and he would grab her, and then the knives would come out in earnest. He closed his eyes, trembling, feeling close to tears. He didn't want this, he thought. He really didn't.

But Kathy fooled him. When she spoke, her voice was surprisingly gentle. "Oh, Peter," she said. "I never meant to hurt you. Please. I love you."

He was stunned. "Love me?" he said wonderingly.

"Please listen. If there is anything at all left between us, please just listen to me for a few minutes. Please."

"All right," he said.

"Peter, I *did* believe in you once. Surely you must remember how good things were in the beginning? I was supportive then, wasn't I? The first few years, when you were writing your novel? I worked, I kept food on the table, I gave you the time to write."

"Oh, yes," he said, anger creeping back into his tone. Kathy had thrown that at him before, had reminded him forcefully of how she'd supported them for two years while he wrote a book that turned out to be so much waste paper. "Spare me your reproaches, huh? It wasn't my fault I couldn't sell the book. You heard what Bunnish said."

"I wasn't reproaching you, damn it!" she snapped. "Why are you always so ready to read criticism into every word I say?" She shook her head, and got her voice back under control. "Please, Peter, don't make this harder than it is. We have so many years of pain to overcome, so many wounds to bind up. Just hear me out.

"I was trying to say that I did believe in you. Even after the book, after you burned it . . . even then. You made it hard, though. I didn't think you were a failure, but *you* did, and it changed you, Peter. You let it get to you. You gave up writing, instead of just gritting your teeth and doing another book."

"I wasn't tough enough, I know," he said. "The loser. The weakling."

"*Shut up!*" she said in exasperation. "I didn't say that, *you* did. Then you went into journalism. I still believed. But everything kept going wrong. You got fired, you got sued, you became a disgrace. Our friends started drifting away. And all the time you insisted that none of it was your fault. You lost all the rest of your self-confidence. You didn't dream any more. You whined, bitterly and incessantly, about your bad luck."

"You never helped."

"Maybe not," Kathy admitted. "I tried to, at the start, but it just got worse and worse and I couldn't deal with it. You weren't the dreamer I'd married. It was hard to remember how I'd admired you, how I'd respected you. Peter, you loathed yourself so much that there was no way to keep the loathing from rubbing off on me."

"So?" Peter said. "What's the point, Kathy?"

"I never left you, Peter," she said. "I could have, you know. I wanted to. I stayed, through all of it, all the failures and all the self-pity. Doesn't that say anything to you?"

"It says you're a masochist," he snapped. "Or maybe a sadist."

That was too much for her. She started to reply, and her voice broke, and she began to weep. Peter sat where he was and listened to her cry. Finally the tears ran out, and she said, quietly, "Damn you. Damn you. I hate you."

"I thought you loved me. Make up your mind."

"You ass. You insensitive creep. Don't you understand, Peter?"

"Understand *what?*" he said impatiently. "You said listen, so I've been listening, and all you've been doing is rehashing all the same old stuff, recounting all my inadequacies. I heard it all before."

"Peter, can't you see that this week has changed *everything?* If you'd only stop hating, stop loathing me and yourself, maybe you could see it. We have a chance again, Peter. If we try. Please."

"I don't see that anything has changed. I'm going to play a big chess game tomorrow, and you know how much it means to me and my self respect, and you don't care. You don't care if I win or lose. You keep telling me I'm *going* to lose. You're *helping* me to lose by making me argue when I should be sleeping. What the hell has changed? You're the same damn bitch you've been for years."

"I will tell you what has changed," she said. "Peter, up until a few days ago, both of us thought you were a failure. But you aren't! *It hasn't been your fault.* None of it. Not bad luck, like you kept saying, and not personal inadequacy either, like you really thought. Bunnish has done it all. Can't you see what a difference that makes? You've never had a chance, Peter, but you have one now. There's no reason you shouldn't believe in yourself. We *know* you can do great things! Bunnish admitted it. We can leave here, you and I, and start all over again. You could write another book, write plays, do anything you want. You have the talent. You've never lacked it. We can dream again, believe again, love each other again. Don't you see? Bunnish had to gloat to complete his revenge, but by gloating he's *freed* you!''

Peter sat very still in the dark room, his hand clenching and unclenching on the arm of the chair as Kathy's words sunk in. He had been so wrapped up in the chess game, so obsessed with Bunnish's obsession, that he had never seen it, never considered it. *It wasn't me,* he thought wonderingly. *All those years, it was never me.* "It's true," he said in a small voice.

"Peter?" she said, concerned.

He heard the concern, heard more than that, heard love in her voice. So many people, he thought, make such grand promises, promise better or worse, promise rich or poorer, and bail out as soon as things turn the least bit sour in a relationship. But she had stayed, through all of it, the failures, the disgrace, the cruel words and the poisonous thoughts, the weekly fights, the poverty. She had stayed.

"Kathy," he said. The next words were very hard. "I love you, too." He started to get up and move toward her, and began to cry.

They arrived late the next morning. They showered together, and Peter dressed with unusual care. For some reason, he felt it was important to look his best. It was a new beginning, after all. Kathy came with him. They entered the living room holding hands. Bunnish was already behind the board, and Peter's clock was ticking. The others were there too. E.C. was seated patiently in a chair. Delmario was pacing. "Hurry up," he said when

Peter came down the stairs. "You've lost five minutes already."

Peter smiled. "Easy, Steve," he said. He went over and took his seat behind the White pieces. Kathy stood behind him. She looked gorgeous this morning, Peter thought.

"It's your move, captain," Bunnish said, with an unpleasant smile.

"I know," Peter said. He made no effort to move, scarcely even looked at the board. "Bruce, why do you hate me? I've been thinking about that, and I'd like to know the answer. I can understand about Steve and E.C. Steve had the presumption to win when you lost, and he rubbed your nose in that defeat afterwards. E.C. made you the butt of his jokes. But why me? What did I ever do to you?"

Bunnish looked briefly confused. Then his face grew hard. "You. You were the worst of them all."

Peter was startled. "I never. . ."

"The big captain," Bunnish said sarcastically. "That day ten years ago, you never even *tried*. You took a quick grandmaster draw with your old friend Hal Winslow. You could have tried for a win, played on, but you didn't. Oh, no. You never cared how much more pressure you put on the rest of us. And when we lost, you didn't take any of the blame, not a bit of it, even though you gave up half a point. It was all *my* fault. And that wasn't all of it, either. Why was *I* on first board, Norten? All of us on the B team had approximately the same rating. How did I get the honor of being board one?"

Peter thought for a minute, trying to recall the strategies that had motivated him ten years before. Finally he nodded. "You always lost the big games, Bruce. It made sense to put you up on board one, where you'd face the other teams' big guns, the ones who'd probably beat whoever we played there. That way the lower boards would be manned by more reliable players, the ones we could count on in the clutch."

"In other words," Bunnish said, "I was a write-off. You expected me to lose, while you won matches on the lower boards."

"Yes," Peter admitted. "I'm sorry."

"Sorry," mocked Bunnish. "You *made* me lose, expected me to lose, and then tormented me for losing, and now you're sorry. You didn't play chess that day. You never played chess. You were playing a bigger game, a game that lasted for years, between you and Winslow of U.C. And the team members were your pieces and your pawns. Me, I was a sac. A gambit. That was all. And it didn't work anyway. Winslow beat you. You *lost*."

"You're right," Peter admitted. "I lost. I think I understand now. Why you did all the things you've done."

"You're going to lose again now," Bunnish said. "*Move*, before your clock runs out." He nodded down at the checkered wasteland that lay between them, at the complex jumble of Black and White pieces.

Peter glanced at the board with disinterest. "We analyzed until three in the morning last night, the three of us. I had a new variation all set. A single sacrifice, instead of the double sac. I play knight takes pawn, but I hold back from the bishop sac, swing my queen over instead. That was the idea. It looked pretty good. But it's unsound, isn't it?"

Bunnish stared at him. "Play it, and we'll find out!"

"No," said Peter. "I don't want to play."

"*Pete!*" Steve Delmario said in consternation. "You got to, what are you saying, beat this damn bastard."

Peter looked at him. "It's no good, Steve."

There was a silence. Finally Bunnish said, "You're a coward, Norten. A coward and a failure and a weakling. Play the game out."

"I'm not interested in the game, Bruce. Just tell me. The variation is unsound."

Bunnish made a disgusted noise. "Yes, yes," he

snapped. "It's unsound. There's a countersac, I give up a rook to break up your mating threats, but I win a piece back a few moves later."

"All the variations are unsound, aren't they?" Peter said.

Bunnish smiled thinly.

"White doesn't have a won game at all," Peter said. "We were wrong, all those years. You never blew the win. You never *had* a win. Just a position that looked good superficially, but led nowhere."

"Wisdom, at last," Bunnish said. "I've had computers print out every possible variant. They take forever, but I've had lifetimes. When I flashed back—you have no idea how many times I have flashed back, trying one new idea after another—that is always my target point, that day in Evanston, the game with Vesselere. I've tried every move there is to be tried in that position, every wild idea. It makes no difference. Vesselere always beats me. All the variations are unsound."

"But," Delmario protested, looking bewildered. "Vesselere *said* he was lost. He *said* so!"

Bunnish looked at him with contempt. "I had made him sweat a lot in a game he should have won easily. He was just getting back. He was a vindictive man, and he knew that by saying that he'd make the loss that much more painful." He smirked. "I've taken care of *him* too, you know."

E.C. Stuart rose up from his chair and straightened his vest. "If we're done now, Brucie, maybe you would be so kind as to let us out of Bunnishland?"

"*You* can go," Bunnish said. "And that drunk, too. But not Peter." He showed his dimples. "Why, Peter has almost won, in a sense. So I'm going to be generous. You know what I'm going to do for you, captain? I'm going to let you use my flashback device."

"No thank you," Peter said.

Bunnish stared, befuddled. "What do you mean, no? Don't you understand what I'm giving you? You can wipe out all your failures, try again, make some different moves. Be a success in another timeline."

"I know. Of course, that would leave Kathy with a dead body in *this* timeline, wouldn't it? And you with the satisfaction of driving me to something that uncannily resembles suicide. No. I'll take my chances with the future instead of the past. With Kathy."

Bunnish let his mouth droop open. "What do you care about her? She hates you anyway. She'll be better off with you dead. She'll get the insurance money and you'll get somebody better, somebody who cares about you."

"But I do care about him," Kathy said. She put a hand on Peter's shoulder. He reached up and touched it, and smiled.

"Then you're a fool, too," Bunnish cried. "He's nothing, he'll *never* be anything. I'll see to that."

Peter stood up. "I don't think so, somehow. I don't think you can hurt us anymore. Any of us." He looked at the others. "What do you think, guys?"

E.C. cocked his head thoughtfully, and ran a finger along the underside of his mustache. "You know," he said, "I think you're right."

Delmario just seemed baffled, until all of a sudden the light broke across his face, and he grinned. "You can't steal ideas I haven't come up with yet, can you?" he said to Bunnish. "Not in this timeline, anyhow." He made a loud whooping sound and stepped up to the chessboard. Reaching down, he stopped the clock. "Checkmate," he said. "Checkmate, checkmate, *checkmate*!"

Less than two weeks later, Kathy knocked softly on the door of his study. "Wait a sec!" Peter shouted. He typed out another sentence, then flicked off the typewriter and swiveled in his chair. "C'mon in."

She opened the door and smiled at him. "I made some tuna salad, if you want to take a break for lunch. How's the book coming?"

"Good," Peter said. "I should finish the second chapter today, if I keep at it." She was holding a newspaper, he noticed. "What's that?"

"I thought you ought to see this," she replied, handing it over.

She'd folded it open to the obits. Peter took it and read. Millionaire electronics genius Bruce Bunnish had been found dead in his Colorado home, hooked up to a strange device that had seemingly electrocuted him. Peter sighed.

"He's going to try again, isn't he?" Kathy said.

Peter put down the newspaper. "The poor bastard. He can't see it."

"See what?"

Peter took her hand and squeezed it. "All the variations are unsound," he said. It made him sad. But after lunch, he soon forgot about it, and went back to work.

A GAME OF VLET

Joanna Russ

In Ourdh, near the sea, on a summer's night so hot and still that the marble blocks of the Governor's mansion sweated as if the earth itself were respiring through the stone—which is exactly what certain wise men maintain to be the case—the Governor's palace guard caught an assassin trying to enter the Governor's palace through a secret passage too many unfortunates have thought they alone knew. This one, his arm caught and twisted by the Captain, beads of sweat starting out on his pale, black-bearded face, was a thin young man in aristocratic robes, followed by the oddest company one could possibly meet—even in Ourdh—a cook, a servant-girl, a couple of waterfront beggars, a battered hulk of a man who looked like a professional bodyguard fallen on evil days, and five peasants. These persons remained timidly silent while the Captain tightened his grip on the young man's arm; the young man made an inarticulate sound between his teeth but did not cry out; the Captain shook him, causing him to fall to his knees; then the Captain said, "Who are you, scum!" and the young man answered, "I am Rav." His followers all nodded in concert, like mechanical mice.

"He is," said one of the guard; "he's a magician. I seen him at the banquet a year ago," and the Captain let

161

go, allowing the young man to get to his feet. Perhaps
they were a little afraid of magicians, or perhaps they
felt a rudimentary shame at harming someone known to
the Governor—though the magician had been out of favor for the last eleven zodiacal signs of the year—but
this seems unlikely. Humanity, of course, they did not
have. The Captain motioned his men back and stepped
back himself, silent in the main hall of the Governor's
villa, waiting to hear what the young nobleman had to
say. What he said was most surprising. He said (with
difficulty):

"I am a champion player of Vlet."

It was then that the Lady appeared. She appeared
quite silently, unseen by anybody, between two of the
Governor's imported marble pillars which were tapered
toward the base and set in wreaths of carved and tinted
anemones and lilies. She stood a little behind one of the
nearby torches which had been set into a bracket decorated with a group of stylized young women known to
aristocratic Ourdh as The Female Virtues: Modesty,
Chastity, Fecundity and Tolerance, a common motif in
art, and from this vantage point she watched the scene
before her. She heard Rav declare his intention of having come only to play a game of Vlet with the Governor,
which was not believed, to say the least; she saw the
servant-girl blurt out a flurry of signs made by the deaf-
and-dumb; she both saw and heard the guards laugh until they cried, hush each other for fear of waking the
Governor, laugh themselves sick again, and finally decide to begin by flaying the peasants in order to relieve
the tedium of the night watch.

It was then that she stepped forward.

"You woke up Sweetie," she said.

That she was not a Lady in truth and in verity might
have been seen from certain small signs and in a better
light—the heaviness of her sandals, for instance, or the
less-than-perfect fit of her elaborate, jewelled coiffure,
or the streaking and blurring of the gold paint on her

face (as if she had applied cosmetics in haste or desperation)—but she wore the semi-transparent, elaborately gold-embroidered black robe Ourdh calls "the gown of the night" (which is to be sharply distinguished from "the gown of the evening") and as she came forward this fell open, revealing that she wore nothing at all underneath. Her sandals were not noticed. She closed the robe again. The Captain, who had hesitated between anticipations of a bribe and a dressing-down from the Governor, hesitated no longer. He put out his hand for money. Several guards might have wondered why the Governor had chosen such an ordinary-looking young woman, but just at that moment—as she came into the light, which was (after all) pretty bad—the Lady yawned daintily like a cat, stretched from top to bottom, smiled a little to herself and gave each of the five guards in turn a glance of such deep understanding, such utter promise, and such extraordinary good humor, that one actually blushed. Skill pays for all.

"Poor Sweetie," she said.

"Madam—" began the Captain, a little unnerved.

"I said to Sweetie," went on the Lady, unperturbed, "that his little villa was just the quietest place in the city and so cutey darling that I could stay here forever. And then *you* came in."

"Madam—" said the Captain.

"Sweetie doesn't like noise," said the Lady, and she sat down on the Governor's gilded audience bench, crossing her knees so that her robe fell away, leaving one leg bare to the thigh. She began to swing this bare leg in and out of the shadows so confusingly that none could have sworn later whether it were beautiful or merely passable; moreover, something sparkled regularly at her knee with such hypnotic precision that a junior guard's head began to bob a little, like a pendulum, and he had to be elbowed in the ribs by a comrade. She gave the man a sharp, somehow disappointed look. Then she appeared to notice Rav.

"Who's that?" she said carelessly.

"An assassin," said the Captain.

"No, no," said the Lady, drawling impatiently, "the cute one, the one with the little beard. Who's *he*?"

"I said—" began the Captain with asperity.

"Rav, Madam," interrupted the young man, holding his sore arm carefully and wincing a little (for he had bowed to her automatically), "an unhappy wretch formerly patronized by the Governor, his 'magician' as he was pleased to call me, but no Mage, Madam, no Grandmaster, only a player with trifles, a composer of little tricks; however, I have found out something, if only that, and I came here tonight to offer it to His Excellentness. I am, my Lady, as you may be yourself, an addict of that wonderful game called Vlet and I came here tonight to offer to the Governor the most extraordinary board and pieces for the game that have ever been made. That is all; but these gentlemen misinterpreted me and declare that I have come to assassinate His Excellentness, the which" (he took a shuddering breath) "is the farthest from my thoughts. I abhor the shedding of blood, as any of my intimates can tell you. I came only to play a game of Vlet."

"Ooooooh!" said the Lady, "Vlet! I adore Vlet!"

"I have been away," continued Rav, "for nearly a year, making this most uncommon board and pieces, as I know the Governor's passion for the game. This is no ordinary set, Madam, but a virgin board and virgin pieces which no human hand have every touched. You may have heard—as all of us have, my Lady—of the virgin speculum or mirror made by certain powerful Mages, and which can be used once—but only once—to look anywhere in the world. Such a mirror must be made of previously unworked ore, fitted in the dark so that no ray of light ever falls upon it, polished in the dark by blind polishers so that no human sight ever contaminates it, and under these conditions and these conditions only can the first person who looks into the mirror look anywhere and see anything he wishes. A Vlet board and pieces, similarly made from unworked stone and without the touch of human hands, is similarly magical and the first game played on such a board, with such pieces, can control anything in the world, just as the user of the virgin speculum can look anywhere in the word. This gentleman with me" (he indicated the ex-body-guard) "is a virtuoso contortionist, taught the art under the urgings of the lash. He has performed all the carving of the pieces with his feet so that we may truly say no human hands have touched them. That gentleman over there" (he motioned toward the cook) "lost a hand in an accident in the Governor's kitchens and these" (he waved at the peasants) "have had their right hands removed for evading the taxes. The beggars have been similarly deformed by their parents for the practice of their abominable and degrading trade and the young lady is totally deaf from repeated boxings on the ears given her by her mistress. It is she who crushed the ore for us, so that no human ears might hear the sounds of the working. This Vlet board has never been touched by human hands and neither have the pieces. They are entirely virgin. You may notice, as I take them from my sleeve, that they are wrapped in oiled silk, to prevent my touch from contaminating them. I wished only to present this board and pieces to the Governor, in the hope that the gift might restore me to his favor. I have been out of it, as you know. I am an indifferent player of Vlet but a powerful and sound student and I have worked out a classical game in the last year in which the Governor could—without the least risk to himself—defeat all his enemies and become emperor of the world. He will play (as one player must) in his own person; I declare that I am his enemies *in toto* and then we play the game, in which, of course, he defeats me. It is that simple."

"Assassin!" growled the Captain of the Guard; "Liar!" but the Lady, who had been gliding slowly to-

wards the magician as he talked, with a perfectly practical and unnoticeable magic of her own, here slipped
the board and pieces right out of his hands and said,
with a toss of her head:

"You will play against *me*."

The young man turned pale.

"Oh I know you, I know you," said the Lady, slowly
unwrapping the oiled silk from the set of Vlet. "You're
the one who kept pestering poor Sweetie about justice
and taxes and cutting off people's heads and all sorts of
things that were none of your business. Don't interrupt.
You're a liar and you undoubtedly came here to kill
Sweetie, but you're terribly inept and very cute and so"
(here she caught her breath and smiled at him) "sit down
and play with me." And she touched the first piece.

Now it is often said that in Vlet experienced players
lose sight of everything but the game itself, and so pas-
sionate is their absorption in this intellectual haze that
they forget to eat or drink, and sometimes even to
breathe in the intensity of their concentration (this is
why Grandmasters are always provided with chamber
pots during an especially arduous game) but never before had such a thing actually happened to the Lady. As
she touched the first piece—it was a black one—all the
sounds in the hall died away, and everyone there, the
guards, the pitiful band this misguided magician had
brought with him and the great hall itself, the pillars, the
fitted blocks of the floor, the frescoes, the torches, everything faded and dissolved into mist. Only she herself ex-
isted, she and the board of Vlet, the pieces of Vlet, which
stood before her in unnatural distinctness, as if she were
looking down from a mountain at the camps of two opposing armies. One army was red and one was black and
on the other side of the great, smoky plain sat the magician, himself the size of a mountain or a god, his lean,
pale face working and his black beard standing out like
ink. He held in one hand a piece of Red. He looked over
the board as if he looked into an abyss and he smiled

pitifully at her, not with fear but with some intense, fearful hope that was very close to it.

"You are playing for your life," she said, "for I declare myself to be the Government of Ourdh."

"I play," said he, "for the Revolution. As I planned."

And he moved his first piece.

Outside, in the night, five hundred farmers moved against the city gates.

She moved all her Common Persons at once, which was a popular way to open the game. They move one square at a time.

So did he.

In back of her Common Persons she put her Strongbox, which is a very strong offensive piece but weak on the defense; she moved her Archpriest—the sliding piece —in front of her Governor, who is the ultimate object of the game, and brought her Elephant to the side, keeping it in reserve. She went to move a set of Common Persons and discovered with a shock that she seemed to have no Common Persons at all and her opponent nothing else; then she saw that all her black Common Persons had fled to the other side of the board and that they had all turned red. In those days it was possible—depending on the direction from which your piece came—either to take an enemy's piece out of the game—"kill it," they said—or convert it to your own use. One signalled this by standing the piece on its head. The Lady had occasionally lost a game to her own converted Vlet pieces but never in her life before had she seen ones that literally changed color, or ones that slipped away by themselves when you were not looking, or pieces that made noise, for something across the board was making the oddest noise she had ever heard, a shrill, keening sound, a sort of tinny whistling like insects buzzing or all the little Common Persons singing together. Then the Lady gasped and gripped the edge of the Vlet board until her knuckles turned white, for that was exactly what was happening; across the board her enemy's little red pieces of Vlet, Common Persons all, were moving their miniature knees up and down and singing heartily, and what they were singing was:

"The pee-pul!"

"The pee-pul!"

"An ancient verse," said Rav, mountainous across the board. "Make your move," and she saw her own hand, huge as a giant's, move down into that valley, where transparent buildings and streets seemed to spring up all over the board. She moved her Strongbox closer to the Governor, playing for time.

Lights on late in the Councillors' House; much talk; someone has gone for the Assassins. . .

He moved another set of Common Persons.

A baker looked out at his house door in Bread Street. In the Street of Conspicuous Display torches flicker and are gone around the buildings. "Is it tonight?" "Tonight!" *Someone is scared; someone wants to go home;* "Look here, my wife—"

Her Tax-Collector was caught and

stabbed in the back in an alley while the rising simmer of the city, crowds spilling, not quite so aimlessly, into the main boulevards

Rav horrified

"We've got to play a clean game! Out in the open! No—"

While she moved the Archpriest

Governor's barricades going up around the Treasury, men called out, they say the priests are behind

And in horror watched him shake his fist at her and stand sullenly grimacing in the square where she had put him; then, before she could stop him, he had hopped two more squares, knocked flat a couple of commoners whose blood and intestines flowed thinly out on to the board, jeered at her, hopped two more and killed a third man before she could get her fingers on him.

"He killed a man! With his own hands!"

"Who?"

"The Archpriest!"

"Get him!"

So she picked up the squirming, congested Arch-priest, younger son of a younger son, stupid, spiteful, ambitious (she knew him personally) and thrust him across the board, deep into enemy territory

Trying to flee the city by water, looks up from under a bale of hides, miserably stinking—

Where the Commons could pothook him to their hearts' content

Sees those faces, bearded and unwashed, a flash of pride among the awful fears, cowers—

"We don't do things that way," said Rav, his voice rolling godlike across the valley, across the towers and terraces, across the parties held on whitewashed roofs where ladies ate cherries and pelted gentlemen with flowers, where aristocratic persons played at darts, embroidered, smoked hemp and behaved as nobles should. One couple was even playing—so tiny as to be almost invisible—a miniature game of Vlet.

"We play a clean game," said Rav.

Which is so difficult (she thought) that only a Grandmaster of Grandmasters attempts it more than once a year. Pieces must be converted but not killed.

The crowd on Market Street is turned back by the troops.

Her Elephant, which she immobilized

Men killed, children crushed, a dreadful silence, in which someone screams, while the troops, not knowing why

and set her Nobles to killing one another, which an inept player can actually do in Vlet

stand immobilized, the Captains gone; some secret fear or failure of will breathes through the city, and again the crowds surge forward, but cannot bring themselves to

She threw away piece after piece

*not even to touch, perhaps thinking: these are our
natural masters? or: where are we going? What are we
doing?*

Gave him the opportunity for a Fool's Kill, which
he did not take

*The Viceroy to the Governor walks untouched
through superstitious awe, through the silent crowds;
he mounts the steps of the Temple—*

Exposed every piece
begins to address the crowd

While Rav smiled pitifully, and far away, out in
the city suburbs, in the hovels of peasant freeholds
that surrounded the real city, out in the real night she
could hear a rumble, a rising voice, thunder; she finds
herself surrounding.

Arrest that man

the Red Governor who wasn't a Governor but a Leader,
a little piece with Rav's features and with the same
pitiful, nervous, gallant smile.

"Check" said the Lady, "and Mate." She did not
want to do it. A guard in the room laughed. Out in the
city all was quiet. Then, quite beside herself, the strange
Lady in the black *gown of the night,* seeing a Red Assassin with her own features scream furiously from the
other side of the board and dart violently across it, took
the board in both hands and threw the game high into
the air. Around her everything whirled: board, pieces,
the magician who was one moment huge, the next moment tiny, the onlookers, the guards, the very stone
blocks of the hall seemed to spin. The torches blazed
hugely. The pieces, released from the board, were fighting in mid-air. Then the Lady fell to her knees, rearrang-
ing the game, surrounding the last remnant of Black,
snatching the Red Leader out of his trap, muttering desperately to herself as Rav cried, "What are you doing?
What are you doing?" and around them the palace
shook, the walls fell, the very earth shuddered on its
foundations.

"Check," said the Lady, "and Mate." A rock came
sailing lazily past them, shattering the glass of the
Governor's foreign window, brought at enormous expense over sea and marsh in a chest full of sawdust, the
only piece of transparent glass in the city. "Trust a mob
to find a window!" said the Lady, laughing. Outside
could be heard a huge tramping of feet, the concerted
breathing of hundreds, thousands, a mob, a storm, a
heaving sea of Common Persons, and all were singing:

"Come on, children of the national unity!
The glorious diurnal period has arrived.
Let us move immediately against tyranny;
The bloody flag is hauled up!"

"My God!" cried Rav, "you don't understand!" as
the Lady—with unLadylike precision—whipped off her
coiffure and slammed it across the face of the nearest
guard. Her real hair was a good deal shorter. "Wonderful things—fifteen pounds' weight—" she shouted, and
ripping off the robe of night, tripped the next guard,
grabbed his sword, and put herself back to back with the
ex-bodyguard who had another guard's neck between
his hands and was slowly and methodically throttling
the man to death. The servant girl was beating
someone's head against the wall. The Lady wrapped a
soldier's cloak around herself and belted it; then she
threw the jewelled wig at one of the peasants, who
caught it, knocked over the two remaining guards, who
were still struggling feebly, not against anyone in the
room but against something in the air, like flies in trea-
cle. None had offered the slightest resistance. She took
the magician by the arm, laughing hugely with relief.

"Let me introduce myself," she said. "My name is
Alyx. I—"

"Look out!" said Rav.

"Come on!" she shouted, and as the mob poured
through the Governor's famous decorated archway,
made entirely—piece by piece—of precious stones collected at exorbitant cost from tax defaulters and con-

victed blackmailers, she cut off the head of an already
dead guard and held it high, shouting, "The Pee-pul!
The Pee-pul!" and shoved Rav into position beside her.
He looked sick but he smiled. The People roared past
them. He had, in his hands, the pieces and board of their
game of Vlet, and to judge from his expression, they
were causing him considerable discomfort. He winced as
tiny lances, knives, pothooks, plough blades, and
swords bristled through his fingers like porcupine quills.
They seemed to be jabbing at each other and getting his
palms instead.

"Can't you stop them!" she whispered. The last of the
mob was disappearing through the inverted pillars.

"No!" he said. "The game's not over. You cheated—"
and with a yell he dropped the whole thing convulsive-
ly, board and all. The pieces hit the floor and rolled in
all directions, punching, jabbing, chasing each other,
screaming in tiny voices, crawling under the board,
buzzing and dying like a horde of wasps. The Lady and
the magician dropped to their knees—they were alone in
the room by now—and tried to sweep the pieces together, but they continued to fight and some ran under the
dead guards or under the curtains.

"We must—we *must* play the game through," said
Rav in a hoarse voice. "Otherwise anyone—anyone who
gets hold of them can—"

He did not finish the sentence.

"Then we'll play it through, O Rav," she said. "But
this time, dammit, you make the moves *I* tell you to
make!"

"I told you," he began fiercely, "that I abhor
bloodshed. That is true. I will not be a party to it, not
even for—"

"Listen," she said, holding up her hand, and there on
the floor they crouched while the sounds of riot and
looting echoed distantly from all parts of the city. The
south windows of the hall began to glow. The poor
quarter was on fire. Someone nearby shouted; some-

thing struck the ground; and closer and closer came the heavy sound of surf, a hoarse, confused babble.

He began to gather up the pieces.

A little while later the board was only a board and the pieces had degenerated into the sixty-four pieces of the popular game of Vlet. They were not, she noticed, particularly artistically carved. She walked out with Rav into the Governor's garden, among the roses, and there —with the sound of the horrors in the city growing ever fainter as the dawn increased—they sat down, she with her head on her knees, he leaning his back against a peach tree.

"I'd better go," she said finally.

"Not back to the Governor," said Rav, shuddering. "Not now!" She giggled.

"Hardly," she said, "after tying him and his mistress up with the sheets and stealing her clothes. I fancy he's rather upset. You surprised me at my work, magician."

"One of *us!*" said the magician, amazed. "You're a—"

"One of them," said she, "because I live off them. I'm a parasite. Don't be too upset, my dear, but I didn't *quite* end that last game with a win, as I said I did. It didn't seem fair somehow. Your future state would have no place for me, and I do have myself to look after, after all. Besides, none of your damned peasants can play Vlet and I enjoy the game." She yawned involuntarily.

"I ended that last game," she said thoughtfully, "with a stalemate."

"Ah, don't worry, my dear," she added, patting the stricken man's cheek and turning up to him her soot-stained, blood-stained, paint-stained little face. "You can always make another virgin Vlet board and I'll play you another game. I'll even trick the Governor if you can find a place for me on the board. Some day. A clean game. Perhaps. Perhaps it's possible, eh?"

But that's another story.

WITHOUT A THOUGHT
(FORTRESS SHIP)

Fred Saberhagen

The machine was a vast fortress, containing no life, set by its long-dead masters to destroy anything that lived. It and a hundred like it were the inheritance of Earth from some war fought between unknown interstellar empires, in some time that could hardly be connected with any Earthly calendar.

One such machine could hang over a planet colonized by men and in two days pound the surface into a lifeless cloud of dust and steam, a hundred miles deep. This particular machine had already done just that.

It used no predictable tactics in its dedicated, unconscious war against life. The ancient, unknown gamesmen had built it as a random factor, to be loosed in the enemy's territory to do what damage it might. Men thought its plan of battle was chosen by the random disintegrations of atoms in a block of some long-lived isotope buried deep inside it, and so was not even in theory predictable by opposing brains, human or electronic.

Men called it a berserker.

Del Murray, sometime computer specialist, had called

it other names than that; but right now he was too busy to waste breath, as he moved in staggering lunges around the little cabin of his one-man fighter, plugging in replacement units for equipment damaged by the last near-miss of a small berserker missile. An animal resembling a large dog with an ape's forelegs moved about the cabin too, carrying in its nearly human hands a supply of emergency sealing patches. The cabin air was full of haze. Wherever movement of the haze showed a leak to an unpressurized part of the hull, the dog-ape moved to skillfully apply a patch.

"Hello, Foxglove!" the man shouted, hoping his radio was again in working order.

"Hello, Murray, this is Foxglove," said a sudden loud voice in the cabin. "How far did you get?"

Del was too weary to show much relief that his communications were open again. "I'll let you know in a minute. At least it's stopped shooting at me for a while. Move, Newton." The alien animal, pet and ally, called an *aiyan*, moved away from the man's feet and kept single-mindedly looking for leaks.

After another minute's work Del could strap his body into the deep-cushioned command chair again, with something like an operational panel before him. That last near-miss had sprayed the whole cabin with fine, penetrating splinters. It was remarkable that man and *aiyan* had come through unwounded.

His radar working again, Del could say: "I'm about ninety miles out from it, Foxglove. On the opposite side from you." His present position was what he had been trying to achieve since the battle had begun.

The two Earth ships and the berserker were half a light year from the nearest sun. The berserker could not leap out of normal space, toward the defenseless colonies on the planets of that sun, while the two ships stayed close to it. There were only two men aboard Foxglove. Though they had more machinery working for them than did Del, both manned ships were mites compared to their opponent.

If a berserker machine like this one, not much smaller in cross-section than New Jersey, had drifted in a century earlier and found men crowded on one planet, there could have been no real struggle and no human survivors. Now, though the impersonal enemy swarmed through the galaxy, men could rise up in a cloud to meet them.

Del's radar showed him an ancient ruin of metal, spread out for a hundred miles before him. Men had blown holes in it the size of Manhattan Island, and melted puddles of slag as big as lakes upon its surface.

But the berserker's power was still enormous. So far no man had fought it and survived. Now, it could squash Del's little ship like a mosquito; it was wasting its unpredictable subtlety on him. Yet there was a special taste of terror in the very indifference of it. Men could never frighten this enemy, as it frightened them.

Earthmen's tactics, worked out from bitter experience against other berserkers, called for a simultaneous attack by three ships. Foxglove and Murray made two. A third was supposedly on the way, but still about eight hours distant, moving at c-plus velocity, outside of normal space and so out of communication with the others. Until it arrived, Foxglove and Murray must hold the berserker at bay, while it brooded unguessable schemes.

It might attack either ship at any moment, or it might seek to disengage. It might wait hours for them to make the first move—though it would certainly fight if the men attacked it. It had learned the language of Earth—it might try to talk with them. But always, ultimately, it would seek to destroy them and every other living thing it met. That was the basic command given it by the ancient warlords.

A thousand years ago, it would have easily swept ships of the type that now opposed it from its path, whether they carried fusion missiles or not. Now, it was no doubt in some electrical way conscious of its own weakening by accumulated damage. And perhaps in long centuries of fighting its way across the galaxy it had learned to be wary.

Now, quite suddenly, Del's detectors showed force-fields forming in behind his ship. Like the encircling arms of a great bear they blocked his path away from the enemy. He waited for some deadly blow, with his hand trembling over the red button that would salvo his atomic missiles at the berserker—but if he attacked alone, or even with Foxglove, the infernal machine would parry their missiles, crush their ships, and go on to destroy another helpless planet. Three ships were needed to attack. The red firing button was now only a last desperate resort.

Del was reporting the forcefields to Foxglove when he felt the first hint in his mind of another attack.

"Newton!" he called sharply, leaving the mike to Foxglove open. They would hear and understand what was going to happen.

The *aiyan* bounded instantly from its combat couch to stand before Del as if hypnotized, all attention riveted on the man. Del sometimes bragged: "Show Newton a drawing of different colored lights, convince him it represents a particular control panel, and he'll push buttons or whatever you tell him, until the real panel matches the drawing."

But no *aiyan* had the human ability to learn and to create on an abstract level; which was why Del was now going to put Newton in command of his ship.

He switched off the ship's computers—they were going to be as useless as his own brain, under the attack he felt gathering—and said to Newton: "Situation Zombie."

The animal responded instantly as it had been trained, seizing Del's hands with firm insistence, and dragging them one at a time down beside the command chair to where the fetters had been installed.

Hard experience had taught men something about the berserkers' mind weapon, although its principles of operation were still unknown. It was slow in its onslaught, and its effects could not be steadily maintained for more than about two hours, after which a berserker was evidently forced to turn it off for an equal time. But while in effect, it robbed any human or electronic brain of the ability to plan or to predict—and left it unconscious of its own incapacity.

It seemed to Del that all this had happened before, maybe more than once. Newton, that funny fellow, had gone too far with his pranks; he had abandoned the little boxes of colored beads that were his favorite toys, and was moving the controls around at the lighted panel. Unwilling to share the fun with Del, he had tied the man to his chair somehow. Such behavior was really intolerable, especially when there was supposed to be a battle in progress. Del tried to pull his hands free, and called to Newton.

Newton whined earnestly and stayed at the panel.

"Newt, you dog. Come, lemme loose. I know what I have to say: Four score and seven . . . hey, Newt, where're your toys? Lemme see your pretty beads." There were hundreds of tiny boxes of the varicolored beads, leftover trade goods that Newton loved to sort out and handle. Del peered around the cabin, chuckling a little at his own cleverness. He would get Newton distracted by the beads, and then . . . the vague idea faded into other crackbrained grotesqueries.

Newton whined now and then but stayed at the panel moving controls in the long sequence he had been taught, taking the ship through the feinting, evasive maneuvers that might fool a berserker into thinking that it was still competently manned. Newton never put a hand near the big red button. Only if he felt deadly pain himself, or found a dead man in Del's chair, would he reach for that.

"Ah, roger, Murray," said the radio from time to

time, as if acknowledging a message. Sometimes Fox-glove added a few words or numbers that might have meant something. Del wondered what the talking was about.

At last he understood that Foxglove was trying to help maintain the illusion that there was still a competent brain in charge of Del's ship. The fear-reaction came when he began to realize that he had once again lived through the effect of the mind-weapon. The brooding berserker, half genius, half idiot, had forborne to press the attack when success would have been certain. Perhaps deceived, perhaps following the strategy that avoided predictability at almost any cost.

"Newton." The animal turned, hearing a change in his voice. Now Del could say the words that would tell Newton it was safe to set his master free, a sequence too long for anyone under the mindweapon to recite.

"—shall not perish from the Earth," he finished. With a yelp of joy Newton pulled the fetters from Del's hands. Del turned instantly to the radio.

"Effect has evidently been turned off, Foxglove," said Del's voice through the speaker in the cabin of the larger ship.

The Commander let out a sigh. "He's back in control!"

The Second Officer—there was no Third—said: "That means we've got some kind of fighting chance, for the next two hours. I say let's attack now!"

The Commander shook his head, slowly but without hesitation. "With two ships, we don't have any real chance. Less than four hours until Gizmo gets here. We have to stall until then, if we want to win."

"It'll attack the next time it gets Del's mind scrambled! I don't think we fooled it for a minute . . . we're out of range of the mindbeam here, but Del can't withdraw now. And we can't expect that *aiyan* to fight his ship for him. We'll really have no chance, with Del gone."

The Commander's eyes moved ceaselessly over his panel. "We'll wait. We can't be sure it'll attack within—"

The berserker spoke suddenly, its radioed voice plain in the cabins of both ships: "I have a proposition for you, little ship." Its voice had a cracking, adolescent quality, because it strung together words and syllables recorded from the voices of human prisoners of both sexes and different ages, from whom it had learned the language. There was no reason to think they had been kept alive after that.

"Well?" Del's voice sounded tough and capable by comparison.

"I have invented a game which we will play," it said. "If you play well enough, I will not kill you right away."

"Now I've heard everything," murmured the Second Officer.

After three thoughtful seconds the Commander slammed a fist on the arm of his chair. "It means to test his learning ability, to run a continuous check on his brain while it turns up the power of the mindbeam and tries different modulations. If it can make sure the mind-beam is working, it'll attack instantly. I'll bet my life on it. That's the game it's playing this time."

"I will think over your proposition," said Del's voice coolly.

"Very well," answered the berserker.

The Commander said: "It's in no hurry to start. It won't be able to turn on the mindbeam again for almost two hours."

"But we need another two hours beyond that."

Del's voice said: "Describe the game you want to play."

"It is a simplified version of the human game called checkers."

The Commander and the Second looked at each other, neither able to imagine Newton able to play checkers. Nor could they doubt that Newton's failure would kill them within a few hours, and leave another planet open to destruction.

After a minute's silence, Del's voice asked: "What'll we use for a board?"

"We will radio our moves to one another," said the berserker equably. It went on to describe a checkers-like game, played on a smaller board with less than the normal number of pieces. There was nothing very profound about it; but of course playing would seem to require a functional brain, human or electronic, able to plan and to predict.

"If I agree to play," said Del slowly, "how'll we decide who gets to move first?"

"He's trying to stall," said the Commander, gnawing a thumbnail. "We won't be able to offer any advice with that thing listening. Oh, stay sharp, Del boy!"

"To simplify matters," said the berserker, "I will move first in every game."

Del could look forward to another hour free of the mindweapon when he finished rigging the checker board. When the pegged pieces were moved, appropriate signals would be radioed to the berserker; lighted squares on the board would show him where its pieces were moved. If it spoke to him while the mindweapon was on, Del's voice would answer from a tape, which he had stocked with vaguely aggressive phrases, such as: "Get on with the game," or "Do you want to give up now?"

He hadn't told the enemy how far along he was with his preparations because he was still busy with something the enemy must not know—the system that was going to enable Newton to play a game of simplified checkers.

Del gave a soundless little laugh as he worked, and glanced over to where Newton was lounging on his couch, clutching toys in his hands as if he drew some comfort from them. This scheme was going to push the *aiyan* near the limit of his ability, but Del saw no reason why it should fail.

Del had completely analyzed the miniature checker game, and diagrammed every position that Newton could possibly face—playing only even-numbered moves, thank the random berserker for that specification!—on small cards. Del had discarded some lines of play that would lead from poor early moves by Newton, further simplifying his job. Now, on a card showing each possible remaining position, Del indicated the best possible move with a drawn-in arrow. Now he could quickly teach Newton to play the game by looking at the appropriate card and making the move shown by the arrow. The system was not perfect, but—

"Oh, oh," said Del, as his hands stopped working and he stared into space. Newton whined at the tone in his voice.

Once Del had sat at one board in a simultaneous chess exhibition, one of sixty players opposing the world champion, Blankenship. Del had held his own into the middle game. Then, when the great man paused again opposite his board, Del had shoved a pawn forward, thinking he had reached an unassailable position and could begin a counterattack. Blankenship had moved a rook to an innocent-looking square and strolled on to the next board—and then Del had seen the checkmate coming at him, four moves away but one move too late for him to do anything about it.

The Commander suddenly said a foul phrase in a loud distinct voice. Such conduct was extremely rare, and the Second Officer looked around in surprise. "What?"

"I think we've had it." The Commander paused. "I hoped that Murray could set up some kind of system over there, so that Newton could play the game—or appear to be playing it. But it won't work. Whatever system Newton plays by rote will always have him thinking the same move in the same position. It may be a perfect system—but a man doesn't play any game that way, damn it. He makes mistakes, he changes strategy. Even in a game this simple there'll be room for that. Most of all, a man *learns* a game as he plays it. He gets better as he goes along. That's what'll give Newton away, and that's what our bandit wants. It's probably heard about *aiyans*. Now as soon as it can be sure it's facing a dumb animal over there, and not a man or computer, it'll attack."

After a little while the Second Officer said: "I'm getting signals of their moves. They've begun play. Maybe we should've rigged up a board so we could follow along with the game."

"We better just be ready to go at it when the time comes." The Commander looked hopelessly at his salvo button, and then at the clock that showed two hours must pass before Gizmo could reasonably be hoped for.

Soon the Second Officer said: "That seems to be the end of the first game; Del lost it, if I'm reading their scoreboard signal right." He paused. "Sir, here's that signal we picked up the last time it turned the mindbeam on. Del must be starting to get it again."

There was nothing for the Commander to say. The two men waited silently for the enemy's attack, hoping only that they could damage it in the seconds before it would overwhelm them and kill them.

"He's playing the second game," said the Second Officer, puzzled. "And I just heard him say 'Let's get on with it.'"

"His voice could be recorded. He must have made some plan of play for Newton to follow; but it won't fool the berserker for long. It can't."

Time crept unmeasurably past them.

The Second said: "He's lost the first four games. But he's *not* making the same moves every time. I wish we'd made a board. . ."

"Shut up about the board! We'd be watching it instead of the panel. Now stay alert, Mister."

After what seemed a long time, the Second said: "Well, I'll be!"

"What?"

"Our side got a draw in that game."

"Then the beam can't be on him. Are you sure. . ."

"It is! Look, here, the same indication we got last time. It's been on him the better part of an hour now, and getting stronger."

The Commander stared in disbelief; but he knew and trusted his Second's ability. And the panel indications were convincing. He said: "Then someone—or something—with no functioning mind is learning how to play a game, over there. Ha, ha," he added, as if trying to remember how to laugh.

The berserker won another game. Another draw. Another win for the enemy. Then three drawn games in a row.

Once the Second Officer heard Del's voice ask coolly: "Do you want to give up now?" On the next move he lost another game. But the following game ended in another draw. Del was plainly taking more time than his opponent to move, but not enough to make the enemy impatient.

"It's trying different modulations on the mind-weapon," said the Second. "And it's got the power turned way up."

"Yeah," said the Commander. Several times he had almost tried to radio Del, to say something that might keep the man's spirits up—and also to relieve his own feverish inactivity, and try to find out what could possibly be happening now. But he could not take the chance. Any interference might upset the miracle.

He could not believe the inexplicable success could last, even when the checker match turned gradually into an endless succession of drawn games between two perfect players. Hours ago the Commander had said goodbye to life and hope, and he still waited for the fatal moment.

And waited.

"—not perish from the Earth!" said Del Murray, and Newton's eager hands flew to loose his right arm from its shackle.

A game, unfinished on the little board before him, had been abandoned seconds earlier. The mindweapon had been turned off at the same time, when Gizmo had burst into normal space right in position and only five minutes late; and the berserker had been forced to turn all its energies to meet the immediate all-out attack of Gizmo and Foxglove.

Del saw his computers, recovering from the effect of the beam, lock his aiming screen onto the berserker's scarred and bulging midsection, as he shot his right arm forward, scattering pieces from the game board.

"Checkmate!" he roared out hoarsely, and brought his fist down on the big red button.

"I'm glad it didn't want to play chess," Del said later, talking to the Commander in Foxglove's cabin. "I could never have rigged that up."

The ports were cleared now, and the men could look out at the expanding cloud of gas, still faintly luminous, that had been a berserker; metal fire-purged of the legacy of ancient evil.

But the Commander was watching Del. "You got Newt to play by following diagrams, I see that. But how could he *learn* the game?"

Del grinned. "He couldn't. But his toys could. Now wait before you slug me." He called the *aiyan* to him and took a small box from the animal's hand. The box rattled faintly as he held it up. On the cover was pasted a diagram of one possible position in the simplified checker game, with a different-colored arrow indicating each possible move of Del's pieces.

"It took a couple hundred of these boxes," said Del. "This one was in the group that Newt examined for the fourth move. When he found a box with a diagram matching the position on the board, he picked the box up, pulled out one of these beads from inside, without looking—that was the hardest part to teach him in a hurry, by the way," said Del, demonstrating. "Ah, this one's blue. That means, make the move indicated on the corner by a blue arrow. Now the orange arrow leads to a poor position. See?" Del shook all the beads out of the box into his hand. "No orange beads left; there were six of each color when we started. But every time Newton drew a bead, he had orders to leave it out of the box until the game was over. Then, if the scoreboard indicated a loss for our side, he went back and threw away all the beads he had used. All the bad moves were gradually eliminated. In a few hours, Newt and his boxes learned to play the game perfectly."

"Well," said the Commander. He thought for a moment, then reached down to scratch Newton behind the ears. "I never would have come up with that idea."

"I should have thought of it sooner. The basic idea's a couple of centuries old. And computers are supposed to be my business."

"This could be a big thing," said the Commander. "I mean your basic idea might be useful to any task force that has to face a berserker's mindbeam."

"Yeah." Del grew reflective. "Also. . ."

"What?"

"I was thinking of a guy I met once. Named Blankenship. I wonder if I *could* rig something up. . ."

A BOARD IN THE OTHER DIRECTION

Ruth Berman

Iskander was senile.

Having no children, he was therefore, of course, entered in a state home. It would not necessarily have made any difference if he'd had any; the homes were lavishly funded, thanks to the votes of the young and guilty. But he might then have had visits and outings to look forward to. As it was, he had nothing to do except look at pieces he no longer knew how to move. On bad days there was nothing but the varying smells of food, deodorant, urine, and feces to occupy his failing senses. On warm days he could go into the garden.

A bright torus, checkered with blue-steel and white-steel magnetic squares, spun on the clear plastic axis attaching it to the clear plastic frame. The plastic was as near invisible as makes no difference, to kibitzers, but to the players it was half-glimpsed curves of light broken into rainbows and reflecting stray bits of color on the board and the blue and white pieces jutting out all over it.

There were some who had said they had seen that Iskander was failing even before Mbara of Uganda beat him, 13 variations out of 20. But others, who knew

Mbara's play better, said that they were both in top form and Mbara had genuinely become the better player. They said it was the shock of losing to a youngster which had ended him.

In fact, Mbara was quite old enough to be tagged as a spinster, married like Iskander to the game alone. It caused quite a stir when she married the following month—and to a nonplayer, at that.

The sunlight was clear and harsh on the dusty park ground. An ordinary chessboard was marked out, but the pieces on it were living men, armed with wooden swords and shields, and sweating heavily under their padding.

Iskander was delighted when he found himself faced with two visitors, at last, on a warm day. Dimly, he heard the words, "Copter ride."

"Yes, yes," he said eagerly. "Copter ride. Most kind of you, Mr. . . . Most . . . Yes." He plucked at the diapers he wore, trying to express his pleasure by freeing himself from the constriction, but they were fastened too securely. He was too excited at the prospect of a ride to mind, however.

But once they were in the copter, one of the men poked him with a needle. He sobbed at this unkindness until he felt himself growing drowsy, and then he went to sleep.

He woke to find himself on a couch in a sunny room. A woman of 65 or so sat rocking opposite him. She looked familiar, but it was not until he tried subtracting years from her face that he recognized her. He sat up slowly, pulling himself on the rim of the couch. "Hello, Miriam. Been a long time. Still in politics?"

"Yes. How do you feel?"

"Fine. And you?" But he had no sooner finished the formality of the exchange than he realized that he did not feel fine. He felt weak and—oddly—happy. The first was not unusual of late. The second seemed strange. It was not as if he had played an interesting game that day.

In fact, he had not played since he could not think when. At that thought, the pawns in his head leaped forward on a dozen different kinds of chessboards, and he knew that he could continue all those games to their ends. Which was as it should be, but not as it had been recently.

The bullet shot over the board. . . . A green knight hop-frogged over a white to take a red pawn. . . . The Fool circled idly around the other pieces and cut down the Moon. . . .

"Well as can be expected," Miriam was saying, and her words took up no more time than Iskander needed to orient himself.

"Testing some kind of intelligence drug on me?" he said as soon as she stopped.

One side of her mouth quirked up, and she leaned forward, saying, "Not exactly. It's an experimental drug which allows the body to tap reserves of energy to overcome the effects of old age."

"Indeed. What happens when the reserves run out?"

She hesitated, and stopped rocking for a moment.

"Death? It's not like you to be sentimental, my dear."

"No, I suppose not." She started the rocker going again. "It's a dangerous drug, certainly. It'll be quite a few hours before you need to worry about unpleasant side effects, though. If you want out of the project, before then, we can reverse it."

"Who do you want me to play?" he said eagerly.

"I didn't say it was chess."

"What else could I possibly mean?"

"That's not a fair way to put it, Zander."

He smiled at her and shrugged. "No. But who do you want me to play? And why?"

She stopped rocking and stretched herself up out of the chair. "You get dressed and come out. I'll show you." She pointed at a suit draped over the end of the couch, and left the room.

Iskander looked down at himself, dressed in diapers,

plastic pants, and sandals. He felt a quick flash of nudity-taboo embarrassment, followed by disgust at the appearance of his body. He tried to suppress that reaction as equally irrational, but failing, ignored his feelings as well as he could and simply began dressing. The suit provided was one of his own from a few years back. It had become a little too large for him, but the looseness of the fabric was pleasant.

"Ready," said Iskander. He stepped through the door into a long, windowless corridor. He blinked for a moment as his eyes adjusted to the change in light.

"Good," said Miriam.

An intense gentleman standing beside her immediately broke into protest. "Madam Chairman," he said, "Have you warned—"

"Yes, of course. Iskander, this is Dr. Hudek. He will be very annoyed with me if anything happens to you."

"Oh, do you play chess, Doctor?" said Iskander, bowing.

"No," said Hudek, obviously puzzled by the question.

"No, he's just a physician," Miriam explained. "This way." She set off down the corridor, and the two men followed.

A Bishop's Pawn opening was unusual, but the QBP was a better fighter than a Live Pawn should be, and worth using as a major piece.

Miriam took them into a small room with a one-way glass wall opposite the door. It looked into a council chamber and was fitted up with outlets for tri-d cameras and tapers, along with pencil sharpeners and the other esoteric paraphernalia of the press.

"Do you plan to broadcast the game?" Iskander asked. He felt out of place, almost a little dizzy at being in a pressroom. He had watched broadcasts of other people's matches often enough, and so he knew what such rooms looked like—or at least what the front sections of them looked like—and he knew that he had been watched many times from such rooms, but he had never been in one before.

"No, we'll only record it," Miriam said. "But there's your opponent."

He glanced quickly at the figure seated at a table going over some papers, and looked back to Miriam, astonished. "It's not Mbara."

"Zander! You're impossible. Why should we risk your life to play her?"

"For the sake of the game?" Iskander made it sound joking, although it wasn't really. "If it's anyone else, why didn't you get Mbara?"

"We would have," Miriam said. "But she died in childbirth a few months ago."

"So I wasn't your first choice," Iskander said regretfully.

"That's irrelevant, Zander. By the way, you still haven't looked at your opponent properly."

Iskander looked. His opponent was . . . a dryad? It had delicate facial bones, like a woman, but a straight-lined body, like a man. It had brown skin, perhaps a little darker than his own, and long green hair, braced up over golden combs on the head, giving a crownlike effect, then falling like a cloak down the back. But even more than the hair, the set of the face and the lines of the body were wrong: the eyes too large and set too wide, the shoulders sloping down too much from the neck, the legs and arms too long. And the most startling wrongness of all was that each of the individual oddities looked right on it. It was not deformed, it was simply not human. And it was beautiful. He found himself tracing designs in the air with one finger. He wanted to get some clay—no, wood was better—and carve a copy of it to be the Magician in a set of Tarotchess pieces or should it be the Fool? But if he carved it dancing like the Fool, how would those long limbs shape themselves to show arrested motion? And what kind of dog would fit with a Fool carved in that likeness?

"Zander?"

"Won't you sit down, sir?" Hudek set a chair behind Iskander, nudging it close enough to touch his legs.

Iskander sat down automatically, then came out of it enough to smile at Hudek. "I'm all right, Doctor. Don't worry."

Miriam sat down in a chair level with his. "Well, Zander."

"From outer space?"

"Right." She nodded, as if granting him a point. "You hadn't heard about the Visitors before, I think?"

"No."

"They represent a confederation of intelligent beings within our Galaxy. They maintain a fleet of scout ships to go around checking promising planets every so often to find peoples ready for membership. The basic criteria are space travel and world government."

"Defined how?" said Iskander.

"Cautious, aren't you? Yes, that's the stinger. Defined as interstellar travel—which, we gather, is most economically managed by treating space-time as four spatial dimensions and traveling cross-time to go places—and a government with some reasonable power to enforce its legislation."

"We don't qualify, then. A pity."

"No, we don't. But we're so close to it, I hate to let the opportunity go. And besides . . . I don't trust people."

Iskander simply nodded, but Hudek's eyes went wide, and for the first time he forgot to address the nominal world leader with respect. "That's a hell of a thing for you to admit!"

"Wait till you're my age, Doctor, and maybe you'll feel the same." She turned back to Iskander. "They made a mistake about us. We were coming along nicely the last time they surveyed us, and they really expected to find us ready for membership this time. Which we almost are, close enough to cause confusion. So they entered openly—in fact, they walked in on a General

Assembly debate." For a moment her eyes gleamed with uncharitable mirth. "I'm afraid that if they find out the truth and reject us, we'll do something silly. Heaven knows, we have enough tense situations threatening to become wars at any moment. If we can fool them and send them away arranging proceedings to invite us into their confederation, I think . . . I hope . . . it'll give us that little extra incentive we need to make peace with each other . . . at last. We've been so close to peace so long, and so close to Armageddon."

Iskander was silent for a moment. "And the space travel?"

"Less important in their reckoning. And easier. We'll get it soon."

"Mmm. Maybe so." Iskander looked into the council chambers at the being, still intent on its papers.

"Or maybe not," Hudek put in. "Maybe the rejection would give us that little extra incentive, as far as that goes."

"Yes. *Maybe*," said Miriam. "And if this gambit doesn't work, let's hope that one does." She looked at him briefly and then turned back to Iskander. "We have all the forms of a world government now—encouraging that mistake is easy. But to keep them thinking we have four-dimensional travel—I'd like you to go out there and play a game of four-dimension chess."

"So. I thought you were leading to that. You really do need Mbara—that variant was her invention. And did anyone ever play it except for her and me?"

"Not a complete game."

"She was a fine player, you know. Playing against her was a kind of heaven, except for losing." He shrugged and half smiled at his own egotism. "But if you don't have her, I'd think a chess-playing mathematician with a specialty in n-dimensional geometry would be your best bet."

"No. You've told me often enough that you can tell a master player from a good one. Our visitor claims to be a master at their equivalent of chess—I gather that it's a good way of spending the time between planetfalls. Both of you will be handicapped, of course, playing an unfamiliar variant, but your familiarity with playing all sorts of variants, I hope, will see you through. You don't have to win, you understand. All you have to do is play well enough to make him think you know what you're doing."

"All right."

The medieval bishop two-stepped its way across the board, to join the slow-moving queen in attack.

They went round by the corridor and entered the council chamber. The alien's big eyes opened even wider. It tossed its head eagerly and cleared away its papers into a sort of briefcase. It said something and a microphone at its throat said, "You are chess master Madam Chairman promised to invite?"

"Yes, how do you do." Iskander bowed.

The alien mimicked the gesture. "White or black?" it said through its mike.

"White," Iskander said without hesitation. He sat down at the table, opposite the alien, and said, "King's pawn-one to king three, level one, cube one."

A board at the side of the room lit up: KP-1, K3-1-1.

"KP-1, K2-2-1," was the answering move.

Iskander nodded. The alien was not going to make orthodox answers, but evidently it wanted to send its pieces out through all dimensions of the "board." But Iskander had chosen white, and he was going to attack so vigorously that the alien would not be able to pursue its own schemes.

Methodically taking his pieces cube by cube across the fourth dimension of the game, he hunted the alien's lesser pieces, first, and then its king. The alien was given to skillful use of the knights, cutting across several dimensions of the board at once, and making it hard for Iskander to keep in his mind the complicated structure of the game's hypothetical playing field. Vaguely, he remembered that he and Mbara had once built a representation of a hyper-cube out of two cubes linked by diagonals which should (if they could have gone in another direction through a fourth dimension) have been perpendiculars. Then they had marked their hyper-cube off into tinier hyper-cubes, making a board to play on, instead of playing the game entirely in their heads. But the board was clumsy, and getting at the pieces was a bore; so in the end they found it simpler to do without it.

Iskander concentrated on getting rid of the dangerous knights. Two he got rid of in equal trades, and one in a trade of bishop for knight. He sacrificed a rook for the fourth, after much hesitation. The rooks, too, made confusing cross-dimension moves, but they only cut across one dimension at a time. He made the sacrifice and looked up to find his opponent's wide grey eyes fixed on him. He met the gaze steadily, wondering if it was respect or curiosity. The alien's eyes fell as it turned to consideration of its next move. Iskander found himself trying to imagine what material could reproduce the shifting colors that made up that grey. It wasn't usual to put eyes into chess figures—they weren't meant to be that realistic—but he decided that a chess piece made to that model ought to include eyes, anyway.

The alien took a strand of its hair in its fingers and fidgeted with it as it thought. The line of green flickered brightly against its skin.

That gesture could not be anything but nervousness, Iskander thought, and he played with renewed confidence.

After four hours or so, it occurred to him that his bladder hurt intolerably. He was surprised. Tournament players were used to sitting without relief longer than that. Then he remembered how long it had been since his last tournament and realized that he felt weak, besides. His head hurt, his chest hurt, his hands and feet were cold. "Excuse me," he said, "I need to stop for a few minutes."

The alien blinked several times, then stood up and

stretched, shivering all its muscles in turn. "Acceptable," it said. It bowed and left through the door opposite the one Iskander had used.

Iskander bowed in turn, cautiously, and looked
around him. He raised his eyebrows at seeing Miriam
still there in the room. "How are you enjoying the
game?" he said facetiously.

"Very much."

On second thought, Iskander corrected himself, she
probably did understand much of what was going on,
following the game through their reactions to the moves.

Dr. Hudek looked frankly bored and unhappy.

Iskander smiled at him and started out. He stumbled
at the doorway, and Hudek promptly came alive, catch-
ing him so swiftly that it looked easy.

"Are you all right, sir?" said Hudek.

"I'm tired, I think."

The doctor looked at him skeptically, but simply said,
"Yes. Rest a little before you start again. That may
help."

When they resumed play, a half hour later, Iskander
felt better, although he could tell that he was weaker
than before, because he could feel the weight of his head.
He propped it in his hands, and it stopped bothering
him.

After two hours more, Iskander announced, "Three
moves to mate." He sat back and let his head droop
against his chest.

The alien looked thoughtfully at the panel recording
their moves and said, "I concede. Thank you. A brilliant
game."

"Thanks," Iskander muttered. He thought perhaps he
should think of a lengthier and more gracious response,
but before he could find one, the alien spoke to Miriam.

"Madam Chairman, I have misapprehended. You
travel to near stars, but you have not fourth-
dimensional drive to go to far ones. So?"

Her smile shriveled into a blank poker face. She hesitated for a moment, then said, "Yes, that's essentially so. How do you know it?"

The alien curved its arm and hand around to point out Iskander. "Chess master's style. He plays as one not used to thinking in all directions at once—takes only three dimensions at a time."

"I see."

The alien curved its hand down to point out its briefcase. "When you have time, Madam Chairman, we will speak more. There is a concept among your peoples I find most difficult to translate: 'national sovereignty'." It used the native term, but its pronunciation was so awkward that they did not recognize the words until after the mike had given them the entire speech.

"It is difficult to understand," Miriam said equably. The diplomatic smoothness of years was back on her face. "We can discuss it later. Doctor. . ." She and Hudek helped Iskander from the room.

Hudek had a wheelchair waiting outside that time. Silently, he trundled Iskander back to the room where he had wakened and laid him down on the couch.

"Thank you," said Iskander, squirming deeper into the soft fabric. "Very kind of . . . Very. . ." He began rubbing at his left arm. "It hurts," he said crossly. He was quiet for a minute, then smiled. "Thanks, Miriam. Lovely game. And now I don't have to go back to the home."

A rook slid over the inside curve of the torus and back up to knock off a knight before the pieces slowed and were still.

Miriam sat down by Iskander and took his right hand. Beside her, Hudek was listening to Iskander's chest. He scowled and took out a needle to inject a painkiller. Then he bent over Iskander's face, breathing air into the lungs. He kept that up for a long time, but nothing happened. At last he gave it up.

"Do you realize you've just killed a man?" he asked, as quietly as he could. "For nothing?"

"For nothing?" Miriam said. She remained as she was for a few moments more. Then she set the hand down and kissed Iskander's cheek. She pulled herself out of the chair and held out her arm to be given Hudek's support as she made her way back to work.

VON GOOM'S GAMBIT

Victor Contoski

You won't find Von Goom's Gambit in any of the books on chess openings. Ludvik Pachman's *Moderne Schachtheorie* simply ignores it. Paul Keres' authoritative work *Teoria Debiutow Szachowych* mentions it only in passing in a footnote on page 239, advising the reader never to try it under any circumstances and makes sure the advice is followed by giving no further information. Dr. Max Euwe's *Archives* lists the gambit in the index under the initial V. G. (Gambit), but fortunately gives no page number. The twenty-volume *Chess Encyclopedia* (fourth edition) states that Von Goom is a myth and classifies him with werewolves and vampires. His Gambit is not mentioned. Vassily Nikolayevitch Kryllov heartily recommends Von Goom's Gambit in the English edition of his book, *Russian Theory of the Opening;* the Russian edition makes no mention of it. Fortunately Kryllov himself did not— and does not yet—know the moves, so he did not recommend them to his American readers. If he had, the cold war would be finished, and possibly the world.

Von Goom was an inconspicuous man, as most discoverers usually are; and he probably made his discovery by accident, as most discoverers usually do. He was the illegitimate son of a well known actress and a prominent political figure. The scandal of his birth haunted his early years, and as soon as he could legally do so he changed his name to Von Goom. He refused to take a Christian name because he claimed he was no Christian, a fact which seemed trivial at the time but was to explain much about this strange man. He grew fast early in life and attained a height of five feet four inches by the time he was ten years old. He seemed to think this height was sufficient, for he stopped growing. When his corpse was measured after his sudden demise, it proved to be exactly five feet four inches. Soon after he stopped growing, he also stopped talking. He never stopped working because he never started. The fortunes of his parents proved sufficient for all his needs. At the first opportunity, he quit school and spent the next twenty years of his life reading science fiction and growing a mustache on one side of his face. Apparently, sometime during this period, he learned to play chess.

On April 5, 1997, he entered his first chess tournament, the Minnesota State Championship. At first, the players thought he was a deaf mute because he refused to speak. Then the tournament director, announcing the pairings for the round, made a mistake and announced, "Curt Brasket—White; Van Goon—Black." A small, cutting voice filled with infinite sarcasm said, "Von Goom." It was the first time Von Goom had spoken in twenty years. He was to speak once more before his death.

Von Goom did not win the Minnesota State Championship. He lost to Brasket in twenty-nine moves. Then he lost to George Barnes in twenty-three moves, to K. N. Pedersen in nineteen, Frederick G. Galvin in seven, James Seifert in thirty-nine, Dr. Milton Jackson (who was five years old at the time) in one hundred and two. Thereupon, he retired from tournament chess for two years.

His next appearance was December 12, 1999, in the Greater Birmingham Open, where he also lost all his games. During the remainder of the year, he played in the Fresno Chess Festival, the Eastern States Chess Congress, the Peach State Invitational and the Alaska Championship. His score for the year was: opponents forty-one; Von Goom zero.

Von Goom, however, was determined. For a period of two and one-half years thereafter he entered every tournament he could. Money was no obstacle and distance was no barrier. He bought his own private plane and learned to fly so that he could travel across the continent playing chess at every possible occasion. At the end of the two and one-half year period, he was still looking for his first win.

Then he discovered his Gambit. The discovery must surely have been by accident, but the credit—or rather the infamy—of working out the variations must be attributed to Von Goom. His unholy studies convinced him that the Gambit could be played with either the White or the Black pieces. There was no defense against it. He must have spent many a terrible night over the chessboard analyzing things man was not meant to analyze. The discovery of the Gambit and its implications turned his hair snow white, although his half mustache remained a dirty brown to his dying day, which was not far off.

His first opportunity to play the Gambit came in the Greater New York Open. The pre-tournament favorite was the wily defending Champion, grandmaster Miroslav Terminsky, although sentiment favored John George Bateman, the Intercollegiate Champion, who was also all-American quarterback for Notre Dame, Phi Beta Kappa and the youngest member of the Atomic Energy Commission. By this time, Von Goom had become a familiar, almost comic, figure in the chess world. People came to accept his silence, his withdrawal, even his half mustache. As Von Goom signed his entry card, a few players remarked that his hair had turned white; but most people ignored him. Fifteen minutes after the first round began, Von Goom won his first game of chess. His opponent had died of a heart attack.

He won his second game too when his opponent became violently sick to his stomach after the first six moves. His third opponent got up from the table and left the tournament hall in disgust, never to play again. His fourth broke down in tears, begging Von Goom to desist from playing the Gambit. The tournament director had to lead the poor man from the hall. The next opponent simply sat and stared at Von Goom's opening position until he lost the game by forfeit.

His string of victories had placed Von Goom among the leaders of the tournament, and his next opponent was the Intercollegiate Champion John George Bateman, a hot-tempered, attacking player. Von Goom played his Gambit, or if you prefer to be technical, his Counter Gambit, since he played the Black pieces. John George's attempted refutation was as unconventional as it was ineffective. He jumped to his feet, reached across the table, grabbed Von Goom by the collar of his shirt and hit him in the mouth. But it did no good. Even as Von Goom fell, *he made his next move*. John George Bateman, who had never been sick a day in his life, collapsed in an epileptic fit.

Thus, Von Goom, who had never won a game of chess in his life before, was to play the wily grandmaster, Miroslav Terminsky, for the championship. Unfortunately, the game was shown to a crowd of spectators on a huge demonstration board mounted at one end of the hall. The tension mounted as the two contestants sat down to play. The crowd gasped in shock and horror when they saw the opening moves of Von Goom's Gambit. Then silence descended, a long, unbroken silence. A reporter who dropped by at the end of the day to interview the winner found to his amazement that the crowd and players alike had turned to stone. Only Terminsky had escaped the holocaust. The lucky man had gone insane.

A few more like results in tournaments and Von Goom became, by default, the chess champion of America. As such he received an invitation to play in the Challengers Tournament, the winner of which would play a match for the world championship with the current champion, Dr. Vladislaw Feorintoshkin, author, humanitarian and winner of the Nobel Peace Prize. Some officials of the International Chess Federation talked of banning the Gambit from play, but Von Goom took midnight journeys to their houses and *showed them the Gambit*. They disappeared from the face of the earth. Thus it appeared that the way to the world championship stood open for him.

Unknown to Von Goom, however, the night before he arrived in Portoroz, Yugoslavia, the site of the tournament, the International Chess Federation held a secret meeting. The finest brains in the world gathered together seeking a refutation to Von Goom's Gambit—and they found it. The following night, the most intelligent men of their generation, the leading grandmasters of the world, took Von Goom out in the woods and shot him. The great humanitarian Dr. Feorintoshkin looked down at the body and said, "A merciful end for Van Goon." A small, cutting voice filled with infinite sarcasm said, "Von Goom." Then the leading grandmasters shot him again and cleverly concealed his body in a shallow grave, which has not been found to this day. After all, they have the finest brains in the world.

And what of Von Goom's Gambit? Chess is a game of logic. Thirty-two pieces move on a board of sixty-four squares, colored alternately dark and light. As they move they form patterns. Some of these patterns are pleasing to the logical mind of man, and some are not. They show what man is capable of and what is beyond his reach. Take any position of the pieces on the chessboard. Usually it tells of the logical or semi-logical plans of the players, their strategy in playing for a win or a draw, and their personalities. If you see a pattern from the King's Gambit Accepted, you know that both players are tacticians, that the fight will be brief but fierce. A pattern from the Queen's Gambit Declined, however, tells that the players are strategists playing for minute advantages, the weakening of one square or the placing of a Rook on a half-opened file. From such patterns, pleasing or displeasing, you can tell much not only about the game and the players but also about man in general, and perhaps even about the order of the universe.

Now suppose someone discovers by accident or design a pattern on the chessboard that is more than displeasing, an alien pattern that tells unspeakable things about the mind of a player, man in general and the order of the universe. Suppose no normal man can look at such a pattern and remain normal. Surely such a pattern must have been formed by Von Goom's Gambit.

I wish the story could end here, but I fear it will not end for a long time. History has shown that discoveries cannot be unmade. Two months ago in Camden, New Jersey, a forty-three year old man was found turned to stone staring at a position on a chessboard. In Salt Lake City, the Utah State champion suddenly went screaming mad. And, last week in Minneapolis, a woman studying chess suddenly gave birth to twins—although she was not pregnant at the time.

Myself, I'm giving up the game.

KOKOMU

Daniel Gilbert

Doorbell: wind-chimes of bamboo and glass gracing a Shinto shrine. But it was not a doorbell, and Samuel Kagami adjusted his thinking. The jamasura, a large procaryotic cell with electronic call-extensors, responded as was its function, chiming when a hand touched the door.

Neither was it a door.

The Tō-screen, a series of unicellular giants linked in symbiotic unity, whose cytoplasm had been design-engineered for tensile strength, weatherproofing, and opacity, formed the splendid arched doorway to Samuel Kagami's home. The arch signified a marvel of neobiotic construction available only to the elite of the Western Nipponese Consolidät. The Tō-screen parted as Kagami approached, and he greeted his visitor.

"Chokki san. May you give me five."

"Kagami san, this is also right on." The plump Neobiotix field representative, clad in conservative grey knickers and shoulder coat, an aluminum brechet at his knee, bowed, signaling an end to the exchange of formal pleasantries. Kagami bowed also and indicated the livingroom with a sweep of his hand.

He hoped the sweep had been well-timed and correct. Chokki removed his platform-zoris and set them on the tatami, suddenly reduced a full fifteen centimeters in height. "I received your call only this morning. Forgive my tardiness."

"No apology necessary. But accepted," said Kagami. "I am most grateful that you have traveled so far to see me. It was not an inconvenience I hope?"

"None. My pleasure."

Kagami smiled uneasily and led his guest into the livingroom. The cochin lanterns and moribana floral arrangements lent the room a traditional appearance, yet Kagami felt, as always, that something still was lacking. "Excuse my forwardness then. May I come to the point and dispense with politic?"

Chokki quickly averted his eyes, allowing no movement or gesture to betray his discomfort. "Certainly," said the small Line Nippon, stiffly. "As you wish."

Though Kagami's grandfather had been a Once American in the days of the Union, no one would dare call Kagami an American now—not, at least, without the offering of swords. Yet the fact that Kagami was only a Nipponese by circumstance—a *sansei,* third generation citizen of the Consolidät—was evident in his desire to rush through formal ceremony. The Line Nippon—of a respected Nipponese ancestry—held the *sansei* in low esteem for this reason.

Ki ni yotte uo o motomu: you ask an elm tree for pears. This was Kagami's heritage; perhaps, in time, he would outgrow this natural impatience.

"It is my southern wall," said Kagami.

"A difficulty?"

"No. Without doubt there is no problem with the manufacture. Neobiotix has done a splendid job with my home. I am most pleased."

"Honored," said Chokki. Kagami poured three deciliters of Mogen David Imperial Sake into an earthenware cup and offered it to Chokki. "*Domo arigato.*"

"Most welcome. Perhaps what I need is a strategy."

"Your wall is weak then?" Chokki sipped gingerly from the cup.

"Near to crumble."

Chokki hesitated for a moment. "And of strategy. Your neighbor has also a consultant?"

"Orgosynthetix Corporation. We have, of course, agreed to unilateral aid." Kagami turned to fill his own cup with sake, hoping to disguise his irritation. Were Kagami not a *sansei,* he knew, Chokki would never have offered such an impertinent inquiry. Had he implied that Kagami might *cheat*?—that he might seek tactical advice illicitly? Both Kagami and his neighbor, Tonàri Ze, had agreed upon allowing professional consultation; Kagami's word need not have been questioned.

Kagami felt the strain of two echelons meeting, the friction of separate and distinct social strata grating as they touched. He smothered the sparks in politic.

"Very fine. Show me then your southern wall." Shyly, Kagami led the Neobiotix field representative through the livingroom and into the tea-room. The Tō-screen parted and Kagami felt embarrassment at the disarray. "*Oya!*"

"Indeed. As you see, the southern wall is nearly surrounded."

Kagami felt shame at the loss of face. Very few *sansei* could afford a neobiotic home, and fewer actually entered in competition. It was said that the ability to play Go—the ancient game of territorial strategy upon which neobiotic play was based—had its roots in ancestry, and though no prohibitions stood between a *sansei* and the game, it was generally agreed that the Line Nippon made the best player. Pitting one's home against another's, using true territory and not a symbolic representation was thought to be a delicate art, and not one to be toyed with lightly.

Chokki inspected the tea room carefully. The tea room wall—built of a flux-organism called *käbe,* a chromoplastic which hardened at some points and undulated at others—was badly buckled. The ceiling sagged under the considerable strain of the damaged wall, and the *käbe* had lost a great deal of its translucency. Without light, the synthetic organism would grow increasingly weaker, unable to repair itself photosynthetically, and the architectural stress would also increase until the tea room fell, or Kagami surrendered.

This, of course, was Ze's strategy; once Ze's northern diningroom wall had surrounded the tea-room and blocked the ultraviolet, he would need only to wait patiently for Kagami's defenses to fall.

Patience was one thing Tonari Ze had plenty of.

"An inventive offensive. Orgosynthetix is a respectable firm," said Chokki, examining the *käbe*-wall with an expert touch. "Or perhaps Ze san is an inventive fellow himself."

Few words. Much said. Samuel Kagami knew that he had attacked foolishly. A quick offensive with which he hoped to gain an advantage in the opening play, had failed, and he found that he had concentrated too much of the house's energy on a single point. He had ignored Ze's threats on many borders, and now those threats had matured and Kagami found himself trapped.

The tea room groaned.

"An honored opponent. What kind of defensive strategy do you recommend to maintain the tea room?"

Chokki laughed mildly. "No, I'm afraid not, Kagami san. One may only extend folly in this way. Incorporate the loss."

"Withdraw?"

"Brute force cannot rise. A fat defense is no answer. Notice how lean is his attacking line." Kagami examined the wall which protruded through the tea room *käbe* in four spots. Indeed, saber thin. "There is no shame in withdrawal." Chokki once again looked away.

Kagami studied the well-mannered Line Nippon. What did this one know of shame? Kagami's grandfather, Charles Carmody, had been a wealthy man and had left Kagami a modest legacy. Thus, Kagami moved in circles usually closed to a *sansei,* played with the luxurious toys of a Line Nippon, and lived as well as many corporate functionaries.

Yet, there were restrictions. Unwritten, politely applied.

Carmody had been killed during the Incorporation. He had called it the Invasion, but politic declared that Kagami refrain from using such terms. As economic crises peaked the Union had been forced to begin auctioning their last resource: Land. Allies were invited to extend their holdings, and the Nipponese, for whom landscape was the only limiting factor to further prosperity, heartily accepted.

Purchasing land in strategic areas they established base colonies on the continent, immigrating in droves. And though they held less than fifteen percent of the actual land area in Once America, their ability to use less—more resourcefully—had quickly insured that their population would exceed that of the Union. Relocation of Union citizens out of Nipponese-occupied territory had been subsidized and expensive, and fiscal ruin had been nothing but forestalled.

It was war that killed Charles Carmody.

There had been no terror jets, no thermonuclear war cries, no multimegaton verbosities. No shouting. The gentleman hordes of Nipponese had attacked politely, armed to the teeth with yen. They incorporated the Union and turned it into a thriving, well-conducted economic sector, which now comprised nearly seventy percent of their vast holdings in the Western Nipponese Consolidät.

Though Carmody had remained a staunch Unionist, resentful and distrustful of the Incorporation from the first (he had insisted that Kagami's given name have at least one *L* in it), his pride had been equal in tenacity to that of the highest ranking Line Nippon.

What they now called politic was not a new custom for Kagami; it had, like so many things, simply changed names. Carmody had been one of those millions whose real estate had been badly bartered, and he'd been forced to sell a manufacturing empire for a fraction of its worth, simply because it lay in Nipponese states. He had retired, rather than attempting to revitalize the business, and had died alone, broken, bitter, soon thereafter.

Kagami studied the half-empty glass of sake, moodily.

"In triumph do not gloat. In defeat do not brood," said Chokki. He pushed a sprig of tomb-black hair from his finely curved face. Why did victors always throw platitudes and maxims in the face of the vanquished? "Reinforce your back line here, in the hallway. Do not extend folly with malicious play. Begin now a forthright attack." Chokki glanced about the room. "Where is your Center?"

Kagami stepped out of the tea room and led Chokki to the *gōban*—the game board. The *gōban* was the hand-crafted component of the large home-computer which controlled the neobiotic play, and resembled a greatly expanded Go board. Kagami's stones were blue diodes on the face of the computerized *gōban*, Ze's red. The square plane was divided into equal sized area; the northern and southern borders were marked with letters, the eastern and western with numbers, and the lines intersected to form a grid. Kagami pointed to the D-8 sector, his tea room. Ze's red glowing stones formed a Tiger's Mouth about the sector and threatened to devour the unit.

"How to play?"

Chokki suppressed a sigh. "One stone, Kagami san, holds infinite power. One stone may alter the outcome of a game. Though surrounded by enemy stones, no soldier is too small or insignificant to affect a victory for his legion. I suggest an outpost here." With a tawny finger, the Line Nippon indicated the N-13 region.

"But I cannot afford any more stones for outposting. I am *kokomu,* surrounded, on many fronts. To withdraw a single stone for outposting will mean the collapse of a unit elsewhere."

"*Mr.* Kagami," said Chokki, "I am a Neobiotix field representative. I can *sell* you an outpost."

Chokki fiddled with his knee brechet and Kagami closed his eyes. Forcing Chokki to make such a tactless remark, to breach etiquette so boldly, made Kagami wonder if Chokki's scorn for the *sansei* was not entirely unfounded. He did not apologize, however, knowing that even such a gesture would only prolong—what must be for Chokki—a very difficult situation.

Neither could he tell Chokki of his financial straits; that his legacy was tied up in the house and that he had been living on equity and small investments for nearly three months, less than the length of one game. One did not discuss such things with intimates, much less business associates. Kagami felt as if he were suffocating.

"I . . . I have . . . I am unable to make such a purchase at this time."

Chokki nodded and both men studied the *gōban* with newfound intensity, each carefully avoiding the other's eyes. Kagami drained his sake. The moment stretched into humiliation.

Finally, Chokki spoke. "I am sorry. Professionally, then, I must judge your situation as hopeless. I suggest you turn game control over to your home-computer and allow it to finish the game mathematically. Perhaps your losses can be minimized."

"Thank you," said Kagami. This was his advice. "More sake?"

Chokki bowed. "Your hospitality is overwhelming. However, I am afraid I must leave. Pressing business of urgency. Take it then in lightness, Kagami san."

"And you also be quite cool." He escorted Chokki to the front Tō-screen, reciting further pleasantries, and bid him good day and fortune. The Tō-screen parted,

In the livingroom, Samuel Kagami studied the *gōban,* poured himself another two deciliters of sake, and considered. He had spent nearly three quarters of his grandfather's bequest (a mere fraction of what it would have been, had it not been converted from dorrars to yen) on the neobiotic home. It was a symbol of that which most *sansei* never hoped to own, and it had indeed elevated his social position. But, like a fool, he had entered into play with a superior opponent, a Line Nippon, Tonari Ze, and was now in danger of losing both home and face. He understood why Chokki had seen him as a stumbling buffoon, an inept inferior, and he detested Chokki for making the distinction so painfully evident.

. . .*must judge your situation as hopeless.* . .

He also realized that it was his third bottle of sake today.

Kagami slid an antique rice-paper partition from the far wall. Seventeen shelves. The true bequest. This was what remained of Charles Carmody.

Memorabilia. Once Americana. Relics. Time-crippled dinosaurs from a day now broken and best set aside. Yet, these items sparked Kagami's imagination, excited him from within, and a day did not pass when he failed to slip aside the rice-paper and fondle one or two of them, evoking memories of days he could not possibly own.

Zane Grey. Ah, the name itself surged with a raw and vital power. Like true anger from the blood-drenched fist of an electric god—what *power* in the name alone, and in the words between the crumbling paper binders.

Dashiell Hammett. Intrigue and adventure! Trench-coated legends who roared and hungered and drank whiskies and did not hesitate to plug one full of lead should circumstances require such. Men who said as they pleased and disregarded politic, laughed in the faces of the world's well-mannered Chokkis.

Louis L'amour. Now here was time as real men had lived it; not packaged time, caged and tamed in a watch or crystal, but time which gouged and vomited and splayed itself upon a man's life like the colored legs of a venomous insect.

Roger Keegan. Andrew North. Hal Kantos.

Kagami traced the rim of the cowboy's hat upon the book jacket. It was Bart Gibson's hat. Bart, a stern and commanding wrangler, lean and supple in denim and steel, and his two brothers, Luke and Roy, stood poised for action as the badmen surrounded the Bar-S Ranch.

Kokomu, three Gibsons? thought Kagami.

He turned to the gōban. Another red stone twinkled to life near the tea room at D-8. Ze had moved, after a three day wait, and the third panel of the referee lighted GO: : :

Kagami's turn. He seated himself before the board.

"I've got you covered, Luke. This town ain't big enough for both of us. Reach for the sky, horsethief!"

Even as Kagami turned to capture the voice, his hand moved autonomously and lifted the stone from the D-7 sector, the last strong stone in the tea room unit.

"Sheriff, the Wilker boys are down at the Bar-S. There's gonna be a whole bunch of shooting!"

His fingers caressed the stone, placing it carefully between index and forefinger, and set it down with a smart click.

"The three Gibson's at the Bar-S, Doc."

"Three Gibsons. Bar-S."

"Bar-S. Three."

The stone clicked at S-3. The GO: : : light winked out and the referee indicated Ze's turn. Samuel Kagami felt dizzy.

He retreated to his lioo-chair and listened to his heart pump furiously, contemplating what had happened and realizing that—whatever had come over him a moment ago—he had made the worst of all possible moves. His delicate garden would now strike at the heart of Tonari

Ze's heavily reinforced den. The garden would be surrounded so quickly. The house would fall.

The sake made Kagami feel ill, and with no hesitation, he switched the game to computer control, as Chokki had suggested, closing his eyes tightly to take one last nap in his neobiotic home before conceding defeat.

By the time Samuel Kagami awoke, he owned all of Ze's territory.

The GO: : : light had winked on four hours earlier, the ever patient electronic referee indicated that it was Kagami's turn. He studied his image in the polished surface of the *gōban*, and listened to the creaking of his den. He stroked his new moustache slowly, thinking that it made his face look more angular, harder, sharper.

Bisho Rinjin was an excellent player, and even with the full force of Kagami's combined territories, he had not answered Kagami's threats to the greenhouse hastily. Instead, he had played around Kagami and attacked the den, a subtle yet stinging offensive which Kagami could not ignore.

Kagami contemplated the *gōban*, recognized gestalts and micro gestalts, conceived patterned formations of stones, computed the intricate futures of both defense and offense. His hands eagerly kneaded the collar of his silk robe, his slippered feet tapped nervously. He poured his fifth cup of Johnny Walker New Tokyo Whiskey and gulped it hurriedly, waiting. He held the book in his lap, his fingers moving anxiously up and down the spine.

Finally: the peculiar spinning sensation. The *gōban* swirled in a splatter of color. He found himself holding a cup, and sighed.

"Please, some water," said the man.

The frail fellow, slumped in a straight-backed chair, groaned. His pock-marked face was a crucifixion of sweat and fatigue, the cracks in his snake-skin lips were made ghostly white by the blinding bulb which hung in the interrogation room.

Kagami reached up, touched the bulb, and it swung ominously above the man's head. This was not Oklahoma, *circa* 1883. What then? When? Kagami looked down at his hands. The book was gone. He noticed his own stocky build, certainly not the slender *sansei* he had been a moment before, the nearly perfect shine on his black leather shoes, the shoulder-holster buckled expertly about his trunk.

"Are you okay, Lieutenant?" said a burly fellow, also wearing a pistol, but leaning against the far wall, smoking in the shadows.

Lieutenant? Kagami glanced at the man slumped in the chair in the center of the room. His wrists had deep red marks in them, and Kagami's hands went to his belt.

Handcuffs.

Kagami left the spotlighted circle and joined the two men at the other side of the room.

"You look tired," said the big fellow.

"Still worried about your brother?" The second man was thin and his voice had a high-pitched nasal quality. He wore a striped shirt with rolled sleeves, and a vest.

"I suppose so," said Kagami.

"Don't worry about Scotty," said the thin man, "he'll kill a couple of Krauts, knock in a few Nip heads, and be Stateside before you know it. He'll be alright."

"Yeah," said Kagami. "You're right."

Nips. That would make it somewhere around 1940, and, judging from the thin fellow's vocal tones, somewhere in the midwest. Perhaps Chicago or St. Louis.

"I don't think Joey's going to tell us anything," said the burly detective, whose badge indicated that his name was Meyers. Yes, there, on the badge: CPD. Chicago then.

"He knows where Calhoun is hiding."

"He ain't telling." Meyers shrugged.

Kagami listened carefully. Yes, this Joey was a prisoner and Murray Calhoun a stick-up man. All the infor-

mation seemed to be seeking and finding its proper
place, as if Kagami had forgotten for only a moment, as
if this man named Samuel Kagami—the *sansei*—had
been but a tremor of stage-fright in a police Lieutenant's
mind.

"I told you, I don't *know* no Murray Calhoun. I don't
know where he is." Joey rotated his head, clamped his
eyes shut in the bright light. Kagami felt a wave of anger
come washing the shores of thought; the man was lying.

Joey's head bobbed, his neck seemed strangely con-
torted, his face a peculiar contrast of harsh light and
shadows. The face seemed so familiar, so real, so close,
so. . .

Kagami pulled back his right hand and smashed the
backside across Joey's face. The sound echoed off the
bare walls of the interrogation room with a reverberat-
ing crack. Joey's head swung sideways with the force of
the blow, then sagged desperately to his chest. A slick
stream of crimson wound its way from his nostril to his
upper lip. The two men in the corner shifted uneasily,
and Meyers lit another cigarette.

Kagami wiggled his fingers and blinked.

The contact . . . the flesh against flesh . . . the surge of
his muscles . . . the yielding of bone . . . it had felt . . .
felt *good*.

"Joey. Where is Murray Calhoun?" said Kagami, and
even his voice was textured and full, precisely the words
he wished to speak, exactly as he wished to speak them.

"I . . . I don't. . . ." Kagami brought his fist back
again. "Wait!"

His clenched hand hung in mid-air, a stop-action
eagle waiting to descend. Joey's eye opened and closed
spasmodically. "I think you screwed up my eye." He
dabbed at the swollen purple cheek with his finger.

"Joey?"

"The Edgewater. He's at the Edgewater. But he'll see
you coming. He ain't dumb, he'll see you and high-tail
it out of there."

"Where at the Edgewater?"

"Room L-3. He's in L-3."

Samuel Kagami smiled. In some strange way, he wished that this Joey had held out just a little longer. The power of the blow, the explosion of contact, the invigorating stinging sensation of his palm—he had never before hit a man. Yes, it was interesting.

"Okay, Meyers, get him out of here," said Kagami. L-3. He had what he'd come for.

"C'mon, Chokey," said the thin man, lifting the shaking prisoner from his seat. Kagami spun about.

"What did you call him?"

The thin man looked at Kagami peculiarly. "Chokey, Lieutenant. Name's Joey Chokey. You know that."

Kagami stared at the man he had struck. Joey Chokey smiled.

By playing the unexpected L-3 position, Kagami had begun an intensive pressing formation on the entire L-group, had turned a corner at H-6, and had quickly devastated Bisho Rinjin. The game of thirty days had not lasted another hour.

The jamasura hummed happily as Kagami greeted Chokki.

"In the midst of another game, I see," said Chokki, entering the livingroom. The northern wall was now greatly expanded, incorporating both dining room and garden in an elegant whole. Chokki nodded in admiration.

"It will be finished in two moves." Kagami wondered what Chokki had come for—he had not called for him —but thought it inhospitable to inquire. He offered sake.

"Many thanks, but no. I cannot stay long." Chokki spoke calmly, but his eyes kept darting about the room, always returning to rest for a moment on the *gōban*. "I have come in my very humble capacity to present a most unusual gift."

"Honored," said Kagami.

"Neobiotix has petitioned the Games Council on your behalf, and we have received permission to raise your status." Chokki paused dramatically. "To *Shihan* Player."

"A Master?" said Kagami. "I am overwhelmed."

"You have respectfully earned the title. I am humbled before your abilities. On my last visit I offered the opinion that your strategic situation was hopeless. Since that time, I have noted two change-of-property titles come through my office. Of course, I immediately offered my resignation to my employer, who graciously declined. Nevertheless, my error was unforgivable." The plump Line Nippon lowered his chin, a sign of submission and shame, but his eyes reflected stubborness and animosity. Was there a small scab on his left cheek? Imagination.

"I differ, Chokki san. You made a most honest analysis. The acts of fate are not yours to predict."

"Not to be argumentative, but this was no hand of God. Superior thinking. However, I am pleased that you do not think ill of me. We wish then to present these tokens of our admiration." Chokki withdrew a slip of paper and a golden ring from his breast pocket and handed them to Kagami.

The ring was cool and smooth in Kagami's hand. He scrutinized it and noticed that it was inscribed with the word *Shinjitsu*—truth, encircled by a single banded line indicating Master status. The check was written for six million yen.

Why?

Kagami knew he was no Master. What had motivated Neobiotix and Chokki to recommend such honor? Indeed, his holdings were significant, particularly when one considered the amount of time in which he had accumulated them, but they certainly did not warrant the ultimate title of *Shihan*. He turned the golden band slowly in his hand.

Did Chokki know?

Impossible. It was his personal madness, his private dream sequence; a fantasy link to his unconscious, or a collective unconscious, or some universal intelligence which favored him. He had not decided which. But it was not shared—it would be impossible for Chokki to be aware of it.

Perhaps, thought Kagami, I do deserve the title. After all, was it not superior strategy which had wrested the L-3 move from the police lieutenant's prisoner? Yes, thought Kagami, indeed. A strategy which the gentlemen sirs have all but forgotten.

"You understand," said Chokki, apparently noting Kagami's hesitation, "that these trinkets are but expressions of our respect?"

Kagami met Chokki's eyes. *Respect?* Respect for a *sansei?* Kagami noticed, in Chokki's expression, the fine and uncooked seeds of condescension, as if he were laughing inwardly at the ignorant *sansei,* at this respect built of wire-mesh, an ornament, paying him off with a fistful of paper money and baubles. Quite suddenly, Kagami understood why.

"I am most flattered," said Kagami, fighting to conceal his anger, "but I cannot accept."

Chokki blinked like a Hiroshiman in the brightness.

"If I am of *Shihan* ability," said Kagami, "I may no longer engage in play. Is this correct?"

"Why . . . of course! Opponents must be of near-equal ability, of matched strength. No one may play a *Shihan.* Advantage does not come in domination of the novice, but in superior thinking with one's equals."

"Or one's betters?" Kagami handed the items back to Chokki, who accepted them unbelievingly. "I am afraid your offer is much too gracious. I shall continue as a player."

A cheap ruse! A child's trick! Did this Line Nippon truly believe that Kagami would be so easily fooled? The transparency of the ploy was grave insult piggybacked upon intended injury. Kagami dug his fingernails into his palms and contained himself.

Chokki began to speak, stopped, began again. "As you wish, though I do not know what we shall tell the Council. No precedent."

"Extend my deepest apologies," said Kagami. "May I catch you later, Chokki san."

Chokki bowed courteously and left the house. Kagami stood by the open Tō-screen and watched Chokki walk briskly down the manicured path, past spacious rock gardens and neatly calendared emperor tulips and Agean windflowers, to his dart. Chokki clambered in to the small vehicle and escalated quietly into the overcast afternoon sky.

"Goodbye," called Kagami, waving with his right hand. His left hand closed and opened behind his back. Then he added in a whisper, "You little Nip."

The words tasted extraordinary.

Samuel Kagami remained on his horse, an impossibly black stallion, and leaned in the saddle to touch the stagecoach driver.

Dead.

The driver's throat was opened in a ragged five centimeter circle. Blood drained slowly, coagulating about his neck and chest, thin strands of fibrin spiderwebbed from his chin. His rifle lay unused in his lap.

"Gawddamn!" said one of Kagami's men—the one he called Moyers, an obese fellow who wore a rancid yellow bandana about his head. Moyers poked an inquisitive finger into the stagecoach driver's neck. "Got him real good, Sammy."

"Open the coach," said Kagami.

A strong wind blew through the pass; sun carved rock and sand about Kagami as it hung like a washed-out lightbulb in the pale morning sky. Samuel Kagami felt strong also; virile, alive. A thin kid in a vest and rolled sleeves dismounted and flung open the door of the coach.

Kagami gestured at the passengers. "Out."

An older fellow, dressed in frock coat and traveling hat, emerged from the coach. He turned and took the hand of a young woman, a girl actually, not more than sixteen, helping her step down. Kagami eyed the girl; her tight bodice accentuated pleasing curves, smooth lines, and Kagami found himself wondering what would please him most.

"Empty your pockets," ordered Kagami.

"Please," said the well-dressed man, his voice trembling with apparent anxiety. "I am escorting my niece to Sioux Falls, for a recital. I am a music teacher. I have nothing you want."

Kagami said nothing, knowing that his reputation here, in whatever time or place this was, read like a headstone. He could tell, simply by the feel of the Kagami he now was.

The man waited a moment, then fished a leather billfold from his frock coat.

"Toss it."

Kagami caught the wallet and opened it, methodically rifling its contents and tossing them one by one to the ground. The wind caught the paper money which Kagami discarded, and whirlpooled it about the feet of his horse.

"Hey!" cried Moyers, as he raced about gathering the money in his hands. Kagami kept pulling items from the billfold.

"If you'll only tell me what you're looking for, perhaps—"

"Shut up!" barked Kagami. Yes, the feel of this one was superb! This Kagami did not take orders, did not heed warnings. This Kagami strode where he pleased, said what he wished, took as he saw fit. He spat tobacco juice in the music professor's face.

The professor wiped at it with a coat sleeve and clamped his jaws together. Kagami continued sorting through the wallet.

There!

This was what he had come for. He withdrew two theatre tickets and waved them at the professor. "Aha! Ya, boys! Here we go. Ya!"

"But those are simply—"

"I know what they are!" shouted Kagami. He walked his horse closer to the music teacher and drew back his leg, driving his spurs into the man's ribcage. The professor reeled backward and tumbled to the sand. Kagami thought of dismounting and having the girl, there, on the ground, with Moyers and the thin kid laughing and the professor shaking violently. He felt no need in his groin, but reminded himself that if he wished to, he could, and the thought of the professor looking on in silent agony pleased him more than he knew the girl would have anyway.

He studied the tickets.

C-16 and C-17. Seat numbers. *Excellent* seat numbers.

The girl knelt by her uncle and wiped his forehead with the hem of her skirt; Kagami was momentarily intrigued by the pale skin exposed on her calf, the compact breasts bound so tightly within the lace blouse, but . . . no time. No need and no time. He had what he'd come for.

"Do you need to further humiliate us, or may we proceed on our way? It seems, quite inexplicably, that you have what you wanted." The professor's breathing was impaired, his voice undercut by the sound of wind cutting cellophane. Perhaps a rib had been broken.

Kagami spat in the man's face a second time. This time, however, the professor did not wipe away the brownish sputum, but stared into Kagami's eyes through the mucusoid film.

"Get on with you," said Kagami.

The girl helped her uncle to his feet and they both walked, he with a slight limp, to the front of the coach. The mutilated driver was slumped in the seat; the girl, having not yet seen him, raised her hands to her lips and stifled a scream.

"Oh, dear Jesus!" she said. "Is he dead, Uncle Choggy?"

The professor turned and looked at Kagami again. He blinked spittle from his eyes and smiled.

"I'm afraid so, Kate," he said. "This time."

"Is there nothing we can offer you then?" said Chokki. The Neobiotix field representative played with the hem of his shoulder coat, avoiding Kagami's eyes.

"No. I shall continue as a player."

Chokki shook his head, sadly. Kagami offered no brandy, but poured himself a large cup—another large cup—and laughed quietly, thinking that certainly a VSOP cognac from the Israeli National States was far too rare for a Line Nippon.

"You are driving us from business, Kagami san. Do you even realize this?"

"I play for victory. I mean no ill to your company's prosperity."

"Yet we find it difficult to sell neobiotic housing any longer. Your reputation has grown too large, customers will not invest knowing that should you challenge, they must accept, and that you shall ultimately conquer their territories. I myself will be dismissed from my employ unless I bring a satisfactory reply, thus, I have nothing to lose and may speak frankly. Neobiotix shall be pleased to furnish you with a check for any amount you estimate you may win."

Kagami drained his glass.

He had waited impatiently all day yesterday, all morning today, for the referee to declare his turn. There was but one crucial move to be made, and though Kagami did not know yet what it was, he did know how to find out. Chokki was nothing more than an annoying insect buzzing about his ears.

"You," said Kagami, "do not *have* what I may win."

"You have crafted an empire, vaster by far than any in the history of the game. Thus, it cannot be material reward you seek. *What then?*" Chokki seemed to be shivering; the muscles in his face tightened, no longer the pleasant oval shape it had been. Kagami had never seen the stoic Line Nippon in such an agitated state, and it greatly pleased him. "Do you believe that further victory and ruthless triumph will make you a . . . a. . . ."

"Line Nippon?" said Kagami, quickly. "Like you, fat little Chokki?"

Chokki's eyes grew wide with astonishment, his mouth hung open like a sprung trap door. "I . . . I did not mean to say—"

"*Damn* what you say! You never say what you mean anyway!" Kagami rose from the lioo-chair and stood above the smaller man, at a distance he knew Chokki would find uncomfortably close. The liquor caused him to sway slightly, like a pear tree in the breeze. "How does it feel then, Chokki? *Mr.* Chokki? How does it make *you* feel? *Kokomu?* Surrounded? Yes? Now it is your turn, my little friend. You are the single stone and I the invader."

"Have you lost your wits?"

"Good! No, excellent! My lost wits against yours. Oh yes, you know, don't you, Chokki? You know, and you are there each time. I *see* you, I know it is you. But this time—oh, *this* time little Chokki, *I* engulf *you*. Or 'incorporate.' Is that a better word?"

"You are mad," said Chokki, softly. He rose and strode toward the front Tō-screen. Kagami followed at his back, his hands waving drunkenly in the air.

"The attacking line, Mr. Chokki! Look out! Here it is —no, there! Now in back of you! Behind you! All about you, ripping into your flesh with pointed politic and gesture, attacking you for what you are, for what you are not, for what you can never be! Do you see it? All around you? Look, my one little stone!"

Chokki touched the Tō-screen and it parted, then he turned slowly to Kagami, standing at the threshold. His composure had not been broken, his face was manicured beautifully, like the Agean windflowers in the garden, yet expressionless. His poise caused Kagami to suddenly step back.

Softly, he said, "One stone holds infinite power, Kagami san. One stone may change the outcome of a game. Malicious play extends folly. Good day."

The small Nipponese stepped through the Tō-screen and was gone. Kagami stood in the immense entryway, holding a snifter filled with expensive liquor in a trembling hand.

The train lumbered through the darkness like a huge slug, crawling past mountains and rivers and plateaus. The box-car vibrated and Samuel Kagami rocked in the corner.

"Damn. Aren't you finished yet?"

"Sorry," said the thin man who knelt by the safe, working the dials in the flashing half-light from the car door. "I can't get that last number, it won't open."

"Get the conductor then. Get somebody!" At Kagami's command, the thin man and the heavy-set fellow named Mayor disappeared into the adjoining car. Kagami found a cigarette in the pocket of his black satin vest and lit it, breathing the smoke through his nostrils and releasing it in a dragon flare. He listened to the even, measured sounds of the locomotive pounding track across the Great Divide. The car smelled musty and a chill wind lashed through the cracks in the floorboards, swinging the oil lantern that hung by the door and sparking Kagami's cigarette.

Samuel Kagami was not interested in the contents of the safe. He was interested in the last number.

The two men reappeared holding a frail old gentleman by the arms. The latter did not appear nervous, a grey shoot of hair slicked across his balding scalp, a natty suit and bow tie. "The ticket-taker," announced Mayor.

"Open it," said Kagami in a rush of smoke.

The ticket-taker shook his head.

Kagami smiled, curling and uncurling his fist. Doesn't he think he's just something? thought Kagami. He slammed the old ticket-taker against the wall of the box-car, and the small fellow smacked against the wood then slid down the wall and sat on the floor. He adjusted his wire-rimmed spectacles which sat crookedly on the bridge of his nose.

"I said open it."

The ticket-taker slowly moved his head from left to right.

Stalling. Blind moves. A field mouse roaring at a cobra. Kagami enjoyed the ticket-taker's resistance; it added an extra dimension to the conquest. He brought his foot up neatly in a large arc, directing his boot into the old man's face.

The spectacles shattered in the ticket-taker's eyes, filling them with blood. The dull thud of cartilage breaking and the sharp crack of the glass lenses filled the car.

Samuel Kagami thought of his empire, his kingdom. He envisioned a pebble lodged in its bright machinery, then, with a *whirr* and a *click,* the machinery grinding to a halt.

"Tell me," he said.

The ticket-taker sat very still.

Kagami forced his boot into the man's groin. Now, in the flickering of lantern light, he noticed just how old the man looked; his outfit a remnant of older, perhaps better days, his thinning hair attempting to deny the in-evitable baldness of his liver-spotted pate. Were these meager wrappings meant to evoke sympathy? Compassion?

Of course.

Kagami shifted his weight to his left leg and ground the old man's testes between his heel and the floorboards. He felt a popping as he pushed.

"You want to die?"

The ticket-taker spoke in spasmed breaths; his words, though, were calm and precise, as if unscathed by physical pain. His mouth, a crescent filled with frothy scarlet, opened slightly. "Nothing to lose," whispered the ticket-taker.

He who has nothing to lose cannot be beaten.

Another hollow platitude from the mouths of the victors. Yet, for the first time, Kagami felt the awesome might of complete surrender, the carefully maintained power of the ticket-taker's position. Kagami could kill him, or the old man would accept any amount of his beating, but because he held to nothing, the ticket-taker could not be threatened, pressed, taken.

Kagami felt fear, as all about him the machine slowed.

One stone, Kagami san, may change the outcome of a game.

Impossible. Kagami had brought to bear a network of holdings so grand that nothing might stop their momentous hurtling toward destiny once they were set into play. Why then did he feel such fright? Why, if the force of this monolith could not be restrained, did he find himself shivering now, staring deep into the eyes of a straw-boned old man?

Blood streaked down the ticket-taker's face like tears. He mumbled.

"What?" said Kagami.

The ticket-taker said nothing. *Your move.* He had heard it clearly enough. It did not bear repeating. Kagami lowered himself to the floor of the box-car and brought his face close to the old man's. His eyes, filmed by a red sauce, held Kagami's unblinkingly.

"It's right to 23, isn't it, Chokki?"

The ticket-taker's lips parted slowly, so slowly that Kagami ached to speed their parting, to reach his hand into the old man's gullet and extract the answer which was rightfully his.

"Please."

The ticket-taker opened his mouth, coughed, and spat two teeth into Kagami's face.

Kagami jumped backward. "Damn you!" He pulled his pistol from his gunbelt and held it level to the ticket-taker's skull. "Now tell me!" Kagami steadied himself on his knees, holding the gun outstretched with both hands. *"Now!"* The veins and arteries in his neck swelled and throbbed, his skin painted with violet.

"Sammy, don't kill him, boy. He's the only one's got the combination."

Bad lines from a bad script. Kagami ignored the clamor of the men and instead focused all his energies into the barrel of his gun. He held the ticket-taker's gaze and knew that soon, very soon, the bad actors would disappear, begone, there would remain that which always remained: the immovable object and the irresistible force.

But this time the object would yield! It had to!

Kagami cocked the pistol and heard his own breathing, out of control, his heart pounding in his ears. Or was it the train?

"Chokki, I don't want to. Please. What is it?"

His extended arms began to shake, he could not hold the pistol straight anymore and the box-car began to swirl.

"Please!"

The deafening noise of the train and his heart did not hide this fact: the ticket-taker was laughing.

"Chokki!" *Malicous play.*

"Chokki!" *Extends.*

"Chokki!" *Folly.*

Kagami pulled the trigger. His arms recoiled in futile protest. He watched the bullet crawl, painstakingly slowly, across the vast space between himself and the ticket-taker, a space which spanned one meter and three thousand years. The ticker-taker's skull separated as if in slow motion, a dream-jar unwinding at the top, the lid splattered against the box-car walls, small parts of bone and flesh suspended in perpetual ballet, swirling, turning, airborne spinners.

Suddenly, the car was quiet.

"Chokki?" Kagami whispered.

He stared at the ticket-taker's body for a very long time, then slowly, he began to weep. He crawled forward, pulling a leg behind a leg, knee to floor, crawling across that great abyss which lay between himself and the corpse, until he reached the body and hugged himself to the bloodied coat and held and stroked the lifeless hand which he did not need to see to know it wore a single-banded, golden ring.

He pressed himself tightly against the used body, squeezing against its chest, mingling his sorrow with blood and bone, pushing and pushing so that laughter might buoy his heart and one day he might still float free.

And in the night, beyond the slow rumble of the train, empires were falling, vaster than one might imagine.

MOXON'S MASTER

Ambrose Bierce

"Are you serious?—do you really believe that a machine thinks?"

I got no immediate reply; Moxon was apparently intent upon the coals in the grate, touching them deftly here and there with the fire-poker till they signified a sense of his attention by a brighter glow. For several weeks I had been observing in him a growing habit of delay in answering even the most trivial of commonplace questions. His air, however, was that of preoccupation rather than deliberation: one might have said that he had "something on his mind."

Presently he said:

"What is a 'machine'? The word has been variously defined. Here is one definition from a popular dictionary; 'Any instrument or organization by which power is applied and made effective, or a desired effect produced.' Well, then, is not a man a machine? And you will admit that he thinks—or thinks he thinks."

"If you do not wish to answer my question," I said, rather testily, "why not say so?—all that you say is mere evasion. You know well enough that when I say 'machine' I do not mean a man, but something that man has made and controls."

"When it does not control him," he said, rising

abruptly and looking out of a window, whence nothing was visible in the blackness of a stormy night. A moment later he turned about and with a smile said:

"I beg your pardon; I had no thought of evasion. I considered the dictionary man's unconscious testimony suggestive and worth something in the discussion. I can give your question a direct answer easily enough; I do believe that a machine thinks about the work that it is doing."

That was direct enough, certainly. It was not altogether pleasing, for it tended to confirm a sad suspicion that Moxon's devotion to study and work in his machine-shop had not been good for him. I knew, for one thing, that he suffered from insomnia, and that is no light affliction. Had it affected his mind? His reply to my question seemed to me then evidence that it had; perhaps I should think differently about it now. I was younger then, and among the blessings that are not denied to youth is ignorance. Incited by that great stimulant to controversy, I said:

"And what, pray, does it think with—in the absence of a brain?"

The reply, coming with less than his customary delay, took his favorite form of counter-interrogation:

"With what does a plant think—in the absence of a brain?"

"Ah, plants also belong to the philosopher class! I should be pleased to know some of their conclusions; you may omit the premises."

"Perhaps," he replied, apparently unaffected by my foolish irony, "you may be able to infer their convictions from their acts. I will spare you the familiar examples of the sensitive mimosa, the several insectivorous flowers and those whose stamens bend down and shake their pollen upon the entering bee in order that he may fertilize their distant mates. But observe this. In an open spot in my garden I planted a climbing vine. When it was barely above the surface I set a stake into the soil a yard away. The vine at once made for it, but as it was about to reach it after several days I removed it a few feet. The vine at once altered its course, making an acute angle, and again made for the stake. This maneuver was repeated several times, but finally, as if discouraged, the vine abandoned the pursuit and ignoring further attempts to divert it traveled to a small tree, further away, which it climbed.

"Roots of the eucalyptus will prolong themselves incredibly in search of moisture. A well-known horticulturist relates that one entered an old drain pipe and followed it until it came to a break, where a section of the pipe had been removed to make way for a stone wall that had been built across its course. The root left the drain and followed the wall until it found an opening where a stone had fallen out. It crept through and following the other side of the wall back to the drain, entered the unexplored part and resumed its journey."

"And all this?"

"Can you miss the significance of it? It shows the consciousness of plants. It proves that they think."

"Even if it did—what then? We were speaking, not of plants, but of machines. They may be composed partly of wood—wood that has no longer vitality—or wholly of metal. Is thought an attribute also of the mineral kingdom?"

"How else do you explain the phenomena, for example, of crystallization?"

"I do not explain them."

"Because you cannot without affirming what you wish to deny, namely, intelligent cooperation among the constituent elements of the crystals. When soldiers form lines, or hollow squares, you call it reason. When wild geese in flight take the form of a letter V you say instinct. When the homogeneous atoms of a mineral, moving freely in solution, arrange themselves into shapes mathematically perfect, or particles of frozen moisture into the symmetrical and beautiful forms of snowflakes, you have nothing to say. You have not even invented a name to convey your heroic unreason."

Moxon was speaking with unusual animation and earnestness. As he paused I heard in an adjoining room known to me as his "machine-shop," which no one but himself was permitted to enter, a singular thumping sound, as of some one pounding upon a table with an open hand. Moxon heard it at the same moment and, visibly agitated, rose and hurriedly passed into the room whence it came. I thought it odd that any one else should be in there, and my interest in my friend—with doubtless a touch of unwarrantable curiosity—led me to listen intently, though, I am happy to say, not at the keyhole. There were confused sounds, as of a struggle or scuffle; the floor shook. I distinctly heard hard breathing and a hoarse whisper which said "Damn you!" Then all was silent, and presently Moxon reappeared and said, with a rather sorry smile:

"Pardon me for leaving you so abruptly. I have a machine in there that lost its temper and cut up rough."

Fixing my eyes steadily upon his left cheek, which was traversed by four parallel excoriations showing blood, I said:

"How would it do to trim its nails?"

I could have spared myself the jest; he gave it no attention, but seated himself in the chair that he had left and resumed the interrupted monologue as if nothing had occurred:

"Doubtless you do not hold with those (I need not name them to a man of your reading) who have taught that all matter is sentient, that every atom is a living, feeling, conscious being. *I* do. There is no such thing as dead, inert matter; it is all alive; all instinct with force, actual and potential; all sensitive to the same forces in its environment and susceptible to the contagion of higher and subtler ones residing in such superior organisms as it may be brought into relation with, as those of man when he is fashioning it into an instrument of his will. It absorbs something of his intelligence and purpose—more of them in proportion to the complexity of the resulting machine and that of its work.

"Do you happen to recall Herbert Spencer's definition of 'Life'? I read it thirty years ago. He may have altered it afterward, for anything I know, but in all that time I have been unable to think of a single word that could profitably be changed or added or removed. It seems to me not only the best definition, but the only possible one.

" 'Life,' he says, 'is a definite combination of heterogeneous changes, both simultaneous and successive, in correspondence with external coexistences and sequences.' "

"That defines the phenomenon," I said, "but gives no hint of its cause."

"That," he replied, "is all that any definition can do. As Mill points out, we know nothing of cause except as an antecedent—nothing of effect except as a consequent. Of certain phenomena, one never occurs without another, which is dissimilar: the first in point of time we call cause, the second, effect. One who had many times seen a rabbit pursued by a dog, and had never seen rabbits and dogs otherwise, would think the rabbit the cause of the dog.

"But I fear," he added, laughing naturally enough, "that my rabbit is leading me a long way from the track of my legitimate quarry: I'm indulging in the pleasure of the chase for its own sake. What I want you to observe is that in Herbert Spencer's definition of 'life' the activity of a machine is included—there is nothing in the definition that is not applicable to it. According to this sharpest of observers and deepest of thinkers, if a man during his period of activity is alive, so is a machine when in operation. As an inventor and constructor of machines I know that to be true."

Moxon was silent for a long time, gazing absently into the fire. It was growing late and I thought it time to be going, but somehow I did not like the notion of leaving him in that isolated house, all alone except for the presence of some person of whose nature my conjectures could go no further than that it was unfriendly, perhaps malign. Leaning toward him and looking earnestly into his eyes while making a motion with my hand through the door of his workshop, I said:

"Moxon, whom have you in there?"

Somewhat to my surprise he laughed lightly and answered without hesitation:

"Nobody; the incident that you have in mind was caused by my folly in leaving a machine in action with nothing to act upon, while I undertook the interminable task of enlightening your understanding. Do you happen to know that Consciousness is the creature of Rhythm?"

"O bother them both!" I replied, rising and laying hold of my overcoat. "I'm going to wish you good night; and I'll add the hope that the machine which you inadvertently left in action will have her gloves on the next time you think it needful to stop her."

Without waiting to observe the effect of my shot I left the house.

Rain was falling, and the darkness was intense. In the sky beyond the crest of a hill toward which I groped my way along precarious plank sidewalks and across miry, unpaved streets I could see the faint glow of the city's lights, but behind me nothing was visible but a single window of Moxon's house. It glowed with what seemed to me a mysterious and fateful meaning. I knew it was an uncurtained aperture in my friend's "machine-shop," and I had little doubt that he had resumed the studies interrupted by his duties as my instructor in mechanical consciousness and the fatherhood of Rhythm. Odd, and in some degree humorous, as his convictions seemed to me at that time, I could not wholly divest myself of the feeling that they had some tragic relation to his life and character—perhaps to his destiny—although I no longer entertained the notion that they were the vagaries of a disordered mind. Whatever might be thought of his views, his exposition of them was too logical for that. Over and over, his last words came back to me: "Consciousness is the creature of Rhythm." Bald and terse as the statement was, I now found it infintely alluring. At each recurrence it broadened in meaning and deepened in suggestion. Why, here (I thought) is something upon which to found a philosophy. If consciousness is the product of rhythm all things *are* conscious, for all have motion, and all motion is rhythmic. I wondered if Moxon knew the significance and breadth of his thought— the scope of this momentous generalization; or had he arrived at his philosophic faith by the tortuous and uncertain road of observation?

That faith was then new to me, and all Moxon's expounding had failed to make me a convert; but now it seemed as if a great light shone about me, like that which fell upon Saul of Tarsus; and out there in the storm and darkness and solitude I experienced what Lewes calls "The endless variety and excitement of philosophic thought." I exulted in a new sense of knowledge, a new pride of reason. My feet seemed hardly to touch the earth; it was as if I were uplifted and borne through the air by invisible wings.

Yielding to an impulse to seek further light from him whom I now recognized as my master and guide, I had unconsciously turned about, and almost before I was aware of having done so found myself again at Moxon's door. I was drenched with rain, but felt no discomfort. Unable in my excitement to find the doorbell I instinctively tried the knob. It turned and, entering, I mounted the stairs to the room that I had so recently left. All was dark and silent; Moxon, as I had supposed, was in the adjoining room—the "machine-shop." Groping along the wall until I found the communicating door I knocked loudly several times, but got no response, which I attributed to the uproar outside, for the wind was blowing a gale and dashing the rain against the thin walls in sheets. The drumming upon the shingle roof spanning the unceiled room was loud and incessant.

I had never been invited into the machine-shop—had, indeed, been denied admittance, as had all others, with one exception, a skilled metal worker, of whom no one knew anything except that his name was Haley and his habit of silence. But in my spiritual exaltation, discretion and civility were alike forgotten and I opened the door. What I saw took all philosophical speculation out of me in short order.

Moxon sat facing me at the farther side of a small table upon which a single candle made all the light that was in the room. Opposite him, his back toward me, sat another person. On the table between the two was a chessboard; the men were playing. I knew little of chess, but as only a few pieces were on the board it was obvious that the game was near its close. Moxon was intensely interested—not so much, it seemed to me, in the game as in his antagonist, upon whom he had fixed so intent a look that, standing though I did directly in the line of his vision, I was altogether unobserved. His face was ghastly white, and his eyes glittered like diamonds. Of his antagonist I had only a back view, but that was sufficient; I should not have cared to see his face.

He was apparently not more than five feet in height, with proportions suggesting those of a gorilla—a tremendous breadth of shoulders, thick, short neck and broad, squat head, which had a tangled growth of black hair and was topped with a crimson fez. A tunic of the same color, belted tightly to the waist, reached the seat —apparently a box—upon which he sat; his legs and feet were not seen. His left forearm appeared to rest in his lap; he moved his pieces with his right hand, which seemed disproportionately long.

I had shrunk back and now stood a little to one side of the doorway and in shadow. If Moxon had looked farther than the face of his opponent he could have observed nothing now, except that the door was open. Something forbade me either to enter or to retire, a feeling—I know not how it came that I was in the presence of an imminent tragedy and might serve my friend by remaining. With a scarcely conscious rebellion against the indelicacy of the act I remained.

The play was rapid. Moxon hardly glanced at the board before making his moves, and to my unskilled eye seemed to move the piece most convenient to his hand, his motions in doing so being quick, nervous and lacking in precision. The response of his antagonist, while equally prompt in the inception, was made with a slow, uniform, mechanical and, I thought, somewhat theatrical movement of the arm, that was a sore trial to my patience. There was something unearthly about it all, and I caught myself shuddering. But I was wet and cold.

Two or three times after moving a piece the stranger slightly inclined his head, and each time I observed that Moxon shifted his king. All at once the thought came to me that the man was dumb. And then that he was a machine—an automaton chessplayer! Then I remembered that Moxon had once spoken to me of having invented such a piece of mechanism, though I did not understand that it had actually been constructed. Was all his talk about the consciousness and intelligence of machines merely a prelude to eventual exhibition of this device—only a trick to intensify the effect of its mechanical action upon me in my ignorance of its secret?

A fine end, this, of all my intellectual transports—my "endless variety and excitement of philosophic thought!" I was about to retire in disgust when something occurred to hold my curiosity. I observed a shrug of the thing's great shoulders, as if it were irritated: and so natural was this—so entirely human—that in my new view of the matter it startled me. Nor was that all, for a moment later it struck the table sharply with its clenched hand. At that gesture Moxon seemed even more startled than I: he pushed his chair a little backward, as in alarm.

Presently Moxon, whose play it was, raised his hand high above the board, pounced upon one of his pieces like a sparrowhawk and with the exclamation "checkmate!" rose quickly to his feet and stepped behind his chair. The automation sat motionless.

The wind had now gone down, but I heard, at lessening intervals and progressively louder, the rumble and roll of thunder. In the pauses between I now became conscious of a low humming or buzzing which, like the thunder, grew momentarily louder and more distinct. It seemed to come from the body of the automaton, and was unmistakably a whirring of wheels. It gave me the impression of a disordered mechanism which had escaped the repressive and regulating action of some controlling part—an effect such as might be expected if a pawl should be jostled from the teeth of a ratchet-wheel. But before I had time for much conjecture as to its nature my attention was taken by the strange motions of the automaton itself. A slight but continuous convulsion appeared to have possession of it. In body and head it shook like a man with palsy or an ague chill, and the motion augmented every moment until the entire figure was in violent agitation. Suddenly it sprang to its feet and with a movement almost too quick for the eye to follow shot forward across table and chair with both arms thrust forth to their full length—the posture and lunge of a diver. Moxon tried to throw himself backward out of reach, but he was too late: I saw the horrible thing's hands close upon his throat, his own clutch its wrists. Then the table was overturned, the candle thrown to the floor and extinguished, and all was black dark. But the noise of the struggle was dreadfully distinct, and most terrible of all were the raucous, squawking sounds made by the strangled man's efforts to breathe. Guided by the infernal hubbub, I sprang to the rescue of my friend, but had hardly taken a stride in the darkness when the whole room blazed with a blinding white light that burned into my brain and heart and memory a vivid picture of the combatants on the floor, Moxon underneath, his throat still in the clutch of those iron hands, his head forced backward, his eyes protruding, his mouth wide open and his tongue thrust out; and —horrible contrast!—upon the painted face of his assassin an expression of tranquil and profound thought, as in the solution of a problem in chess! This I observed, then all was blackness and silence.

Three days later I recovered consciousness in a hospital. As the memory of that tragic night slowly evolved in my ailing brain I recognized in my attendant Moxon's confidential workman, Haley. Responding to a look he approached, smiling.

"Tell me about it," I managed to say, faintly—"all about it."

"Certainly," he said; "you were carried unconscious from a burning house—Moxon's. Nobody knows how you came to be there. You may have to do a little explaining. The origin of the fire is a bit mysterious, too. My own notion is that the house was struck by lightning."

"And Moxon?"

"Buried yesterday—what was left of him."

Apparently this reticent person could unfold himself on occasion. When imparting shocking intelligence to the sick he was affable enough. After some moments of the keenest mental suffering I ventured to ask another question:

"Who rescued me?"

"Well, if that interests you—I did."

"Thank you, Mr. Haley, and may God bless you for it. Did you rescue, also, that charming product of your skill, the automaton chess-player that murdered its inventor?"

The man was silent a long time, looking away from me. Presently he turned and gravely said:

"Do you know that?"

"I do," I replied: "I saw it done."

That was many years ago. If asked today I should answer less confidently.

RENDEZVOUS 2062

Robert Frazier

In the season of chrysanthemum,
Players align like tiles along a great ivory wall,
Matching velocities with Halley's,
Which ascends as an immense flaming dot
With tail as of a fighting kite
On winds from the North reaches of our solar system.
On an East wind rides a satellite shaped
Like a Chinese character.
From the West wind a souped-up shuttle
Resembling a bamboo bird.
From the South wind a U.N. solar sail,
Shining white dragon with mylar scales.
Drawing and discarding data,
The players shift hands
Until the United Nations melds.
They board the comet under the Starfaring Provisions,
And as it swings around Sol, the heart of Ma Jong
And all games of man,
They chip away the icy packing
From an ancient alien artifact. . .
They have played out a rare honors hand:
"A moon from the bottom of the sea".

REFLECTIONS ON THE
LOOKING-GLASS: AN ESSAY

Fred Stewart

Almost everybody has heard of Lewis Carroll's *Alice in Wonderland* and knows most of its characters are a deck of cards. Far fewer have read Carroll's *Through the Looking-Glass*, which is organized around a chess puzzle. Alice's adventures as she proceeds to the Queening square are not as memorable or exciting as those in Wonderland even though the poem "Jabberwocky" is the most famous passage of Carroll's work. Meeting Tweedledum and Tweedledee, Humpty Dumpty, the Lion and the Unicorn, and various animals, insects and chess pieces do not seem to charm us as the earlier book did. Yet when Alice steps through the mirror in her Victorian drawing-room into the world beyond, finds the world outside the Looking-Glass house is a huge chess board, and takes her place in the game as a White Pawn, we can see that Carroll is using the chess game as a symbolic commentary on the whole of human existence.

But what an unchessic game it is! Among its many odd characteristics, the only one critically unexplained (as far as I know) is the fact that White makes 13 moves to Red's three! I believe even this can be explained by a close look at Carroll's puzzle and translating its chess

aspects into the commentary on human life that it really
is. The clearest metaphor is that Alice's side wins; she
becomes Queen, makes an important capture, and de-
livers mate to the Red King. Carroll shows through
Alice that human beings do have a major role in shaping
their (chess) game of life.

I.

I do not believe Charles T. Dodgson (Lewis Carroll)
meant his *Alice* books to be mere codes to be broken or
logical games as so many of his non-fictional works
were. However, I do believe he put his fiction together
with much more left-brain activity than most literary
artists; that is, the meanings in his works are far more
accessible to abstract thought since they are so purposefully symbolic. The *Alice* books are not themselves
dreams, though they are set in dream context. Carroll
never lets us forget that he is controlling the march of
symbolic characters and actions across the page.[1] So I
believe Carroll would approve of my puzzling over the
chess motif that structure *Through the Looking-Glass*.
To consider this chess situation *as chess* is to find he has
framed his view of the deepest puzzle of all—the nature
of human existence.

When Alice climbs through the mirror, she finds
herself operating within a chessboard world. At first the
chess pieces she encounters, in her normal size, ap-
prehend her existence only as "a volcano" which can
pick them up and toss them about.[2] Soon after, she enters the garden of the Looking-Glass house and saw "in
all directions" a countryside broken into squares,
hedges lining each file and brooks each rank; " 'just like
a large chessboard,' " she declares (207). When she as-
sumes her place on the board as a White Pawn, her
perspective is from then on limited to the squares immediately to her left and right; "she sweeps a narrow
track," as A. L. Taylor puts it.[3]

Carroll sets his chessboard situation before us as a

frontispiece, together with the moves of the pieces:

Diagram #1
RED

WHITE

White Pawn (Alice) to play, and win in eleven moves.

1. Alice Meets R. Q.
2. Alice through Q's 3d *(by railway)* to Q's 4th *(Tweedledum and Tweedledee)*
3. Alice meets W. Q. *(with shawl)*
4. Alice to Q's 5th *(shop, river, shop)*
5. Alice to Q's 6th *(Humpty Dumpty)*

1. R. Q. to K. R's 4th
2. W. Q. to Q. B's 4th *(after shawl)*
3. W. Q. to Q. B's 5th *(becomes sheep)*
4. W. Q. to K. B's 8th *(leaves egg on shelf)*
5. W. Q. to Q. B's 8th *(flying from R. Kt.)*

6. Alice to Q's 7th (forest)	6. R. Kt. to K's 2nd (Ch.)
7. W. Kt. takes R. Kt.	7. W. Kt. to K.B's 5th
8. Alice to Q's 8th (coronation)	8. R. Q. to K's Sq. (examination)
9. Alice becomes Queen	9. Queens Castle
10. Alice Castles (feast)	10. W. Q. to Q. R's 6th (soup)
11. Alice takes R. Q. and Wins	

In his "Preface" Carroll addresses the problems that would immediately occur to anyone even vaguely familiar with the game of chess:

> As the chess-problem, given on the next page, has puzzled some of my readers, it may be well to explain that it is correctly worked out, so far as the *moves* are concerned. The *alternation* of Red and White is perhaps not so strictly observed as it might be, and the "castling" of the three Queens is merely a way of saying that they entered the palace: but the "check" of the White King at move 6, the capture of the Red Knight at move 7, and the final "checkmate" of the Red King, will be found, by any one who will take the trouble to set the pieces and play the moves as directed, to be strictly in accordance with the laws of the game. (p. 171)

Some of Carroll's "moves" are not chess moves at all —"Queens Castle" (9th move for Red) requires two pieces to move on the same turn and merely indicates that both Queens enter their castle though staying within the same square each had been on the move before. On her 10th move Alice also enters the castle. Her 9th move ("Alice becomes Queen") takes place a move *after* she reaches the eighth rank—clearly some "moves" are essential to the narrative plot rather than to chess rules and strategy. Carroll clearly shows that there is more to his chess situation than chess, but setting the *real* chess moves will help separate plot from chess:

WHITE	RED	WHITE	RED
1. . . .	Q-KR4	8. Q-QB8	. . .
2. P-Q4	. . .	9. P-Q7	N-K2 ch
3. Q-QB4	. . .	10. N x N	. . .
4. Q-QB5	. . .	11. N-KB5	. . .
5. P-Q5	. . .	12. P-Q8-Q	Q-K1 ch
6. Q-KB8	. . .	13. Q-QR6	. . .
7. P-Q6	. . .	14. Q(Alice) x Q	mate

Three things will be noticed immediately by the chess aficionado—there are more real chess moves than the eleven indicated by Carroll; White moves 13 times to Red's 3 (including one string of 8 straight!); and the original White Queen makes real move 13 even though her White King is in check from the Red Queen:

Diagram #2

12._____, Q-K1 Ch.W will next move 13. <u>Q-QR6</u>

The first problem has an easy solution. As Carroll's

notes to his "moves" show, the eleven "moves" refer to portions of the narrative plot of the book—21 separate occurrences that happen to Alice as she moves across the board. There are only 16 separate real chess moves (13 by White, 3 by Red) by the pieces themselves.

The second problem proved to have an historical solution. Ivor Davies found that, at his death, Carroll owned a copy of George Walker's book *The Art of Chess-Playing: A New Treatise on the Game* (1846). Law XX in Walker states, "When you give check, you must apprize your adversary, by saying aloud 'Check'; or he need not notice it, but may move as though check were not given." Davies notes that chess rules, as Walker sets them forth, "are the Rules of St. George's Chess Club, London, drawn up in 1841 and still in force in England when *Through the Looking-Glass* was written in 1871." Davies notes that the Red Queen does not say "Check":

> Her silence was entirely logical because, at the moment of her arrival at King one, she said to Alice, who had been crowned Queen eight, "Speak when you are spoken to!" Since no one had spoken to *her* she would have been breaking her own rule had she said, "Check."[4]

There is no doubt that the Looking-Glass characters are consistent, and those in *Alice in Wonderland* are not; and I accept Davies' analysis why the Red Queen did not announce check. Still, there remains a light problem —one of point-of-view: chess pieces *give* check, but they do not *announce* check, in the real game. The Red Knight does gallop up to Alice and yell "check!" on Red's second move (Carroll's 6th plot-move, chess move 9). But, as Marlin Gardner, editor of *The Annotated Alice,* points out, when the White Knight captures the Red Knight, he "absentmindedly shouts, 'Check!'; actually he checks only his own King" (294). The strange puzzle as to why and how the chess pieces are responsible for their own moves and strategy can be resolved in considering the third problem—White's having ten more moves than Red.

Davies takes four stabs at solving this most vexing peculiarity:

Four possible explanations suggest themselves. Firstly, Red might move the White pieces by mistake. Under Law IX White could insist that the moves stand. Secondly, according to Law XIV, if White were moving out of turn Red could insist that the moves stand. Neither of these contingencies is very likely in view of the number of consecutive moves made by White. Thirdly, the game might be played at odds. Both Walker and Staunton devote much space to various methods of giving odds to a weaker player. But the order of the moves—one Red, eight White, one Red, three White, one Red, two White—would imply an impossibly difficult mathematical basis for the giving of odds.

There remains a fourth possibility. Book V of Staunton's *Companion* is entitled "On Odds." Staunton begins with a discussion of the origins of chess and remarks that at first the giving and receiving of odds was unnecessary because the game was not one of pure skill. At the remote period of its birth in India it belonged to the widespread family of human games based on chance and "the moves were governed by the casts of dice". These significant words occur in the very first sentence of the treatise Staunton wrote and Lewis Carroll bought. They provide a key that turns easily in the lock of the door to Alice's secret garden. White has more moves than Red because White wins on the throw of the dice more often than Red!

"They don't keep this room so tidy as the other," thought Alice to herself when she arrived behind the looking-glass and discovered a world beyond the care of providence or the decrees of fate. How disturbing if Carroll is suggesting that this 'other world' is, after all, the real one and that it is ruled by the principle of uncertainty! A pawn's progress towards the eighth rank is hazardous in the hands of a skilled chess player. In looking-glass chess its survival depends on the casting of unseen dice by an invisible master. No wonder Alice cried as she threw herself down on the last square, "Oh, how glad I am to get here!"

None of these four suggestions resolves anything about the moves because none explains either the character or implications of the game itself. Only the fourth suggests a real solution—the game is controlled by "an invisible master" and "is ruled by the principle of uncertainty!" Gardner more narrowly implies the same: "Carroll may be suggesting . . . that the knights, like Punch and Judy, are merely puppets moved by the hands of the invisible players of the game" (295). Richard Kelly can assess the same evidence and come to the complementary conclusion that "in the Looking-Glass world life is completely determined and without choice."[5]

These men come to different conclusions about the character of the game either because they are either examining different objects, or the same object from differing points of view. Actually, they are doing both. Davies and Gardner view Carroll's chess puzzle as a *game*, using a player's point-of-view totally beyond the game and finding the game symbolizes the uncertainty of human existence. Kelly sees the puzzle as a chess *problem* and takes the point-of-view of the pieces. Kelly finds this world narrow, limited, and totally determined.

What is our puzzle—*problem* or *game*? Alice calls it a "huge game of chess that's being played—all over the world—if this *is* the world, you know" (207-8). However, Carroll has already called it a "chess-problem" in his "Preface" (172).

If we look at our puzzle carefully, we will find that it *is* both *game* and *problem*, and that this paradox is the solution to the highly symbolic narrative plot.

II.

In his fine book *The Enjoyment of Chess Problems*, Kenneth S. Howard makes an essential distinction between the chess *problem* and the chess *ending*:

> There is an essential distinction between a chess problem and a composed endgame. In an endgame the solver has to demonstrate a win or draw for white against a superior, or at least an equal, force, and is allowed an indefinite number of moves in which to do so. The point of the endgame is based on the difference in the apparent relative material strength of white and black. In a problem it is not a question of relative strength but of the possibility of showing a mate against any defense in a limited number of moves. In an endgame the solver is fighting against *material* odds; in a problem he is fighting against *time*.
>
> The modern chess problem is an illustration of some particular powers of the chess men in their interaction with one another. The chess problem is not primarily merely a puzzle.[6]

However, in neither the *problem* nor the *ending* is the solver actually playing against another mind. He is acting *within* the rules of the *problem* situation, and for the most efficient win or mate in the game-like *ending*. If a *problem* mate can be escaped or solved in fewer moves than required, the problem is said to be "cooked." In the *ending*, the situation must be a win or draw for the appointed side or it too is ruined. For both *problem* and *ending,* one's opponents are the pieces, rules, and the situation set forth on the board. The *game* of chess pits two minds against each other, the board situation remaining at their mercy.

Carroll's Looking-Glass *problem* is "cooked": it has overlooked early mates (3, Q-K3 mate), captures avoided by Red, and no plot reference to the White Rook at KB1. As Edmund Miller notes, "This chess problem is completely arbitrary and so does a wonderful job of organizing everything else in the nonsense book."[7] If the puzzle-plot is considered as *problem,* the reader is confined to the limited perspective of the chess pieces which only know what they must do and little or nothing of the complete plot/solution. Alice (as Pawn) and the other chessmen see only some of the play; the Queens know the rules, but the other pieces do not speak of them. As Taylor points out, Alice never grasps the purpose of the game; at the eighth square she asks if the game is over.[8] It is not over, of course, until later when she herself captures the Red Queen.

Martin Gardner is correct: "the mad quality of the chess game conforms to the mad logic of the looking-glass world" (172). The moves of the game (Gardner will call it a "chess problem" on p. 336) are correct and meaningful if seen within Alices' limits on the board—the logic is that of the moves laid out in Carroll's diagram; that is, the narrative plot and the chess *problem* are identical. As *problem,* only the placement of pieces and their "character" (narrative and chessic) determine its moves and thus limit our view to their own; the moves therefore do not matter *as chess.* The logic of the puzzle and of each piece makes the *actual* chess moves unobservable from within the *problem,* and the plot-moves seem both logical and real.

If we view our puzzle as absolute outsiders, as a chess *game,* the absurdity of the moves are apparent. Who is really playing the game is unknown, even to Alice; the

Red King "was part of my dream, of course—but then I was part of his dream, too!" (344). Whoever the unseen player may be—Carroll, God, Alice, the Red King—from his view mistakes, errors, blunders, lost chances, and illegal moves are obvious. In a chess *game,* rules are never to be violated willfully, foolishly, or made part of the puzzle.[9]

We have resolved the chess paradox: one puzzle is both *game* and *problem,* for we see it from both points-of-view at once—as player/reader, and as Alice/chessman. The puzzle has also resolved itself as a symbol of human existence. If Carroll had totally ignored the rules of chess, his allegory would then suggest human existence is blind, directionless, and meaningless, like a child moving chessman without purpose. But purpose is accomplished—the Red King is mated, though Alice is unaware until she is awake and *outside* the game (until, in human terms, she is wise and mature enough to see) and changes her point-of-view.

On the other hand, if Carroll had presented perfectly straightforward chess (game or problem), he would imply human existence lacks freedom, spontaneity, and charm. As a Church of England clergyman and as teacher of math and logic at Christ Church, Oxford, the Reverend Dodgson could not believe in blind chance or transcendental puppetry as descriptive of the nature of human life. He believed in God, logic, and science; and these beliefs he translated into a charming literary puzzle.

Carroll's story provides the same problems and resolution for the nature of human existence as Emmanuel Kant had done in his *Critique of Practical Reason:* man lives in two realms at once—the realm of Nature in which all facets of his existence are completely determined and explained by mechanical causation (the chess *problem)*; and the transcendental realm of freedom in which he is a free, unconditioned cause acting on the world, bringing novelty and uncertainty into being (the chess *game*). For Lewis Carroll, the game of human existence presents a deep problem which he resolved in a happy ending in *Through the Looking-Glass*.

FOOTNOTES

[1] Carroll himself admits changing the Black pieces to Red for the purpose of religious symbolism, though the change violates the color scheme of the pair of kittens (one white, one black) which were responsible for part of the character of Alice's "dream."

[2] Lewis Carroll, *The Annotated Alice*, ed. Martin Gardner (NY: Clarkson N. Potter, 1960), p. 188. Further reference to *Through the Looking-Glass* will be from this edition.

[3] A. L. Taylor, "Chess and Theology in the *Alice* Books," in *Alice in Wonderland*, ed. Donald J. Gray (NY: W. W. Norton, 1971), pp. 365-377; quote is on pp. 367-8.

[4] Ivor Davies, "Looking-Glass Chess," *The Anglo-Welsh Review*, 15 (Autumn 1970), pp. 189-91.

[5] Richard Kelly, *Lewis Carroll* (Boston: Twayne, 1977), pp. 97-99.

[6] Kenneth S. Howard, *The Enjoyment of Chess Problems* (Philadelphia: McKay, 1943), p. 3. Howard's definition confirms the idea that viewing our puzzle as a problem would confine our point-of-view to the board of character of the pieces.

[7] Edmund Miller, "The *Sylvie and Bruno* Books as Victorian Novel," in *Lewis Carroll Observed*, ed. Edward Guiliano (NY: Clarkson N. Potter, 1976), p. 140.

[8] Taylor, p. 368.

[9] Davies finds that some aspects of our puzzle here are derived from an old form of chess using a "Marked Pawn," as described in a book owned by Carroll at his death; see "Queen Alice," *Jabberwocky*, 2 (Autumn 1973), pp. 10-11. I also reject A. S. M. Dickins' "Alice in Fairyland," *Jabberwocky* 5 (Winter 1976), pp. 3-24. Dickins, an international judge on Fairy Chess, uses these wilder rules of this chess offshoot to show our puzzle to be a "parody of chess morality."

WHY WASTE
YOUR PRECIOUS
PENNIES ON GAS OR
YOUR VALUABLE
TIME ON LINE
AT THE BOOKSTORE?

We will send you, FREE, our 28 page cata-
logue, filled with a wide range of Ace
Science Fiction paperback titles—we've
got something for every reader's pleasure.

Here's your chance to add to your personal
library, with all the convenience of shop-
ping by mail. There's no need to be without
a book to enjoy—request your *free* cata-
logue today.

 ACE SCIENCE FICTION
P.O. Box 400, Kirkwood, N.Y. 13795   A-05

CONAN

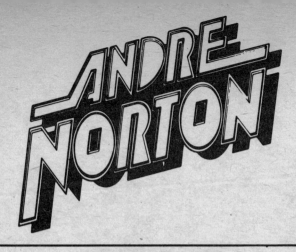

WITCH WORLD SERIES